GW01375278

## Deadly score

'For Christ's sake, don't look round! Turn and face the road as though you're just enjoying a stroll . . . I'm too late . . . Warn him . . .'

Mark Holland, Geneva-based manager of classical musicians, is accompanying a young American pianist on a concert tour of Japan when, with a barrage of bullets and a body on the tarmac, his past life catches up with him.

Holland, once a high-level operative in the shadowy world of international espionage, has lived with vital secrets that could endanger his life. The desperately whispered message in a Tokyo back street recalls a long-ago assignment in the Ticino area of Switzerland, and primes the fuse for an electrifying sequence of events ten years later.

Returning to Europe, he is summoned to Berlin by a celebrated conductor, who has learned that some lost scores by Gustav Mahler have been discovered stored away in a deep cellar in Dresden. Against his better judgement, Mark accompanies a beautiful German girl into East Berlin to purchase the manuscripts illegally, only to find that he is once again drawn into a spider's web of violence and intrigue. Nothing is ever quite what it appears to be as he unravels mysteries that were set in motion a decade earlier and pieces together the horrifying facts.

Paul Myers's fifth 'Mark Holland' adventure combines exciting action with authentic knowledge of the international music scene and proves, once again, that he is a story-teller to revel in and a master of suspense.

*By the same author*

Deadly variations (1985)
Deadly cadenza (1986)
Deadly aria (1987)
Deadly sonata (1987)

# DEADLY SCORE

Paul Myers

Constable London

First published in Great Britain 1988
by Constable & Company Ltd
10 Orange Street, London WC2H 7EG
Copyright © 1988 by Paul Myers
Set in Linotron Palatino 10 pt by
Rowland Phototypesetting Ltd
Bury St Edmunds, Suffolk
printed in Great Britain by
St Edmundsbury Press Ltd
Bury St Edmunds, Suffolk

British Library CIP data
Myers, Paul
Deadly score.
I. Title
823'.914[F]

ISBN 0 09 468470 7

For Nicholas and John

## Author's note

In the late 1960s and 1970s, when he was Editor and Publisher of that august bible of the record industry, *The Gramophone*, Tony Pollard and his wife used to give an annual summer party in their house and garden, to which they invited the many writers who had contributed to the magazine as well as representatives from the various record companies. Those parties, which provided a rare opportunity for record men to meet record reviewers, are remembered with great affection.

On one such occasion, I met Deryck Cooke, whom I had long admired for his superb explanation and analysis of Wagner's system of *leitmotifs* in the historic Decca recording of *Der Ring des Nibelungen*, but even more for his extraordinary reconstruction and realization of Mahler's unfinished Tenth Symphony, which I believe to be a masterpiece.

It was a warm and somewhat sultry evening, and I seem to remember that we had both wined and dined rather well. While reminiscing, Mr Cooke told me that in the 1930s he had held the scores of several unpublished Mahler symphonies in his own hands while on a visit to Dresden, and that the manuscripts had tragically disappeared in the following years, presumably destroyed during the bombing raids that almost completely annihilated that city. He told the story dramatically, and I was suitably moved, but that might have been partly attributed to the Pollards' generous hospitality.

It was a memory of that conversation that suggested this story. Sadly, Deryck Cooke died some years ago, so it was not possible to check the details with him. I hope he would have forgiven me for using the musicological information in such an odd context.

P.M.

Tokyo, 1986

# 1

Mr Nozaki raised his glass, smiling and nodding deferentially. '*Campai!* I hope you have enjoyed your first visit to Japan, Mr Holland.' Then he turned to Alvin Hudacek. 'I am sure this will be the first of many visits for you. Your recital was a great success, and the Tokyo Symphony have already called to ask if you will return for another concerto.' He paused for a moment, unwilling to drink before his guests. 'You do not, perhaps, like sake?'

'Of course.' Mark Holland raised his cup in salute and drank a mouthful of the tepid liquid. It had a vaguely alcoholic flavour. The young American pianist at his side wrinkled his nose and sipped cautiously. They had both accepted Mr Nozaki's invitation to try the rice wine out of courtesy, although Mark noted that their host was drinking Japanese whisky. The expression on Alvin's face revealed the anticlimax he felt. Sake was an acquired taste. Formalities being dispensed with, Mr Nozaki barked several rapid instructions to three waitresses, dressed in traditional obis, who had been awaiting his orders.

They were sitting in a restaurant in the heart of Tokyo's Rappongi district, well known for its entertainment and night life. Most of the customers were Japanese, but Mark could see a number of other Western diners. The room was decorated in simple, polished natural woods, with translucent screens to separate the tables. On loudspeakers playing at a discreetly reduced volume, a koto was plunking its way through the ubiquitous *Sakura*, which seemed to be the only Japanese melody reserved for foreign visitors. The restaurant was obviously a popular tourist attraction. Perhaps that was why it was called, incongruously, La Vie En Rose.

Mr Nozaki turned to face them. 'This is a *shabu-shabu* restaurant. It is a special way of preparing food.'

Alvin looked nervous. Since arriving in Tokyo, he had scarcely ventured out of the Okura Hotel except to perform, and his diet had remained determinedly American. 'Does that involve raw fish?'

For a moment, Mr Nozaki's smiling composure was disturbed. 'I thought we would start with *sashimi*, but that can be changed. Would you like soup?' Before Alvin could reply, he called to one of the waitresses and snapped new instructions. She fled to the kitchen.

They had been in Tokyo for five days, marking Alvin's Japanese debut. Mark had used the appearances to make contact with the Japanese musical world. He was only just beginning to become accustomed to the enormous, dense city, with its quasi-Western atmosphere and endless activity. On first impression, it was an ugly, unattractive place: concrete overhead highways, choked with traffic, and squat, utilitarian blocks of cement and glass. He had mistakenly anticipated a mixture of the modern blended with the old Japan of delicate prints and lithographs, but that seemed to have been swallowed up by the vast, sprawling new city. During long taxi rides, when every place seemed to be at least half an hour from the last, an occasional glimpse down a narrow side street, revealing a row of tiny wooden houses, had reassured him that even this huge metropolis had retained some of its past. The time change had affected him more than he had expected, leaving a feeling of slight malaise after sleepless nights, and the humid atmosphere of mid-June was ennervating.

Alvin appeared to be surviving the experience better, but he had cloistered himself from his surroundings, turning up the air-conditioning in his room and concentrating on his music. His only complaint had been on arrival at Narita airport after a spine-jarring non-stop flight of fifteen hours from New York, to learn that there was still an eighty-kilometre taxi ride into the city. He had retired to bed immediately, to sleep round the clock, leaving Mark and Mr Nozaki to dine together. On one occasion, he had accompanied Mark down the Ginza, but the busy shopping street, its windows filled with beautiful silks and ceramics, had left him unimpressed. He had been relieved to find a Colonel Sanders Kentucky Fried Chicken and a McDonalds. As far as Alvin was concerned, he could just as easily have been in Canton, Ohio.

Mr Nozaki continued to smile as a waitress darted forward to refill the tiny china sake cups to the brim. It was hard to guess the promoter's age. His face was smooth and expressionless, but there were traces of grey in his hair at the temples, where the metal arms of his rimless glasses cut into them. He was dressed in a severely cut pinstripe suit, with a tiny white triangle of handkerchief visible in the breast pocket.

'I hope you will enjoy *shabu-shabu*. Some of my visitors call it a do-it-yourself dinner.' It was a joke he had obviously used before, and Mark smiled encouragingly. Alvin remained wary. 'You see, we will cook the meat and vegetables ourselves in a pot of boiling water, and at the end of the meal, we drink the soup we have prepared. It is very simple and quite original, don't you think?'

Mark decided not to mention that *fondue orientale* was a popular dish in Switzerland, based on the same principle. One of his favourite Lausanne restaurants, in a small street just off Beaulieu, served it nightly. It was a pity to spoil Mr Nozaki's treat, and for all he knew, it might shame the man. He was still discovering the thin veneer of occidental behaviour beneath which there remained a powerful Eastern culture. The Japanese might have perfected their electronics and technology to the point where they led the world, but they were still in the imitative stages of Western thinking. That morning, Mark had been shown round a giant electronics factory, whose thousands of smartly disciplined workers assembled complicated equipment at long rows of workbenches. His guide had explained how each employee, from top executive to the humblest floor sweeper, was looked after almost from the cradle to the grave. 'Every person begins at age eighteen and works until age sixty-five, with regular paid holidays, here and overseas.' (That explained those mass invasions of Europe.) 'Even then, when he has retired on a good pension, he comes back every three months, to see how his successors are working in his place.'

'Do you ever have to dismiss anyone? Surely, there must be times when employees go bad on you.'

A slight pause. 'Not very often.' The question had taken the man by surprise.

'But when that happens?'

'Ah. Then we move the employee to another job.'

'Does that always solve the problem?'

'No. You do not understand.' His mentor had been puzzled by Mark's lack of comprehension. 'If the employee is moved and it is not a promotion, then he must resign. You see, he loses face!'

Alvin was impressed with his soup, a consommé with diced vegetables arranged in the bottom of the bowl to form intricate flower patterns. 'How the heck do they get them to stay in place like that?'

Mr Nozaki smiled serenely, but Mark explained. 'They put the vegetable patterns between sheets of rice paper, and pour the broth over them just before serving it. The rice paper melts by the time it reaches you.'

Mr Nozaki nodded approvingly. 'Bravo! I think you are an astute man, Mr Holland.' He spoke excellent English, having lived in London for several years, and did not appear to be troubled by the perennial Japanese problem of distinguishing between 'l's and 'r's. Mark had also discovered that the Japanese did not like to pronounce two consonants together. A word like 'necktie' presented difficulties, and even Mr Nozaki was inclined to pronounce Hudacek's first name 'Al-a-vin'.

The pianist was sipping steadily from his sake cup, which was immediately refilled, and began to relax noticeably. Mark suspected that the rice wine was stronger than the young man realized. His long dark hair was slightly tousled, and there were beads of sweat on his forehead. The heat from the small gas ring in the centre of the table, on which the steaming *shabu-shabu* bowl was placed, made the confined space uncomfortably warm. Mark loosened his tie, wondering whether he was also feeling the effect of the sake. Only Mr Nozaki remained impeccably correct. He seemed to remember that the Japanese seldom perspired.

At his side, Alvin giggled suddenly. 'How the hell am I going to dunk the meat in that water? I can't handle chopsticks.' His comment delighted his waitress, hovering nearby, and she bent over him, placing his fingers round the thin wooden instruments and accompanying the lesson with a bird-like patter of pidgin English.

Taking advantage of Alvin's preoccupation, Mr Nozaki said, 'I hope you have been satisfied with all the arrangements, Mr Holland?'

'Very. I've enjoyed the visit.' The fees had been better than Mark had anticipated, and the audiences at the recital and the orchestral concert had been enthusiastic.

'I am very pleased. Of course, the concerts would have been

better sold if Mr Hudacek had been more famous. Next time, there will be no empty seats.' He leaned forward, lowering his voice slightly. 'You see, it is very important that you are satisfied. I am aware that you also represent maestro Konstantin Steigel. We were very disappointed when he did not accept our last invitation.' Mr Nozaki hesitated, slightly embarrassed. 'Now that you have been here to see for yourself, I was hoping you would be persuaded to ask the maestro on our behalf.'

'I'll be pleased to.' They had made numerous unsuccessful approaches to Konstantin Steigel. Mark knew that the old conductor hesitated before travelling halfway round the world because he questioned whether Japanese audiences were truly sophisticated enough to appreciate his readings of Brahms and Mahler: 'There are plenty of others, my dear, only too eager to jet to any point on the globe, and their audiences won't notice the difference!' Steigel's wife, Heidi, worried for different reasons. Although he would not admit to it, the conductor had grown very frail in the past few years, and it was a long way from home if he should be taken ill.

'I would be greatly indebted to you, Mr Holland.' Nozaki cut across his thoughts. 'It would be a great honour to hear Konstantin Steigel conduct a Japanese orchestra.' He hesitated again. 'If Mr Hudacek were able to come with him, I believe you would be happier than on this occasion.'

'I'm sure I would.' Mr Nozaki was referring obliquely to the young American conductor who had directed the concerto the night before. Mark had heard him on several previous occasions, and had been similarly unimpressed. The conductor's career had been over-sold by his New York manager who, as chief of one of America's largest agencies, had used his power and influence to accelerate a career which was destined to be, at best, second-class. The Japanese promoter could not refuse the conductor in question; otherwise, the New York office would withhold their major artists.

Aware of Mr Nozaki's dilemma, Mark smiled. 'Even if maestro Steigel refuses yet another offer, I am sure there are a number of other suitable conductors who would be more . . . sympathetic.'

Mr Nozaki nodded slowly, unwilling to criticize New York openly, and to Mark's delight said, 'Ah so.' It was just like being in a film! 'I did not wish to appear too critical, Mr Holland, but that young man seemed . . .' He was at a loss for words.

'Unsatisfactory, to put it kindly. Unfortunately, the music world – especially New York – has to survive a certain amount of power politics. I'm sure you have the same problems.' The promoter nodded silently. Presumably, New York would go on pushing the young man until the next whiz–kid came along. For a moment, he was tempted to tell Mr Nozaki that Abe Cohen, his American partner, hearing that they were to be saddled with the young conductor, had scowled and grunted, 'You know the difference between that kid leading the Tokyo Symphony and a bull? A bull has horns at the front and an asshole at the back!' Perhaps not. Mr Nozaki was still very formal, and conundrums probably did not translate into Japanese.

'Very well.' Mr Nozaki became businesslike. 'I will rely on you to arrange matters, Mr Holland. If you think it is possible, I will also arrange television and a recording. It would be a very important occasion.'

'That sounds excellent.' Mark smiled. 'But I haven't persuaded him to come yet.'

'I trust your abilities, Mr Holland. You see, in Japan we are very conscious of the history of European music. So, if we are to hear the great composers, we would prefer to hear them conducted by Europeans.' He glanced apologetically towards Alvin. 'I know this may sound very simplistic to you, but Japanese audiences ask for European conductors. They feel it is more authentic.'

'I suppose so, but surely there are a number of American conductors who are greatly admired in Japan. Look at Lorin Maazel.'

For a moment, Mr Nozaki was startled. 'But we thought he was a European!'

Towards the end of the meal, Mr Nozaki excused himself from the table, heading towards the front desk. It was considered more polite to settle the bill away from one's guests. Alvin leaned back. 'I really enjoyed that, even though I didn't expect to. I guess I might try some Japanese restaurants when I get home. Listen, can't I talk you into going on to Hong Kong with me? I sure as hell hate to go there alone, especially if there are going to be any more cracks about European musicians being better than Americans.'

'Mr Nozaki didn't mean to offend you. He was apologizing for the Japanese. I have to get back to my office. I'd love to take the time, but I'm needed in Geneva.'

Alvin sighed. 'OK. It's funny, but I can never get used to hearing you talk about Geneva as "home". What's an Englishman like you doing in Switzerland?' The sake had made him more voluble than usual.

'It's a long story. I was tired of the work I was doing in London, so I moved to Switzerland and started the agency.' He rarely thought about his old life. It was like another existence.

'You mean you weren't a manager back in London?'

'No. I had a job in the Arts, but I was a sort of civil servant.' London Arts had always been their cover. It was vague enough to suggest a wide variety of activities.

'A civil servant?'

'Yes. I worked for the Government.' Put that way, it was almost the truth. 'Anyway, I'm sure you'll enjoy Hong Kong. Sammy Chang is supposed to be an excellent promoter. From what I've heard, he'll look after you from the moment you step off the plane.'

'If you say so.' Alvin drained his sake cup. 'This stuff's great. It doesn't taste of much, but it sure soothes you. I guess I'll take tomorrow easy. Maybe I'll do a little sightseeing after all.'

'I expect Mr Nozaki will be delighted to show you round. There's a lot to see.'

'It's fantastic. Did you know there are five downtown areas?' Mark nodded. 'The view from my window at night is spectacular, with all those neon signs. I guess they're only saying "Smoke Seven Stars Cigarettes" and stuff like that, but they look neat in Japanese.'

'You should try to see the National Museum. It has the best collection of Chinese art in the world.' Alvin looked less enthusiastic. 'Better still, take the train over to Kyoto, and see all the shrines.'

'Maybe next time. I thought I'd price out some of those portable compact-disc players.'

Mr Nozaki rejoined them, and they made a ceremonious exit from the restaurant to a chorus of sing-song farewells from their three smiling waitresses, who bowed in unison and looked for all the world as though they were about to break into a chorus of 'Three Little Maids from School'.

Mr Nozaki beamed. 'It is still quite early, so I thought we would visit a club. Do you like jazz, Mr Hudacek?'

'Sure.' Alvin looked at Mark uncertainly. Perhaps he feared Mr Nozaki was about to take them to a geisha house or, worse still, a public communal bath. His impressions of Japan had been coloured by old films on television.

'Excellent. We have many good night clubs in this district. It would be a shame to visit Tokyo without going to one.'

Mark looked at his watch. 'If you'll forgive me, I think I'll go back to the hotel. I'm leaving quite early in the morning, and I still have to pack.'

'Ah, then let me find a taxi, and we will take you there first.'

'Don't worry. I'd prefer to walk for a while. After such an excellent meal, the exercise will do me good. It's not very far to the hotel from here.'

Mr Nozaki inclined his head. 'As you wish. I will call for you in the morning in my car. Perhaps we can discuss a few matters on the way to the airport. Are you sure you will not be lost?'

'Sure.'

The Japanese promoter smiled. 'A man of your height will certainly see over the heads of everyone, Mr Holland! Do you know which direction to walk?'

'Yes, thank you. If I do get lost, I'll find a taxi.'

'Don't worry about Mr Hudacek. I will be pleased to look after him.'

Alvin appeared to be torn between natural mistrust and a false sense of adventure, probably inspired by generous refills of sake.

After the heat of the restaurant, the night air was pleasantly cool and refreshing, with a noticeable drop in the humidity. Mark walked in the direction of the hotel, choosing narrow streets in which every doorway seemed to be the entrance to a cafè or bar. It was modern, and yet it seemed to have some of the flavour of the Japan he had hoped to find. At one point, he passed a *pachinko* hall, brightly lit and filled with players and he paused to watch as row upon row of men stood before the vertical pinball machines, similar to the penny slot-machines that he had played on seaside piers in his childhood, solemnly paying in coins and flicking the metal levers that sent the chromium balls flying round the track. It seemed an odd recreation for adults.

The streets were busy, and the pavements crowded with sightseers. From the number of Westerners among them, it was obvious that this was Tokyo's entertainment district. He had driven through other sections of the city that were populated exclusively by the Japanese and where foreigners were noticeable by their absence. Taxis edged their way cautiously down the narrow roads, stopping constantly to set down passengers. There was something slightly eerie about the way the drivers operated the rear doors with a lever inside the car, so that they appeared to open and close automatically. Mark was also conscious of curious glances in his direction. At least a head taller than the average Japanese man, and with blond hair in a land where everyone was a brunette, he felt conspicuous. Passing a group of teenage boys and girls, he heard one of them make a comment which caused his companions to giggle. The boy had been looking at him as he spoke, but there was no malice in his voice, and Mark smiled at him.

The street widened out to pass the gaudily neon-lit entrance to a night club the size of a theatre. A huge hoarding, running the length of the façade, advertised a chorus line of scantily dressed girls, and two burly commissionaires, large by Japanese standards, paraded in Ruritanian uniforms lavish with gold braid. Some local entrepreneur, many years earlier, must have been impressed by the showplaces in Pigalle and had returned to Tokyo to recreate the same thing, correct to the last detail. There was also a Maxim's restaurant which, by all reports, exactly reproduced its Parisian cousin. Perhaps that was why the Japanese always travelled with cameras, photographing everything in case their memories failed them.

He was coming to the edge of the district and quickened his pace, walking through quieter streets. On a slight rise before him, partly masked by the overhead highway, he could see the Okura Hotel, and aimed towards it. Passing under the giant concrete supports of the road, it was like moving into another town, and the lights and the noise faded behind him, with only a low rumble of distant sound. He climbed the hill towards the hotel, finding himself on a curving driveway, in a quiet road bordering the hotel gardens. It was contrastingly peaceful after the bustle of the Rappongi district.

About forty yards from the hotel entrance, Mark paused under a streetlamp to light a cigarette. At that moment, a voice quite close but in the direction of the bushes, called his name. Astonished, he spun round, scanning the shadowy foliage.

'For Christ's sake, don't look round!' The voice was urgent. 'Turn and face the road as though you're just enjoying a stroll.' Mark hesitated. 'Please!'

It was as though an instinct from the past took over, and Mark turned slowly, facing the empty driveway. He drew on the cigarette, exhaling slowly.

'What do you want?' Mark kept his voice low. Glancing casually in either direction, he saw no one. 'Who are you?'

He thought he heard a groan, and started to turn, but the voice returned. 'Don't look round. Please! You can't do anything for me. It's too late.' The sound was strained.

Moving very slowly, Mark edged backwards, to be closer. 'Who are you? How did you know my name?'

'Chance. I saw you in the restaurant . . .' The man was speaking with difficulty. 'I hung around until you came out . . . When I heard you say you were walking back to the hotel, I ran on ahead of you. That's when they saw me . . . Oh Christ!' He groaned again, and was silent.

'What's wrong with you? Are you hurt?'

In reply, there was a shallow laugh. The man seemed to be having difficulty breathing. 'I'm hurt.'

Mark dropped his cigarette, grinding it underfoot and using the movement to turn and peer towards the darkened bushes. 'Where are you?'

'Don't come closer!' The voice was suddenly urgent. 'We're being watched . . . I haven't much time left.'

'What do you mean?'

'I've been hit . . . two or three . . . I'm not going to make it.' His voice was strained with pain.

'The hotel's only a few yards up the road. I'll get help . . .' Mark turned away.

'No! There isn't time. Look, if they're watching, they're going to get suspicious of you, so I can't waste . . .' After another pause, he said, 'I'm Bailey.'

'What?' The name struck Mark like a physical blow.

'Bailey . . . from London. For Christ's sake, don't you remember who I am?'

'I remember.' For a moment, Mark was silent. 'What the hell's . . . ?'

20

'Don't interrupt. For God's sake, let me talk! I can't hang on much longer. You've got to get a message through to Quentin Sharpe in London. Thank God I spotted you.'

'Why are you here?'

'It's not important . . .' Each sentence seemed to be an effort. 'I was following a lead . . . they must have realized . . . I've been on the run for three days.'

'But . . .'

'Let me talk, for God's sake!' The exertion seemed to drain him, and he was silent. When he spoke again, his voice was little more than a hoarse whisper. 'Call Quentin . . . soon . . . Tell him what's happened . . . Tell him I'm sorry . . . They must have seen me when I . . .' His voice died away again.

'Let me get someone . . .'

'No! I can't hold on . . .' He seemed to be making a final effort. 'Tell Quentin we've got to get him out of Dresden before . . .'

Mark waited. A pulse seemed to be beating in his temple. The darkened driveway was still deserted. The overhead streetlamps were weak, but a circle of light splashed across the road further down, indicating the hotel entrance. It was only a few seconds away if he ran. Throwing caution aside, he stepped closer to the bushes. 'I'll get you out of there.'

'No! It's more important that you reach Quentin . . . I'm too late . . . Tell him . . . Get a message as soon as . . . Warn him . . .'

'Who?'

'In Dresden . . . We've got to warn him . . .'

'Warn who?'

Bailey muttered, but Mark could not hear what he said.

'*Who* must Quentin warn?'

There was a rustling of leaves and breaking twigs. Bailey was gasping for air, and Mark had the impression that he was trying to pull himself to his feet. 'Get out of here! Get to a phone . . . Call Quentin!'

Mark stood back. 'All right, but who should he warn?'

'Hyatt . . . Richard Hyatt.' The words were whispered, spoken with desperation.

'But he can't!' Mark paused.

'Tell him! For Christ's sake, tell him!'

'Are you . . . ?'

'Call Quentin . . . please!' Bailey forced the words. 'Don't let anyone . . . there's security leak . . . Quentin knows . . . He must warn Hyatt!' The rustling increased, and Mark could hear branches tearing. Suddenly, a figure crashed through the leaves, staggering forward across the pavement. It was Bailey, his face smeared and bloody, and with a narrow stream of dark liquid flowing from the corner of his mouth across his chin. In the poor light, it looked black. Mark recognized him immediately. He was wearing an open-necked shirt which had once been pale-coloured, but the front was now soaked with blood. The stain looked like a dark, uneven shadow, covering his chest and stomach.

Bailey tottered forward, pressing his arms against his chest as though to hold the flesh back, then stumbled and fell, lying motionless on the road. He did not move again. Mark stepped forward, but as he did so, he heard the sharp crack of a rifle shot and the whine of a bullet as it hit the pavement in front of him. A powdery cloud of cement exploded where it struck. He threw himself backwards into the shadow of the undergrowth, and a second bullet thudded into the earth, close to his feet. An uneasy silence followed, and he waited. The shot had come from the direction of the far corner, away from the hotel entrance. On the pavement, Bailey's body was immobile. He lay, face down, sprawled and flattened, as though in a deep sleep.

Mark waited a few more seconds, then moved fast. Running to left and then right in a wide zigzag, he raced towards the circle of light at the hotel entrance. There were two more shots. He did not hear where the first landed, but the second ricocheted off the road a few feet ahead of him with an ugly squeal. There might have been a third, but the blood pounding in his head deafened him. Moments later, he threw himself through the hotel door, vaguely conscious of a startled doorman jumping back to allow him in. As he struggled to regain his breath, gasping for air, a single thought dominated his mind. How could he tell Quentin Sharpe to warn Richard Hyatt? The bastard had been dead for ten years.

# 2

The policemen had commandeered a small conference room in the hotel. A long, polished refectory table occupied most of the space, and there were enough chairs to seat twenty people. Mark had counted them several times while he awaited the results of each hasty conference taking place at the far end of the room. At his side, a portable easel held a blackboard on which columns of Japanese ideograms and letters accompanied blocks of figures. From the look of it, the previous tenants must have been holding a sales conference. He wondered vaguely what they had been selling. There was no other information, and the room was suitably anonymous. Like so many international facilities, it could have been in a hotel anywhere in the world. He lit another cigarette and looked at his watch. Surprisingly, it was only a little after midnight.

His four interrogators had retired to the other end of the room for the fifth or sixth time, and were speaking in hushed voices. It was difficult to decide whether they were arguing. The Japanese, especially in Tokyo, talked very quickly, always giving the impression of great animation. Two of the men were plain-clothes detectives, dressed rather formally in business suits. They had been called in by the other two – a night manager from the front desk and one of the hotel's security men – shortly after Mark's spectacular entrance through the front door of the hotel. The night manager was wearing a dinner jacket, but the security man was in slacks with an open-necked sports shirt. Beyond these four, a uniformed policeman stood by the door, his eyes fixed on a point on the opposite wall. He looked rather bored, but his stare never faltered.

From time to time, the night manager stole a quick glance towards Mark, then rejoined the lively discussion. He wondered why they chose to lower their voices when it was more than apparent that he could not understand what they were saying. The first of the two plain-clothes men had advised Mark rather sibilantly that he spoke English, but it had become painfully apparent that his vocabulary was limited to about thirty words, forcing him to rely on the night manager.

At length, the delegation returned to his end of the room. The night manager, as spokesman, took two paces closer. He smiled politely.

'The Inspector would like to know whether you would like to change any of the details you have given, Mr Holland.' He pronounced it 'Horrun', but Mark had grown accustomed to the title. 'We have already shown you that there is nobody outside, and certainly no dead men.' He simpered slightly at the idea. The Okura was definitely not that sort of hotel.

'I told you what happened.'

'Ah.' The night manager turned to the other three and snapped the translation. Their conversation became animated again, and from time to time, each of them looked at Mark. There were several long, low vowel sounds in their speech, and perhaps because his nerves were still tightly stretched, Mark suppressed a sudden, guilty urge to laugh. It was like being in a Kurosawa movie.

The mini-conference came to an end, and the night manager turned back to Mark. He seemed to be having trouble maintaining his smile. 'The Inspector suggests you describe what happened again.' One of the detectives nodded, and seated himself at the table, opening a notebook.

Mark took a deep breath. 'Very well, but this is the third time I've been through it.'

'Yes, sir.' The night manager's voice had hardened slightly. 'The Inspector offers you his apologies, but he has shown you personally that there is nobody outside. Do you wish to look again?' Mark shook his head. 'We could find no sign of a disturbance in the road. Everything is quite normal.'

'It's too dark to see anything properly.'

'Yes, sir, but there are two policemen searching the road where you showed them. They cannot find anything unusual.'

It was true. When Mark had flung himself through the hotel door, calling for help, the staff had sprung into action. Accompanied by the night manager and the security man, he had returned to the street, retracing his steps, but the driveway had been empty and deserted. There was no sign of Bailey. When the police arrived, they had returned again, walking slowly along the pavement to inspect the place where Mark had stopped. He was not even certain which streetlamp he had stood under, and had walked from one to the next, trying to find some tell-tale piece of evidence. The police had produced powerful torches, shining them on the ground and under the bushes, but they had revealed nothing. After a fruitless half-hour, they had returned to the hotel, where Mark gave the first of his statements, slightly revised for their benefit. He had given no indication of knowing Bailey, and made no reference to Quentin Sharpe or Richard Hyatt.

Mark spoke slowly, recounting the events in a monotone, and the policeman wrote in his notebook as the night manager maintained a running commentary in Japanese. Mark was beginning to regret calling for their help. They did not believe him, and he had nothing to offer as proof.

When he had finished, the room was silent. The two detectives stared at him. Without taking his eyes off Mark, the senior man spoke quietly to the night manager, who translated.

'Why are you in Japan, please?'

'I came here with Alvin Hudacek, an American pianist who is staying at this hotel. I am his manager. Mr Hudacek gave two concerts in Tokyo this week. The last one took place yesterday, with the Tokyo Symphony Orchestra.' Mark paused, waiting for the laborious translation and the next question. It seemed to take longer in the other language.

'Did you know the man who called to you from the bushes?'

He tried not to answer too quickly. 'No.'

'Then why did you stop?'

'He asked me to help him. He sounded desperate.'

'What did he tell you?'

'That he was hiding from gunmen and needed help.'

'How long did you talk?'

'I don't know; about a minute I should think.' That was all he could risk saying.

'Why didn't you run to fetch help?'

'I did.'

'Immediately?'

'Almost immediately. The man fell out of the bushes at my feet, and then someone opened fire at us. It sounded like a rifle shot.'

'How do you know that?'

Mark hesitated. 'I didn't know for sure, but it was too far away to be a revolver. A bullet hit the pavement near my foot. You should be able to see the mark in daylight.'

'We have already looked many times, Mr Holland. Perhaps the daylight will help. Did you look at the wounded man carefully?'

'No, I couldn't. They opened fire almost as soon as he came out of the bushes.'

'They?'

'Whoever shot at me. It could have been just one person.'

'Then why did you say "they"?'

'Because the man said "they". He said something like: "They're after me", so I assumed there was more than one.'

'Can you describe the man again, please?'

Mark closed his eyes. 'He was medium height, slightly built, with dark hair. By his accent, he sounded English.'

There was a delay while the Inspector spoke at length to the hotel man. 'How did this man know you were English, Mr Holland?'

'I don't understand.' Mark was suddenly wary. He hoped it was not apparent.

The night manager shrugged. 'We are in Tokyo. He could see that you are not Japanese, of course, but he did not know anything else about you, did he?'

'No.'

'But he addressed you in English.' The policeman, obviously pleased with himself, nodded vigorously.

Mark shrugged. 'I suppose he took a chance that I was either English or American.'

The hotel man translated, and the two policemen nodded assent. The senior man looked disappointed.

'How did the man appear to you?'

'He was badly wounded. He was bleeding from the mouth, and the front of his shirt was soaked with blood. He said he had been shot several times.'

'Yes?'

Mark shrugged helplessly. 'That's about all I saw. He collapsed on the pavement in front of me. As I went forward to help him, someone started firing. The shots came from near the bend in the road, where the hill comes up from below.'

'What did you do?'

'I moved into the shadow of the bushes, so that I'd be less visible.'

'How long?'

'A few seconds. I was frightened.' His interrogators nodded again. 'Then I decided to make a run for it. They fired several more shots at me, but I was lucky. You know the rest.'

There was a short silence. The senior Inspector muttered something, and the manager continued. 'The Inspector says it is very strange. If the man was bleeding in the way you describe, there would be a mark on the road, where he fell. We did not find one.'

'No.' Mark had puzzled over that, too.

'How would you explain it, please?'

'I can't. I can only assume that whoever was following him must have removed the body as soon as I entered the hotel. Perhaps they had a car. I didn't see one, but I didn't stop to look round!'

'Ah. A moment, please.' The four men returned to the end of the room for a further caucus. It was shorter than previous conferences, and the night manager returned almost immediately.

'Where is Mr Hudacek?'

'He's with Mr Nozaki, the promoter who arranged his concerts. I left them together outside a restaurant in the Rappongi district, and walked here. The restaurant is called La Vie en Rose.' His interrogators nodded. 'I came back early because I wanted to pack. I'm supposed to fly home tomorrow.' He glanced at his watch. 'Mr Hudacek should be back by now. You can check his room.'

'Thank you.' The night manager did not seem eager to continue questioning, but the senior Inspector appeared to be prompting him. 'Excuse me, but did you drink very much at the restaurant, Mr Holland?'

'I don't think so. We drank sake with the meal.'

Recognizing the word 'sake', the policemen exchanged knowing glances. One of them whispered in the night manager's ear. 'You are quite sure you did not drink very much?'

'Not more than average. It's rather hard to tell. The waitresses refilled our cups whenever we drank.'

'Ah.' The night manager looked pensive, and the policeman murmured to him again. 'You do not think, perhaps, that the sake had a bad effect on you, Mr Holland? It is very strong, even though it does not appear to be.'

For a moment, Mark could feel his temper rising, but he

controlled his voice. 'I see what you are trying to suggest, but I don't think I was drunk. Besides, I'd just walked back to the hotel. That would have been enough to clear my head.'

'Perhaps. Sometimes, there is a delayed effect.'

'What are you trying to suggest?'

The night manager looked sheepish, avoiding Mark's eyes. 'The Inspector wonders whether you might have suffered a small attack from the alcohol, causing a moment's unconsciousness. He wonders whether you could have imagined meeting this Englishman while you were in such a state. Dreams are sometimes very vivid.'

'I see. And did I imagine I was being shot at, too?'

The night manager shrugged. 'Perhaps the backfiring of a car's exhaust? It can sound like a gun sometimes . . .' He did not look very convinced.

It occurred to Mark that there was no point in prolonging their meeting. Bailey had gone, and unless he was prepared to reveal their conversation, the police would never be persuaded. A bitter thought struck him: My God, even now, those bastards have got me working for them! Besides, it was time to find a telephone and call Quentin.

The night manager coughed politely to regain his attention. 'Do you think such an explanation is possible, Mr Holland?'

Mark hesitated, lowering his head. 'It's possible, I suppose. I find it hard to believe.'

The man was patently relieved. 'It is not so hard to understand. Sake is very strong, especially if you are unaccustomed to it.' The policemen nodded.

'I see.' Mark paused. 'I seem to have made a fool of myself.' Being English had one distinct advantage: he did not give a shit about losing face!

The night manager was enthusiastically sympathetic. 'Ah no, sir, it is very understandable. I am very sorry if you have been inconvenienced.' He spoke at some length to the other three, who listened attentively. At one point, the hotel security man grinned broadly, but a sharply snapped comment removed any expression from his face. At length, the manager turned to Mark. 'We are sorry you have had such an unpleasant experience.'

'Thank you.' Mark smiled wryly. 'I think I am the one who should apologize. I seem to have caused everyone a great deal of trouble.'

'That is no problem, sir. The Inspector was pleased to be of assistance.'

'That's very understanding of him. I'm supposed to leave Tokyo tomorrow. If you think . . .'

'There should be no reason to delay your departure, sir.' The night manager was professionally in control again. 'I am sure that when you have had a good rest, you will be feeling quite recovered. The Inspector says he will send a man to check the street again when it is daylight, but you should not change your plans. He has your statement in full.' He led the way to the door, where the uniformed policeman, springing to life, turned the handle and stepped to one side with military precision.

Mark faced the four men. 'Please accept my apologies. I am sorry to have caused such a nuisance.'

The four men bowed gravely, the night manager's head reaching almost level with his waist. Mark managed an exaggerated nod, and headed towards the hotel elevators.

In his room, he called the Long Distance operator, and gave her Quentin Sharpe's old number in London. It was amazing how easily he remembered it. Within seconds, he heard the phone ringing.

A girl spoke. 'Hello. London Arts.' The tone was surprisingly clear.

'Can I speak to Quentin Sharpe, please.'

'He's not in, I'm afraid. Who's calling?'

'Mark Holland.'

'Just a moment, please.' The line was silent for half a minute. When the girl returned, she was cheerfully apologetic. 'Sorry to keep you waiting. I'm afraid Mr Sharpe's away at the moment. He's not expected back for several days. Can anyone else help you?'

Mark hesitated. 'No. I need to speak to him directly. It's urgent. Do you know where he can be reached?'

'I'm awfully sorry, but I'm afraid not. He's on holiday this week.'

'I see.'

'He sometimes calls in. Can I give him your number?'

'No. I won't be here after tonight. I'm calling from Tokyo.'

'Really?' She sounded impressed.

'I'll be leaving in the morning, and with the time changes I'm not quite sure where I'll be.'

'Would Mr Sharpe have a number where he can reach you?'

Mark's face was set, but he kept his voice light. 'Yes, I'm sure he would.'

'Well, perhaps he can try to get back to you in a day or two. Will you be returning home?'

'Yes.' A sudden thought struck him. 'No, as a matter of fact, I may be delayed *en route*. I may break the journey in San Francisco, so perhaps I'd better try again from there.'

'All right. We'll tell him you called.'

'Thank you. Would you be sure to tell him I called from Tokyo.'

'Yes.' She sounded puzzled. 'I'll make a note of it.'

Mark hung up, and sat on the edge of the bed for a moment, staring into space. Then he took his battered old address book and searched through it for a number. He could not remember whether he had kept it. He had not spoken to Ernie Sullivan for more than ten years . . . God! Was it that long ago? He remembered an address in Muir Woods, somewhere outside San Francisco. Ernie had always talked about giant sequoia trees in his back garden.

For a moment, Mark paused, closing the book. Should he involve Ernie? Bailey had said something about a security leak. No, it couldn't matter, after all these years. What the hell had happened to Bailey? There had been no trace, and he had checked for himself. They must have had a car. Another thought came, and he crossed the room to double-check the lock on his door. With Bailey out of the way, was he the next target on the list? But whose list, and why, for God's sake?

Ernie's number was there, and he dialled the operator again. Within moments, he could hear the American call-tone. It rang several times before someone picked up.

'Ernie?'

'Yeah. Who is this?' He recognized the gravelly tones and the slow drawl. Ernie Sullivan's Irish ancestry had long disappeared from his voice.

'Mark Holland.'

'Mark? Why, you son of a gun!' He sounded pleased. 'How are you, and where the hell did you show up from?'

'It would take too long to explain. It's good to hear your voice again.'

'Je-sus, Mark, you sure know how to disappear. I heard you quit the business.'

'I did, years ago. How about you?'

'Me?' Ernie laughed comfortably. 'I'm retired. Don't you folks stop when you hit sixty-five?'

'Yes.' He had forgotten that Ernie was more than twenty years his senior.

'Well, I'll be hitting seventy in a couple of years.' He spoke with pride.

'I forget how the years pass.'

Sullivan chuckled. 'Specially when you're having fun? Listen, am I going to lay eyes on you, or d'you just make a friendly phone call every decade?'

'I'd like to come and see you, Ernie, if you have the time.'

'Time's just about all I do have these days. Martha died two years back, you know.'

'I'm sorry.'

'It's OK; one of the things you have to get accustomed to at my age. I still miss her, though. D'you want to come stay for a few days? Longer if you like.' The warmth in his voice indicated his sincerity. 'I have plenty of room.'

Mark hesitated. 'No, thank you, Ernie, but I would like to see you. I could be in San Francisco the day after tomorrow, if that suits you.'

'Suits me fine. I'll meet you at the airport.'

'I'm not sure of the flight times. Perhaps it would be better if we met in town. I'm sorry to sound vague, but I haven't checked the flights and arrival times.'

'No sweat.' If Ernie had questions, he did not ask them. 'Where do you want to meet?'

Mark thought for a moment. 'How about Ghirardelli Square?'

'Sounds OK.'

'Eleven o'clock, the day after tomorrow?'

'Sure.' Ernie chuckled again. 'I'm intrigued, Mark. Do I hold my breath until I see you.'

'It might be better.'

'I'll be pretty red in the face by then, son.'

'I'm sorry. I didn't mean to make it sound so mysterious. I wanted to talk to you about a man called Hyatt. Richard Hyatt.'

The line was silent for a moment. 'I haven't heard his name mentioned for a long time. I thought he died years back.'

'So did I.'

'Then I'm more intrigued than ever.' Sullivan's voice became softer. 'Didn't you just get through telling me you quit the business?'

'Yes, a long time ago.'

'But you want to talk about Richard Hyatt?'

'Yes. I'll explain when I see you.'

'Whatever you say, Mark. I'll look forward to it. You know, you just made my day.'

'Really?'

'There's not a lot happens around here any more, son. It'll be good to catch up on old times. I'll be looking for you.'

Mark replaced the receiver, and lit a cigarette. There was a daily flight from Tokyo to San Francisco, and by crossing the international date-line, he would arrive within what appeared to be a few hours of his departure from Japan. In a while, he would make the reservation.

Damn Quentin! He had picked the worst possible time to be on holiday. With any luck, he would call in. He was much too ambitious to absent himself for more than a few days without wanting to know what was going on at the office. Maybe he could explain the reappearance of Hyatt. It was the last name Mark ever wanted to hear again, but there was no mistake. Bailey had been quite clear. He had repeated it twice, together with the message he was desperate to pass on. God, the young man had been prepared to die for it! Where did Dresden come into it?

He stubbed out the cigarette angrily. The Japanese police did not know what they were doing, and they did not want to be involved. The hotel was worse. Too much sake! He had just watched a man die, and they were trying to call it a bad dream!

But why Hyatt? Almost unconsciously, Mark lit another cigarette and settled back on the bed, trying to piece together his memories. Ten years was a hell of a long time to recall, and yet . . .

Hamburg, 1976

# 3

He stood, his hands thrust deep into his trouser pockets, and stared out of the window at a narrow, shadowy backyard. The rain was falling in windblown sheets from a leaden sky, and he could see the spatter of drops bouncing off the grey concrete of the building on the other side of the well. From somewhere above, a broken drainpipe spewed a steady stream of dirty water across half the windowpane, distorting the view. Such inefficiency was surprisingly un-Teutonic, but Hamburg had its shabby side. It was nearly midday, but there were lights burning in the windows across the yard.

'What's the matter with you, then?' Harry Price looked up from the papers he had been shuffling round his desk for the past half hour. He was sucking on an old pipe which sputtered and crackled, punctuating the silence, and a thin fog of tobacco smoke hung round him like an unhealthy mist.

Mark did not bother to reply, and continued to gaze moodily into space. The single room allocated as their office was quite large, with ample space between their desks and a row of filing cabinets, but the drab colours and pale overhead lighting made it feel oppressively claustrophobic.

'You're never going to get that report out by this evening.' Harry pretended to be busy again. 'Rome wasn't built in a day, was it?'

Despite himself, Mark smiled. The man had a rare talent for choosing the wrong aphorism or finding an inappropriate simile. Combined with his irritating salf-of-the-earth bonhomie, it could have been a source of entertainment if only there were someone else to share it. At least, it distracted him from his gloom.

'Nobody gives a damn whether I finish the report or not. They're not going to read it when they get it.'

Harry looked offended. 'I don't think you should assume something like that. I'll grant it's not very dramatic, but the details could fit together with other material that could be vital. You never know. We're all part of one big cogwheel, aren't we?'

'I think what you're trying to say is that we're all little cogwheels in one big machine, Harry, except that some of us are littler than the rest.'

'You know what I mean.' When Harry blushed, pink patches appeared on the bald area above his forehead. 'You young college lads like to show off your expensive education.' Harry had worked his way up through the ranks, and was due to retire in a year or two. That was why London had put him out to graze in the Hamburg 'drying-out' house. Somebody had to act as a permanent caretaker for the transient staff.

'In the first place, I didn't go to college; and in the second, I was thirty-five last month, so I'd hardly qualify as young, but let it pass. As for the lousy report, all I'm supposed to do is list the names of freighters currently in the Hamburg docks. They can get that from the newspapers, for God's sake!'

'But you have to verify the information.'

'Well, I'm damned if I'm going to drag out in this bloody weather.' Mark moved towards a radiator under the window. 'I've only just dried out.'

'You should buy yourself a proper raincoat, instead of that leather jacket. It's no wonder your clothes are soaked.' Harry rode to work on a motor-cycle every morning, swathed in transparent plastic, and the first five minutes of the day were spent in an elaborate disrobing, from which he emerged, like a misshapen Venus, in a shiny brown suit with an off-white shirt and a wrinkled tie. He looked uncomfortable, staring at Mark's crumpled trousers. 'I know I've mentioned it before, but I really think you should wear a jacket and tie to the office, Mark.'

'Why?'

'You never know who might come in.' Harry bridled. 'It doesn't look right.'

'Who the hell's going to come in, Harry? I've been here three weeks, and the only person we've seen is Kurt, who couldn't care less.' Kurt was Harry's local contact, a sad-looking messenger in his late fifties who supplemented his income as janitor of the building by running errands for them. Mark suspected that Harry employed him because, even after years in Germany, his command of the language was limited to a few schoolboy phrases. Not that anyone cared. The Hamburg office was a dead end, and the Department had for long centred its operations in Berlin.

'We shouldn't give the wrong impression. Germans are very touchy about appearances, and we ought to put on a good face and clean suit.' He repeated it like a catechism. 'We do represent Britain.'

'God help Her Majesty!'

'You shouldn't joke about things like that, Mark. It's one thing when you're in the field, but this is an office. Anyway, I wasn't thinking about Kurt. I meant outsiders.'

'Oh, come on, Harry, you don't really expect any, do you? We're not listed anywhere, and the nameplate on the door downstairs is so inconspicuous you need a magnifying glass to find it. We wouldn't know what to do with a genuine visitor if we had one!'

'That's not true. We get a new set of brochures every month.' Harry pointed to the printed forms lying on a polished table by the door. 'London supplies them as regular as clockwork.'

Mark nodded. Once a month, a parcel arrived from Britain, containing free brochures and flyers from a tourist bureau, advertising the various concerts, plays and other activities that would be taking place in Britain. As employees of British Arts, a branch of London Arts, Harry and Mark purported to be cultural missionaries to North Germany, but Head Office strictly forbade direct contact with any of the local organizations, in case their presence generated interest. There was not even a budget to cover tickets for local Hamburg events. The whole point of a drying-out house was to be anonymous.

'You never know.' Harry was relighting his pipe, sending new clouds of Three Nuns into the gloomy atmosphere. 'There was a fellow in last month.'

'What did he want?'

'Nothing much. I gave him a handful of brochures, and sent him to a travel agent.' He paused and lit a second match. 'He was American.'

'CIA?'

'Not unless they're recruiting them younger than ever! He was some sort of student. Seems he saw the shingle downstairs, and came in for a look-see.'

'It must have made your day!'

Harry shrugged. 'It's best to be prepared. You never know what the day will bring. We could get a surprise visit from Head Office. They're not likely to give us any warning. One of these days, we could be sitting here when Tricky Dicky walks in.'

Mark laughed. 'Richard Nixon?'

'No.' Harry waved away the thought, clearing pipe smoke. 'Richard Hyatt, the Director General. There's more than one Tricky Dick, I can tell you.'

'I've never heard him called that.'

'Ah, that's because you haven't been around as long as I have.' Harry looked knowing.

'Why tricky?'

'Because he was always a bit smarter than the rest, and a bit quicker off the mark. That's why he's where he is, at the top of the flagpole.'

The image amused Mark. *'Guinness Book of Records?'*

'Come again?'

'Nothing. I've never met Hyatt. My work doesn't go beyond that little shit Willis.'

Harry looked offended again. He believed in absolute loyalty among the rank and file. 'That's because you're still a field man. You'd need a spell at Head Office before you meet the high-ups.'

'How do you come to know him?'

'Various places. I haven't been here all my career, you know. I've had a few postings myself.' He leaned back in his chair, so that his shoulders touched the wall. It was a familiar pose, and there was a greasy patch on the imitation cloth wallpaper to mark the spot. 'I first met Dick Hyatt in Berlin, just after they put up the wall. He was a field man himself in those days, and asked me to show him around.' The memory pleased him.

'Really?'

'Yes. Dick Hyatt worked his way up the ladder, with his own initiative, unlike some of those Whitehall wizards who get to the top with business lunches and contacts in all the right clubs.' These was a trace of bitterness in Harry's voice. 'He was one of us, and he did it the hard way. I dare say they would like to have kept him in the field for a few more years, but he was too smart for that.'

'Tricky?'

'Not really. It was more of a nickname than a criticism. He was good in the field, but he always made sure he kept in touch with the right people at Head Office.' Harry's voice was wistful. 'He was going places, all right. They sent him off round the Commonwealth for a while, making sure all the outposts of Empire were running shipshape. That was the start of it, really. He was seconded to half a dozen different security organizations. You can imagine, there was a bit of jealousy among his contemporaries.'

'I suppose so.' Mark wondered whether Harry had been one of them.

'After that, he was attached to the Americans for quite a long time. He acted as a liaison man between us and them. He did Washington for three years.'

'You seem to know a lot about him.'

'It was all in his bio when he was made DG. Don't you read the circulars?'

'Not often. I usually look at the top line, and skip the rest if it doesn't affect me.'

'You ought to keep abreast of what's going on, lad. It could affect your own future, too.'

Mark thought, What happened to yours, Harry?, but remained silent.

Harry tapped out the remains of his tobacco. 'It was quite a shock when he was appointed, I can tell you.'

'Why?'

'Because there were plenty of old boys in the old boys' brigade who thought they should have got there first. He was much younger than most of them, but he outsmarted them.'

'Tricky Dicky?'

'That's about it, and he's held on ever since. Done a good job, too.'

'Perhaps.'

'What does that mean?'

'Maybe he should take a look at one or two of the people running desks for him at the moment; Willis, for instance.'

'H.W.? He's supposed to be good. Brilliant, I've heard him called.'

'Not by me.' Mark's voice was hard.

Harry shook his head. 'It doesn't do you any good to talk like that, Mark. You'll never get on if you do.'

'I'm not looking to. I want to get off.'

'It's just a phase, lad – lull before the storm, and all that sort of thing. H.W.'s one of the best.'

'I think he's got a screw loose.'

'Go on!'

'You seem to forget that I work for him, Harry.' Price looked sceptical. 'I was in Austria before they shipped me here. You want to know what my last job was, Harry?' When the other man did not reply, Mark continued, 'I was there to make sure that one of our own men was nabbed by the Czechs, and taken back to Prague. Our own man, Harry. It was Willis's plan. They saved me the trouble, and got him before I could.' For a moment, Mark remembered the man running across open ground towards the frontier, and the sudden, shattering sound of rifle fire as the border guards picked him off. 'I was supposed to . . .'

Harry raised a large hand, its fingers tobacco-stained. 'I don't want to know, lad. You've read regulations, haven't you? That's restricted information.' His voice softened. 'I must say, I wondered why they shipped you over here.'

'Well, now you know, more or less. I told Willis I wanted out, but he asked me to think it over and sent me here to dry out.' He glanced towards the windows. 'Dry out! It's been pissing with rain ever since I got here!'

'April's a wet month.'

'Don't tell me. I'm supposed to sit around here, cooling my heels and thinking about my future. I told Willis I'd decide by the end of the month. If it goes on like this, I'm packing it in.'

'Sounds a bit drastic. Why don't you think it over?'

'What the fuck do you think I'm doing?' Harry looked wounded. 'I told him I wanted some time off, but he's too bloody chintzy to give me any, unless I want to use up my holidays.' He sat at the desk. 'Which is why they've packed me away here, to fill in a bunch of useless bloody reports!' Mark scattered papers across the surface.

'What would you do?'

'I don't know. I'm not trained for anything very useful, am I? There's got to be something else.'

Harry tapped his pipe against a heavy glass ashtray. 'I could see you'd been under a bit of a strain . . .'

'Not half as much as sitting around here, doing nothing.'

'You should relax a bit; let yourself go. You might as well enjoy your stay. Hamburg's not so bad. Who knows what you'll be doing next?'

'That's what worries me. Let's face it, Harry. There's not a lot to do in this dump. I'd go more often to the opera, but with prices like theirs and a salary like mine, I can't afford to.'

'I noticed you'd been to the opera house.' Harry grimaced. 'I can't imagine what you see in that: a bunch of old bags, caterwauling at each other! I wouldn't have thought it was your kind of thing.' Although he read all the monthly brochures assiduously, Harry thoroughly disapproved of the arts, secretly convinced that they were an extension of the perverted tastes of sexual deviants in what he regarded as 'the upper classes'. He glowered. 'Load of rubbish!'

'It's about the only thing that keeps me sane.'

'There's plenty of entertainment, especially for a good-looking young fellow like you. Find yourself a nice young Fräulein . . .'

'I've got a nice young Fräulein, Harry, but she lives in London.' He grinned crookedly. 'Well, to pass the time . . .'

'No, thanks!' Harry's current companion was an ageing bar-girl from one of the many clipjoints on the Reeperbahn, who had been demoted to serving drinks and working behind the bar while her younger colleagues tempted the clientèle. They had spent a disastrous Saturday evening together shortly after his arrival, when Ilse had shown up with a friend for Mark: a blowsy companion to make up an alcoholic foursome. He had gone home early, leaving Harry, giggling drunk, promising to accommodate them both. He had never mentioned it again.

Harry sighed philosophically. 'Well, I don't know what to tell you, lad. It's a shame to give it all up. Good jobs are hard to find . . .'

'You call this one good?'

'It has its compensations. I'm not complaining.' He looked at his watch. 'My God, look at the time! I should be having my lunch. If I don't watch my routine, my stomach gets all upset. You want to come for a bite?'

Mark returned to his papers. Harry's 'bite' was usually liquid, in one of the seedier bars in the neighbourhood. The invitation was a formality, and neither wanted the other's company. 'I'd better finish my report. The rain might clear later.'

'As you like.' Harry peered out of the window. 'It looks better than earlier. If you do go out before I'm back, remember to switch off the lights. London sent me a rocket about the last electricity bill.'

When the phone rang, it took Mark by surprise. He could not remember receiving an outside call since his arrival, and as Harry had forbidden any outgoing calls unless they were local, he had almost forgotten the existence of the instrument.

'British Arts.'

'To whom am I speaking?' The voice was crisp and authoritative.

'Mark Holland.' For a moment, he wondered whether the caller expected him to add: 'Sir'. The hell with that! 'Who are you?'

'Richard Hyatt.' There was a slight edge to his voice. 'I trust the name rings a bell somewhere?'

'Yes.' Poor Harry! He would be mortified when he heard about it. Screw Harry! Mark grinned suddenly. What the hell! 'In fact, if you listen carefully, you'll hear my heels clicking together.' As an afterthought, he added, 'Sir.'

The caller was silent for a moment. Then Mark heard a low chuckle. 'You know, I have the feeling I asked for that! Are you alone in the office at the moment?'

'Yes. You just missed Harry Price. He went out to lunch. Did you want to speak to him?'

'Not really, although it's always nice to catch up on old times. We go back a long way.'

'He told me.'

Hyatt offered no further comment.

'Is there anything I can do?'

'Yes, I think there is.' He paused. 'I'm in Hamburg at the moment, at the Vier Jahreszeiten.'

'That's just around the corner from here. Would you like me to come over?'

'No.' He paused again. 'I don't think that would be a good idea. I wonder, can you take a little time away from the office this afternoon? It might be better if we discuss the matter in absolute privacy.'

'Yes, of course.' It seemed an odd inquiry for the Director General of the Department to make. Officially, Mark was still on active duty. For a moment, he remembered Harry's comments about his clothing, and wondered whether he would have time to change. On the other hand, why the hell should he care? 'Where would you like me to be?'

'As a matter of fact, I've borrowed a house from a friend of

42

mine. It's on Reichskanzlerstrasse. That's out in the Hochkamp district. Do you know where I mean?'

'Yes.' It was one of the wealthier suburbs of the city, a fifteen-minute train ride from the centre.

'Why don't we make it there, at three o'clock, then?' His voice had warmed considerably, as though they were arranging lunch at one of Harry's despised clubs. 'I'd take the S-Bahn out, if I were you. You'll find the street is right next to the Hochkamp stop.'

'All right.' Mark glanced at his watch. There was plenty of time to change after all. It irritated him that he cared.

Hyatt gave the number of the house. 'I imagine I'll be there well before you arrive. You'll find the front door is on a little path along the side of the house. You can't miss it. The number's on the gate.'

'Right.' Mark had the impression that Hyatt wanted to say something further, but the man remained silent. He was about to hang up, when Hyatt spoke again.

'Listen, I'd be grateful if you'd keep all this to yourself.' He spoke mildly, but the instruction was implicit.

'As you wish.'

'Good man.' He seemed embarrassed. 'It doesn't really affect old Harry, as you'll see, so there doesn't seem much point in bringing him in on it, does there?'

'I suppose not.' Why was Hyatt asking his opinion?

'Good old Harry! How's he getting along these days? I haven't seen him for a long time.'

'Very well.'

'He must be due to retire quite soon.'

'Yes. I believe he has a couple of years to go.'

'Really? One forgets how the time goes by. He was very helpful to me at one time, you know. He showed me the ropes in Berlin when I first got there.'

'Yes, he mentioned it.'

'Anyway, I think you'll understand my reasoning for leaving him out of this, once we've had a chance to talk. I understand you were in Austria and . . . that part of the world recently?'

'Yes.' Mark could feel himself growing tense.

Hyatt's voice remained friendly. 'I'd like to hear about it if there's time. It's a part of the world I used to know rather well.'

'I'll be happy to tell you what happened.'

'Good. We'll try to make a point of it. I'm looking forward to meeting you, Mr Holland. I've heard quite a lot about you.' Mark said nothing. 'Three o'clock, then?'

'Yes.'

Hyatt paused again, then gave a low laugh. 'And please don't bother to click your heels. You may very well find yourself back on active duty again, but there's really no need to get carried away!'

The line went dead.

# 4

Harry –

I may not be in for a few hours this afternoon. I have a couple of personal errands, and if the rain clears, I'll go down to the docks.

Cheers, Mark.

As an afterthought, he added a postscript:

H – Thanks for the talk this morning. It helped.

He wondered why he should bother to seek his colleague's approval. Perhaps it was the perverse pleasure of misleading the man. The frustrations of working for the Department brought out the worst in him.

It was hard to explain why the prospect of meeting Hyatt lightened Mark's mood. He indulged in the luxury of a taxi home, to change into a blazer and slacks, and selected the shirt and tie carefully. Examining himself in the mirror, he scowled. 'You crawler! Under the surface, you're as eager to please as that idiot Harry!' He removed the tie, leaving the shirt casually unbuttoned at the collar.

The Hochkamp stop on the S-Bahn reminded him of one of those smaller stations serving the wealthier suburbs of New York and Long Island: a leafy platform, swept clean and hidden among trees and bushes, carefully located so that the noise of trains would not disturb the pleasant retreats provided by large houses and substantial gardens. But then, so much of contemporary

Germany reminded him of the Eastern United States, from the well planned suburbs to the new, characterless glass and concrete cities. Perhaps the Americans had left it as a legacy of their presence in the war, or perhaps it was just that they had both enjoyed a building boom during the same era. The rebuilt centre of Frankfurt was similar to any number of 'downtown' areas in Pennsylvania or Ohio. They were depressingly uniform.

He was the only passenger to alight, and descended steps to a quiet road hemmed in by tall trees and thick bushes that marked garden boundaries and hid the houses from inquisitive passers-by. It gave the impression of being rural, but the setting was slightly artificial: the hedges too carefully trimmed and the trees placed at intervals that were too regular. It was very pleasant, but not quite the countryside, and he knew that, nearby, there was an American-style highway, with roadside shops and services. He walked up a slight incline beneath dripping branches that were shedding the last of the rainfall. No cars passed, and the empty road, its grass verges neatly trimmed, was deserted. Somewhere behind one of the hedges, he heard a dog barking and, looking over a wrought-iron gate, he saw a large square-cut house dating from around the turn of the century. He had expected to find a building from a later, post-war date. Presumably, the suburb was far enough from the centre of Hamburg to have escaped the constant bombings. Mark walked slowly, checking his watch. He was irritated with himself for being punctual. It was as though the Department was still manipulating him. For a moment, he debated whether to walk on, killing time, but the gesture seemed pointless. He was already at the gate of the house he wanted.

Richard Hyatt opened the door almost immediately, and Mark suspected that he had probably watched his approach along the gravel path at the side of the house. He was shorter than Mark had anticipated, with broad shoulders tapering to a narrow waist. He had a young man's face, rugged rather than handsome, with iron-grey hair that would have been curly had it not been cut short and parted, then combed close to his head. His three-piece suit was discreetly Savile Row.

'Hello. I'm Hyatt.' His grip was firm. He glanced at a heavy grandfather clock, its pendulum swinging majestically, and nodded approvingly. 'I'll lead the way, shall I?' Hyatt spoke with the deference of a man in command who knows that he will be obeyed, and moved away swiftly, leaning slightly forward, without bothering to see if Mark would follow.

They passed through an airy living room, furnished in pale colours. The modern white chairs and sofa formed solid blocks on the ivory carpeting. Standing under a special artificial light, there was a superb indoor bonsai tree, trained in the *moyogi* style. It looked like a species of fig, and from the colour and markings on the bark, it was probably forty or fifty years old. Hyatt had stopped by some French windows leading into the garden, and followed the direction of Mark's eyes.

'You like those things?'

'Very much. I've always promised to buy myself one, when I can afford it.'

Hyatt shrugged. 'I suppose they're beautiful, but a little unnatural. I don't think I'd have the patience for all that pruning and training.' The subject was dismissed. 'Shall we walk in the garden? It's less . . . confined.' When he smiled, his face was charming. 'You're probably too young to remember all those wartime posters about walls having ears.' He did not wait for Mark's reply, and stepped through the doorway onto a small patio overlooking a broad expanse of grass, bordered by a distant hedge of tall, impenetrable firs. It had a curiously empty look. There were no flower beds or flowers, and Mark suspected that the owner spent little time in it. Either that, or he disliked gardening.

Hyatt stood with his hands locked behind his back, inhaling deeply, like a proud landowner surveying his property. 'Thank God that bloody rain stopped. I was beginning to wonder whether it ever would!'

Mark nodded silently, standing next to him. Why did the English always feel it was necessary to open a conversation by talking about the weather?

When he turned to Mark, Hyatt's stare was unblinking. 'You were highly recommended to me by an old friend of yours: Ernie Sullivan. He said you were good.' He smiled again. 'I think his words were to the effect that you were the best!' His tone was slightly bantering.

'That was kind of him. I haven't seen Ernie for a long time.' Mark had worked with Ernie for several months when the CIA man had been based in London. 'How is he?'

'Well enough.' Hyatt offered no further information. There

was a cinder path by the edge of the lawn, and he stepped onto it, waiting for Mark to join him. 'I understand you just came back from a tour of duty in . . . Austria?'

'Near enough.'

'Yes.' He paused for a moment, staring towards the distant trees. 'I had a chat with Willis about it. From what he said, the whole operation was a rather convoluted business, wasn't it?'

'Yes.' In his mind, Mark saw the dead man, lying face-down on the frost-covered ground, and the two Czech guards, their rifles slung, stooping to drag him by the heels towards their jeep. At the time, he had wanted to open fire. It would have been easy to finish both of them before they had time to take cover, but that would have spoiled Willis's plan.

'Well –' Hyatt resumed walking – 'that's another matter. I suggested that we might try something a little subtler in the future. It seemed an unnecessary waste of manpower, but it's too late to do anything about that now.' Once again, Mark had the impression that the subject was closed to Hyatt's satisfaction, and that he would not expect it to be raised again. He had kept his promise to discuss it. After a silence, he looked again at Mark. 'Tell me, do you know anything about electronics or computers?'

'No.' His laugh felt gruff. 'Virtually nothing.'

'Neither do I.' Once again, the charming smile. 'I'm assured it's the thing to know about from now on. Frankly, I don't understand how computers work, although a lot of people have gone to some lengths to explain them to me. I'm inclined to get lost as soon as they start shooting out words like Pascal and binary at me. Mathematics wasn't my subject.'

'Nor mine.'

'It's not important.' Hyatt reached into his pocket for a silver cigarette case. He seemed to select a cigarette with care, tapping it briskly against the side of the case, and gave a wry smile. 'My doctor's forbidden me these things, but I think he knows he's wasting his time.' The smile became forced. 'If you listened to doctors all the time, you'd never get out of bed in the morning.' He lit the cigarette, and coughed as soon as he inhaled, turning his body away from Mark and making an effort to control the spasms. Eventually, he straightened, and with a grimace threw the cigarette away. 'Silly, isn't it, the way we punish ourselves? I might just as well obey the man, for all the pleasure the damn things give me!'

Mark said nothing. Hyatt's face had coloured unhealthily, and his eyes seemed more shadowed than before.

The Director General sighed. 'Listen, you can smoke if you want to. Perhaps it will make me feel more virtuous if you do and I don't. Bloody doctors! If you want to know the truth, I faked my last medical, on condition that I promised to be a good boy and take things easy.' He eyed Mark. 'We all have problems of one sort or another.'

Mark nodded. It appeared that Hyatt was taking time out for a small departmental pep talk.

'Where were we?' His manner became brisk again. 'Oh yes; computers. I was asking you whether you knew anything about them, and you don't.' He smiled.

'Something like that.'

'It's not important. Actually, I'm not so interested in the instruments themselves as the technology that goes into them. If I have the right jargon, it's what the Americans call the spin-off that interests me, like all those non-stick cooking pots that came out of developing space vehicles.' He grinned. 'It's a hell of an expensive way to improve kitchen utensils, isn't it?'

'I suppose so.' Mark had to admit there was something charming about the man. He had the trick of appearing to take one into his confidence. It was easy to understand how he had earned his sobriquet.

'We started putting computers into general use long before most other countries, you know. They're amazing machines. I visited a place last week, with an enormous great monster clicking away, living in its own specially air-conditioned room behind glass walls. It seems they're very sensitive to dust or changes of temperature. They're as demanding as prima donnas!' He stared at the distant pine trees. 'Britain's often first in the field. Not bad for a handful of small islands off the coast of Europe that are supposed to be nothing more than a second-class power. You'd have thought our American friends would have wanted to be in front.'

'They usually are.'

'Not really. I'm always astonished by how long they take to adapt to change. Look at telex machines. Here we are in the mid 'seventies, and we've got them installed in every highstreet bank and office, while the Yanks are still time-sharing and using cables. You'd be amazed at how conservative they are, despite the big talk. They'll catch up and surpass us in a couple of years, I'm sure, but they're a long way behind at the moment. Give them time, and they'll have it all.'

'Bigger and better?'

'That's it.' Hyatt took out his cigarette case again, then with a quick shake of the head, returned it to his pocket. 'Actually, it's smaller and more efficient that interests me.'

'In what way?'

'In a few years' time, all those enormous great temperamental machines will be replaced by tiny ones that will run twice as effectively and do ten times – a hundred times – the work, or so I'm told. Apparently, it's all a matter of printed circuits and microchips. Given time, they'll be putting something the size of a wardrobe into a box no bigger than a portable typewriter and weighing a few ounces. God knows how it's done. I sometimes wish I'd taken science instead of languages when I was at Cambridge. I feel like something out of the Dark Ages when the boffins start talking.'

'I'm afraid I'm no better off. I can just about understand how my transistor radio works, but that's the extent of my knowledge. The Japanese seem to be the experts.'

Hyatt stopped walking. 'Funnily enough, they're not. I must admit I always thought they were, but it seems we're both wrong.'

'Really?'

'Oh, they're good at it, all right, but only when it comes to putting things to practical use. They've got the labour force, and they're incredibly nimble when it comes to miniaturization: all those little Japanese ladies peering through magnifying glasses all day! The research and the invention comes from elsewhere – Europe, mostly.' He walked on.

'I didn't know.' Mark followed Hyatt along the path. It seemed an odd conversation to be holding with a Director General, but it was preferable to a damp tour of Hamburg's dockland.

Hyatt glanced at him. 'Philips research in Holland, Siemens in Germany, English Electric – they're all working on it. So are the Americans, of course. That's how they got themselves on the moon. Basically it's always the same principle: how to make it smaller, lighter, more energy-efficient. You don't have to have too much imagination to see how the technology could be adapted to other uses.'

'And presumably Eastern Europe's doing the same?'

Hyatt smiled. 'You can count on it! They're pretty good, too, but it's a matter of brute force and unlimited numbers in their case. God knows how many failures they've had on the way. When it comes to computer technology, they're curiously lagging, which is why they're so interested in what's being developed on this side of the fence. They're monitoring just about everything they can learn about, and they're prepared to spend a hell of a lot of cash to get their hands on the information they need.' He hesitated, lowering his voice slightly. 'It's one of the things that has kept me on the move for the past few years.'

'Harry mentioned that you had travelled a great deal.'

Hyatt nodded sombrely. 'Someone has to handle the co-ordination. The left hand doesn't always know what the right hand is doing. Before I took up my present job, I had the feeling I was living on a plane . . .' He stopped walking. 'Which is one of the reasons why I suggested this meeting.' He turned to face Mark. 'I understand you're thinking of packing it in.'

'Yes.'

'Why?'

Mark shrugged. 'You appear to know what happened last month on the Austrian border. I'm not prepared to take on another assignment like that.'

'It was clumsy, I agree.'

'It wasn't clumsy; it was cold-blooded murder.' Mark could feel the old anger rising to the surface. 'And for what: a few weeks of misdirection? A couple of points to us? No, not any more!'

'All right.' Hyatt's voice was hard. 'I've already told you that Willis has been cautioned. It was an ill-conceived plan. What are you asking for: written guarantees? I'm not prepared to discuss policy every time an operation is mounted.'

'I'm not suggesting you do. I'm simply saying that, as far as I'm concerned, I don't want any further part of it.'

There was a long silence. A few drops of rain fell, heralding another shower. They seemed to distract Hyatt, who looked up with a frown, then turned back towards the house. At length, he smiled. 'This conversation isn't going quite the way it was planned. I was supposed to be offering a few kindly words of fatherly advice, coupled with a mild rocket for being out of line, but I'm a bit late for that, aren't I?' He sighed. 'All right, if I give you my word that Willis has been instructed to back off, and that

I'm to be personally informed before he undertakes any new operations, does that satisfy you?' His voice was impatient.

'I suppose so.'

'Good. You'll be posted back to London at the end of the month, to resume normal duties. I assume you'd rather be there?'

'Yes.' Despite himself, Mark smiled. 'Hamburg's something of a dead end.'

'I hope so; otherwise, it isn't serving its purpose. Frankly, I sometimes wonder why we keep the office open, unless it's to give poor old Harry somewhere to put his feet up until he goes.' Hyatt stared at the gathering clouds. 'We'd better go back inside, walls or no walls. I'm damned if I'm going to get soaked for the sake of unnecessary security.'

In the living-room, sprawled on the sofa, Hyatt finally lit a cigarette, drawing on it carefully. He did not cough. 'That's better. Not being allowed to smoke doesn't do much for my temper!' For a moment, he appeared preoccupied. 'It's odd, really. You never think about your health until it starts to play tricks on you.' He looked up. 'I don't suppose that's a problem for you?'

'No.'

'Be thankful for small mercies.'

Mark sat on the arm of one of the heavy chairs. 'Do I really need to wait out the month before I go back to London?'

'What's the matter: Harry's awful pipe smoke getting to you, or is it that endless stream of folksy maxims?'

'Both and neither. I hate the idea of doing nothing. It feels like a waste of time.'

Hyatt nodded. 'That's one of the reasons I suggested this meeting, but I wanted to be sure you wouldn't walk out on us. I take it I can assume that's settled?'

'For the moment, yes.'

'Don't do me any favours, for God's sake! The Department will survive with or without you. You're not the first man to have pangs of conscience, damn it!'

'I know, but . . .'

'But nothing! I've given my word that Willis and his desk will be answerable to me from now on. If that isn't enough, you'd better go.'

'It's enough.'

'Good.' Hyatt stubbed out the cigarette and paced across the room, pausing by the bonsai to examine it. When he turned to face Mark, his smile had returned. 'I have the feeling you can be as bloody-minded as I am, if you try. Perhaps that's why Ernie Sullivan likes you.' When Mark did not reply, he continued, 'The reason for my little lecture on computer technology is that it seems there's already been something of a breakthrough.'

'Here in Germany?'

Hyatt shook his head. 'Believe it or not, in Italy. As I said earlier, everyone's in the same race. There's a small electronics firm in Milan, called Marini, or Marelli, or something like that. It doesn't really matter. They're employed as consultants by all sorts of clients – anything from washing-machine manufacturers to car designers – to improve on the electronic components they use. I'd never realized there was so much gadgetry being built into modern machinery. It hardly seems to justify the expense, does it?' He returned to the sofa.

'Have you spoken to them?'

'No, not exactly.' Hyatt stared at his well manicured hands for a moment. 'The man in charge of their research is a certain Doctor Franco Stratta. He's been in touch with us, in a rather roundabout way.' Mark looked puzzled, and Hyatt grinned. 'In addition to being a very able scientist, Dr Stratta's no fool. He realizes he's come up with something very valuable, worth much more than his annual salary, and he's putting his discovery up for sale on the open market to the highest bidder.'

'How about his employers?'

'They know about his work, and they're very excited. Needless to say, they believe they're going to benefit enormously from it, but they don't realize that the good Doctor has a few commercial plans of his own.'

'Why not warn the company, and make a deal?'

Hyatt shook his head. 'Easier said than done. Stratta's cagey. He hasn't told them how far he's progressed. We probably know more about it than they do. Our only problem is to get there first, before the competition, which now includes a couple of interested buyers from the Kremlin.'

'But surely that can be prevented.'

'Perhaps. Dr Stratta's smart. He's interested in hard cash, and he doesn't really care where it comes from. The main thing we have going for us is that he feels safer negotiating with London. We have easier access to hard currency.'

'Who else is in the market?'

Hyatt shrugged. 'Just about everyone: the Americans and the Japanese for starters, and there could be others. I want to get there first.'

Mark hesitated momentarily. 'If it's not too indiscreet a question, why? Why not bring the Americans in, too, and buy him out?'

Hyatt frowned. 'Several reasons. The first is that they don't always share all their information. The "special relationship" is inclined to be a one-way affair a lot of the time. Besides, if we're going to buy their hardware at a later stage, we could probably reduce the price considerably if we add the final ingredient. I have other reasons.'

In the silence that followed, Mark thought he could hear the steady ticking of the clock in the hall. 'What do you want me to do?'

'Not very much, and I think you'll find it a pleasant change, since it will take you out of Hamburg.' He leaned forward. 'Do you know the Ticino area of southern Switzerland?'

'No.'

'It's a nice part of the world, very Italian in flavour, although most of the residents seem to be retired German industrialists nowadays. They're the only ones who can afford to live there! I've arranged for Dr Stratta to meet you next Sunday in a little village called Camedo, on the Italian border, up in the mountains above Lake Maggiore. You'll be taking him a down payment in cash, and he'll hand you the papers. Provided we're satisfied with what he gives us, we'll pay the rest in to a bank in Lugano for him. It's a simple sort of transaction.' He looked at Mark closely. 'Why are you smiling?'

'It sounds as though all the arrangements have already been made. You must have been very certain I would agree to stay on.'

Hyatt's face was expressionless. 'Not entirely, and arrangements can always be altered. If necessary, I'm prepared to look after it myself, but there are other matters to settle. Nobody's indispensable.' He became businesslike. 'The meeting's arranged for next Sunday at two o'clock. There's a little café with a terrace overlooking the valley. You can't miss it; it's the only one in the village. You're to wait there for him.'

'Where will he be coming from?'

Hyatt seemed to relax. 'Milan. He'll drive up from Domodossola and cross the border just before he reaches you. It's a very quiet road, and Stratta often goes that way, returning to the city along the lake road. He's an ardent Sunday driver.'

'Will he know me?'

Hyatt nodded. 'Close enough. I've given him a rough description of you, and as long as you're already waiting there, he'll find you. It's a pretty sleepy little place at the best of times.'

'All right. Today's Monday. When should I leave?'

'Thursday's soon enough. You can tell Harry you've decided to take a few days' holiday, but please don't tell him where you're going.'

'He'll want to know. Harry's a stickler for correct procedures.'

Hyatt brushed aside the comment impatiently. 'Make something up. Tell him you're going on walking trip and you'll call in. Use your imagination!'

'I'll think of something.'

'Good. As a matter of fact, I like the idea of a walking holiday. Take the train down to Locarno, and book yourself into a hotel there. There's a rather fancy one near the station.' He grinned. 'Don't worry, you're on expenses!'

'Why don't I drive?'

The question seemed to irritate the Director General. 'Because car registration numbers can be remembered, especially if they're foreign. I'd prefer you to be as anonymous as possible: just an ordinary English tourist on a walking holiday in the Centovalli.' He paused. 'Tell me, do you have a second passport?'

'Yes.' Mark felt himself colouring slightly. 'I keep it for emergencies.'

'Good. I'd like you to use it. What name?'

'Peter Williams.'

'I'll remember.'

Mark hesitated. 'I think I should mention that it's not an official departmental one. I organized it for myself a few years ago, in case . . .'

'I won't tell the Home Office about it! Actually, it suits my purpose very well. You see, I'd rather London didn't know about this trip for the moment. Understood?' Hyatt watched him. 'You don't look very sure.'

'I don't feel very sure. Why shouldn't London know?'

Hyatt was silent for a moment. 'I'm afraid you've caught me

out in an act of rather childish vanity.' He took out another cigarette, lighting it slowly. 'You see, it appears that my term of office is probably coming to an end quite shortly.' He stared at the glowing tip of the cigarette. 'When I told you that I faked my last medical, it was the truth, but I'm not fool enough to believe I can get away with it a second time. I'm also not conceited enough to believe I'm indestructible.' He paused. 'I have a private doctor at home, and I can't fake anything with him.'

'I see.'

'No, I doubt whether you do. Sooner or later, my resignation is going to be . . . unavoidable.' His face became expressionless again. 'I've no doubt that will be greeted with a certain amount of satisfaction in some quarters. Nobody really likes a golden boy!'

'I'm sorry.'

'Oh, please spare me your condolences. You've only just met me, so you have very little reason to feel one way or another. I'm sorry, but I'm rather touchy on the subject.' He was silent for a moment, and Mark watched him. 'I'm not complaining, and I've had a pretty good run for my money, everything considered, but I'd still like to pull this one off.'

'I think I can understand that.'

'I hope so. You're right, though. I do owe you an explanation for the secrecy. I don't really know how much longer I'll be running things, so this Stratta business will give me a great deal of pleasure. It's a little like holding the last trump in the pack when your opponents need the final trick.' He shook his head slowly. 'Moment of glory! There's really no need to look suitably sympathetic. When the time comes, I'm sure everyone's going to be embarrassingly solicitous and very kind, with perhaps a little mention in the Honours List – nothing too ostentatious! Frankly, I'd sooner go out with a bang than a gong, and I'm equally sure that Whitehall has a dozen replacement candidates lined up, so it's all a very minor kind of victory.' He smiled to himself. 'On the other hand, I may outlast them longer than they think.'

'Thank you for telling me.' Mark felt self-conscious. 'And I'm still sorry, even on short acquaintance.'

Hyatt nodded. 'In that case, it would be ungracious of me not to accept.' He looked at his watch. 'I'll have to leave soon. Before you go, I'll give you a money belt to hand over to Stratta. It contains fifty thousand dollars, so I'd be grateful if you'd look after it carefully. There's also an envelope to cover your expenses.

It's quite generous, and you won't be asked to fill in a report. Just don't draw any attention to yourself. The Swiss customs won't even give you a second glance unless they think you're smuggling drugs. They're quite accustomed to undeclared amounts of money.'

'I suppose so.'

'You're sure you're clear on the meeting? Two o'clock next Sunday, and be there first. There's only the one café, with a terrace jutting out over the hillside. If it's sunny, sit under one of the red umbrellas. The view's lovely.'

'What shall I do with Stratta's papers?'

'Bring them to me in London.' Hyatt stood. 'If you can't reach me, I suppose you could give them to –' He frowned. 'No. Don't worry. I'll be there. Just try not to make yourself conspicuous. You can fly from here to Zurich, but take the train from there. Remember, you're supposed to be on holiday. You can reach me at the office when you return. There's nothing very much to it, is there?'

'No.'

'Then I hope you enjoy yourself. The weather should be better than here, if nothing else.' He glanced across the room. 'You never know, if you watch your pocket-money carefully, there should be enough left over to buy yourself one of those fancy Japanese trees.'

Locarno, 1976

# 5

The view from the balcony of his bedroom was magnificent. Bright sunshine glittered on the gently rippling waters of Lake Maggiore, burning off the last of the morning's mist, and the crisp air felt fresh and clean. On the far side of the lake, with the sun behind them, the mountains were grey and shadowed, but the brilliant light picked out the white of solitary houses nestling within the folds of their slopes. In front of the lake, he could see terracotta roof-tops and the long spit of land that jutted out into the water. Directly below were the landscaped gardens of the hotel, ringed by a hedge which separated them from the town. Looking down, Mark watched an old gardener as he slowly wheeled a barrow across the carefully tended lawn. The Park Hotel's gardens occupied several valuable acres of real estate, preserving a dignified air of luxurious Swiss tranquillity. The gardener stooped for a moment at the edge of the grass, and a giant sprinkler came to life, throwing a fine spray of water in a steadily widening arc. Rays of sunlight created miniature rainbows in it. Mark stretched comfortably, enjoying the warmth. It seemed to cut through the pallor of Hamburg that clung to his skin.

He had arrived late the preceding afternoon, tired and uncomfortable in the unexpected heat of southern Switzerland. The journey had been pleasant enough, but he had been in no mood to be seduced by the prospect of a few days' vacation. At each point – the flight from Hamburg, the station in Zurich, changing trains at the small town of Bellinzona, where the main line branched off to Lugano and Como – he had mentally prepared himself to do battle with officialdom and to encounter problems, and when there were none, he had been left with a feeling of frustration, as though he had been cheated of the opportunity to vent his anger on some minor irritation of bureaucracy. Swiss efficiency had foiled him. Perhaps the prospect of yet another mission for the Department, no matter how simple Hyatt claimed it would be, had left his nerves on edge. When he had collected his suitcase at Kloten airport, the money-belt seemed to cut painfully into his waist, but there had not been a customs officer in sight.

He had hesitated on the platform of the station, debating whether to find a cheap *pensione* in the town or choose the expensive hotel. Hyatt's allowance was generous, more than enough to cover the four days of his visit, and the hotel won. As a compromise, he walked from the station, saving on the taxi fare. The uniformed doorman at the Park Hotel had seemed taken aback by his arrival on foot, and had run forward to the entrance gate to take possession of his luggage.

The place was almost empty. Easter was still two weeks away, and the first flood of tourists had not yet arrived. The Ticino district was too far north to attract the genuine sun-worshippers, and too far south for the last of the season's skiers. The young girl at the reception desk explained that he would be charged off-season rates for his double room overlooking the lake. In the evening, the large dining room had been occupied by a handful of guests: an elderly American couple, who asked for a detailed translation of the menu, two Swiss businessmen, who scarcely spoke; a dark-skinned Middle-Eastern man who read an Arab newspaper; an old Frenchwoman with a young companion who was either an employee or a granddaughter, and a young English couple who sat very close together, occasionally holding hands. Mark guessed that they were on their honeymoon. The dining room was designed to accommodate at least two hundred people, but there were more waiters than guests.

The balcony on which Mark was standing was part of a terrace which had been divided into separate sections, running the length of the floor. He was about to return inside to telephone for breakfast when the sound of music, much too loud, came from the adjoining balcony. It was the opening March from Stravinsky's *Histoire du Soldat*, and he could not resist the temptation to peer round the partition. The young Englishman whom he had seen the night before was seated at a table laid for breakfast. He was dressed in pyjamas and a very new-looking dressing-gown, and was fiddling with a portable tape-recorder. The sound was suddenly reduced.

Before Mark could retreat, the young man looked up. 'I'm awfully sorry. I hope I didn't disturb you.'

Mark smiled. 'I think I'm the one who should apologize. I don't think I'm supposed to peep round these partitions.'

'I'm afraid I was making a hell of a racket. I'm still sorting out how to work this thing, and must have pushed the wrong button.' He nodded towards the tape-recorder, which was now playing unobtrusively.

'Is it new?'

'Yes. Actually, it was a wedding present.' The man looked self-conscious. 'We're on our honeymoon.'

'Congratulations.' Stravinsky's tale of the Devil's efforts to steal a young soldier's violin-soul seemed an unusual choice for one's first days of wedded bliss.

'Thanks. We saw you having dinner last night, and I guessed you were English.' Mark nodded. 'It's a sort of game we've been playing. I hope you don't mind.' He had dark hair, cut rather long, which he tended to push aside with a nervous gesture. 'Are you on holiday?'

'Yes, just for a few days. I thought I'd do some walking.'

'Marvellous place, isn't it? I was here years ago with my parents, and always wanted to come back. I thought it would be a lovely choice for Jill . . .' He looked self-conscious again. 'My wife.'

'Yes.' For a moment, Mark thought about his girl in London. He should have telephoned her and invited her to join him. God knows what Hyatt would say to that!

'I'm so sorry about the noise I was making. I hope you don't mind music.'

'On the contrary. I suppose I was curious to see which of my fellow guests had a taste for Stravinsky.'

'Oh, you know it?'

'Yes. You picked the right country, but the wrong lake.'

'How's that?'

'Stravinsky wrote it in Switzerland, when he was living outside Lausanne on Lake Geneva.'

'I didn't know.' The young man stood up. 'My name's Taylor, by the way, John Taylor, but everyone calls me Jack.' He smiled.

'You can imagine all the jokes when I went and married a girl called Jill!' He walked forward.

Mark reached past the partition and shook his head. 'I'm Peter Williams.'

'Nice to meet you. Sorry about the din.'

At that moment, his young wife appeared in the doorway. She was dressed only in a translucent nightdress and, seeing Mark, quickly placed her hands over her breasts and backed away. Jack, apparently unaware of Jill's embarrassment, beckoned to her. 'Come and say hello to our neighbour, darling.' Her reply was muffled, and Jack grinned guiltily, whispering, 'I didn't notice!'

Mark said, 'Don't let me disturb you.'

'That's all right. We've done nothing but talk to each other for the past four days. It makes a change to hear another English voice. It's a long drive from London.'

'Really?'

Jack smiled. 'It is if you're in a Deux Chevaux. My poor old wreck starts complaining if I go anything over fifty. On a couple of the passes, I thought I was going to have to ask Jill to get out and push! Did you drive down?'

'No, I took the train.'

'Sensible man.' Jill reappeared, wearing a faded cotton dressing-gown. She was small and blonde, with fluffy hair. In the interim, she had dabbed pale pink lipstick on her mouth, but her face, devoid of make-up, was pasty. It was apparent to Mark that she did not enjoy being discovered in such a state of disrepair.

Jack placed a protective arm around her shoulders, urging her forward. 'This is Peter Williams, darling. He came for a few days of walking.' She nodded and smiled with an effort. 'I was just telling him what a lovely area this is.'

'We're a bit near the station.' Jill was not prepared to be mollified. 'They were shunting carriages at six o'clock this morning. It woke me up.'

'You were sleeping like a log when I got up.' Jack gave her shoulder an extra squeeze.

'That's because I was awake earlier.'

'Well, I didn't hear a thing. I was dead to the world all night.'

'You usually are!'

Mark raised his hand. 'Don't let me interrupt you. Your breakfast will get cold.'

Jack seemed eager to prolong the conversation. 'Perhaps we'll see you later?' Jill looked less enthusiastic.

'I expect so. I only arrived yesterday evening, so I'll spend the day looking round the town. I want to find a few good maps of the district.'

'I've got several. You can borrow them if you like.'

'Don't worry.' Jill was looking pointedly at the breakfast table.

'No trouble. I found mine at an excellent book shop on the main street. I'll show you where it is.'

Jill's voice was cool. 'I thought we were supposed to be driving over to Lugano today . . . darling. You said we'd need an early start, especially if there are any hills.'

'Oh, yes.' Jack looked hopefully at Mark. 'Have you been there?'

'Not yet. I'm looking forward to exploring Locarno today.'

'I suppose so.'

Jill's expression towards Mark softened. 'Jack wants to have a look at a model village, rather like the one at Bekonscot. It's a whole town of miniature houses, each one representing a famous Swiss building.' Her smile was forced. 'Jack loves that sort of thing, you know. It reminds him of his childhood.'

'I'm sure you'll both enjoy it. See you later.' Mark backed away to the safety of his balcony. From the tone of the voices behind the partition, it appeared that Jack and Jill were having their first marital disagreement.

Locarno was busier than he expected, after the peaceful isolation of the hotel. The main street was crowded with shoppers, mostly tourists, who filled the *pâtisseries* and souvenir establishments, comparing prices in several languages and currencies. Mark found the bookshop and stationer's recommended by Jack Taylor, and chose a good large-scale map of the district which indicated footpaths as well as major roads. The road from Locarno to Camedo was bigger than Hyatt had suggested, but there were a number of parallel paths which made him wonder whether the ever-efficient Swiss had replaced the old thoroughfare through the hills with a modern highway.

While he was making his purchase, he noticed the Middle-Easterner from the hotel, who was inspecting a newspaper stand by the door of the shop. It was filled with journals from around the world. The majority of them were German – no doubt to satisfy the needs of the émigré population – along with the ever-present *International Herald Tribune*, but there were several printed in Arabic. His eyes met the other man's, and he nodded slightly in recognition before continuing his selection. He assumed the man must be an Arab from his choice of reading, although apart from his dark complexion, it was impossible to tell where he came from. He was dressed in a lightweight tan-coloured suit, with an open-necked shirt. Mark wondered for a moment what an Arab would be doing in a small Swiss town like Locarno, but ever since the oil crisis a few years earlier they had appeared, almost overnight, in every part of Europe. He remembered how the sky-rocketing house prices in London bore witness to their presence, and it was more than likely that they had had the same effect on every other country.

It was pleasantly warm, and he strolled through the town towards the broad strip of land that jutted into the lake. There was a park, planted with flower beds, and beyond it, hidden amid trees, a camping area. He was surprised by the number of cars and caravans already installed. Some of the hardier settlers and their children were even wading in the cold waters of the lake, which was filled at that time of the year by rushing streams swollen with melting snow from the mountain tops. There was a narrow ribbon of discoloured sand by the water, occupied by those who were hoping to develop the first suntan of the season. In an open space behind the trees, a gang of men in overalls was erecting a large marquee with a gaudy sign. As Mark passed, a small English child, half running to keep pace with his mother, was tugging her sleeve.

'Can we go to the dolphin show?'

'It hasn't opened yet. They're still putting up the tent.' She glanced at her husband for support, but he pretended not to hear.

'When they have, can we? Please!'

'We'll have to see. We may have left by then.'

'Can't we stay? I've never seen a real, live dolphin.'

'We'll see. You've already spent all your pocket money. It may be very expensive.' The last remark was directed towards her husband, who shrugged silently and lengthened his stride.

Mark turned back towards the ornamental park. The camp site stretched a long way, spoiling the scenery, but at least the Swiss had the good sense to hide it under the trees. There were whole bays on the Somerset coast, once deserted and beautiful, that now looked like gypsy camps. He found a sunny bench overlooking the water, and sat for a while, studying the map. It was difficult to estimate the exact distance from Locarno to Camedo, but a rough guess made it fourteen miles – about a four-hour walk. There was also a *Schmalspurbahn*, which he guessed to be a branch line, between Locarno and Domodossola, and he made a mental note to check the train times on a Sunday, in case the weather changed. Despite Hyatt's instructions, there was little point in trudging through the rain, especially if he was supposed to remain inconspicuous. Once Stratta had made the exchange, he would take the next train back. Perhaps Hyatt was right. It all looked simple enough, and the exercise was a pleasant alternative to the drab routine of Hamburg.

'Do you mind if I share your bench?' The voice startled him. It was the Arab again, and he had not heard the man approach. 'It is such a sunny day.'

'No, of course not. Help yourself.'

'Thank you.' The man was now wearing heavy sunglasses which masked his eyes, so that Mark could not be sure whether he was looking directly at him. He turned his face towards the lake, which reflected the dark blue of the sky. The breeze had lightened, and the surface of the water was mirror-calm. 'It is very beautiful, Switzerland.' He glanced towards the open map that Mark had been reading. 'You are on vacation?' His voice was slightly sibilant, and his accent was pronounced.

'Yes. I hope to do a little walking.'

'Ah, that is something I do not know very much about. In my country, it is too hot to walk, and there is very little to see except sand.'

'Where are you from?'

'Oman.'

'And are you also on holiday?'

'No.' He hesitated. 'Not really. I come to Switzerland from time to time. My company has a number of investments . . .' He did not finish the sentence, and settled himself more comfortably on the bench, facing the bay.

'I'm only here for a few days.' Mark lit a cigarette. 'I'd like to explore the district.'

'Where will you walk?'

'I don't know. Anywhere, I suppose. I should have asked if the shop had any local guides. I'll probably try Ascona, and walk on to Ronco and Brissago along the lake road. It should be pretty.'

'Ah, you may be a little disappointed. I have driven along that road, all the way down to Pallanza and Stresa in Italy. The lake side is completely taken up by villas and apartment buildings. You rarely see the water.'

'That's a pity.'

'It is understandable. The property overlooking the water is very valuable. Perhaps you should try the mountains.'

'I may do.' Mark smiled. 'It will all be new to me, but I don't plan anything too strenuous.'

'I am told the Centovalli is most charming. There is a road that runs through the mountains to the Italian border.'

Mark looked at the man, but his expression had not changed. He kept his voice casual. 'I noticed it on the map.'

'You may find that it is more interesting.'

'You could be right.'

'My company is considering some property there, depending upon the price.' He turned to face Mark, but seemed to hesitate before speaking again. 'The land is attractive, and because it is in the hills, it is less expensive. I will go there myself in the next day or two.' Behind the dark glasses, Mark could not see the expression in his eyes, but there was a faint smile on his lips. 'I will be driving a car. I do not have the time or the energy to walk!'

'I suppose not.' Mark looked at his watch. 'I think I must be on my way.'

'Yes. Perhaps we shall meet again at the hotel?'

'I expect so. It's not very busy.'

'No. I prefer that. It is so much easier to negotiate without being disturbed.'

'It must be.' Mark rose from the bench, and the Arab opened his newspaper.

He walked slowly back to the hotel, glancing over his shoulders when he reached the edge of the park. The Arab appeared to be deeply engrossed in his paper. Mark frowned. Hyatt had suggested that Stratta had been approached by other interested buyers. Why not from the Arab world? In which case, was this man one of them? It was hard to tell. His reference to the Centovalli was very direct. There was a hint of warning in his voice, or was he simply choosing his words carefully because of the language? He shook off the thought. Fourteen miles was a long way, and the mountain road was an obvious alternative to the lake shore.

At the hotel, he called Harry Price.

'Mark! I'm glad you called. I was just wondering how I was going to find you. I said you shouldn't go off like that, without a contact number.' He sounded anxious.

'What's the problem?'

'You know you should make yourself available at all times, even on holidays.'

'Yes, I know, but it's not always possible. What's up?'

'It's London. They've been on the blower, asking for you. They were very upset when I couldn't tell them where you were. You know the drill.'

'For God's sake, Harry! I'm entitled to a few days to myself. They don't own me! I told you I'd call in.'

'I know, lad, but you're still supposed to be reachable at all times.'

'Not when I'm on holiday! Anyway, I'm walking from place to place, so there's no way to reach me. I don't know where I'm going to be until I get there.'

'Where are you, then?'

Mark thought quickly. 'Salzburg, but only for the day. It's much too expensive for me! I'm going to move on before the evening and find somewhere on the road. What does London want?'

'You, from what they said. It looks like the old prodigal son treatment. They want you back in London by the end of the month, so all's forgiven and forgotten.'

'Not by me!' It appeared that Hyatt had kept his word. 'Anyway, it's good news. When do I leave?'

'End of the month, as far as I could tell.' Harry sounded resentful. 'I got a right bollocking for not knowing where you were. You could have picked a better time to disappear!'

'I haven't disappeared, Harry. I've just taken a few days off. The Department isn't going to come to a standstill without me. Do they want me to call them?'

'No I don't think so. They didn't say anything about calling in.'

'Then there's no need to make such a fuss about it. I'll call you tomorrow from wherever I am.'

'Tomorrow's Saturday, Mark. I won't be in the office.'

'Give me your home number. I didn't bring it with me.'

There was a pause. 'I'm not exactly sure where I'll be.' He was embarrassed. 'You see, tomorrow's my birthday –'

'Many happy returns!'

'Thanks, but it's not that. Ilse's planning some sort of a blow-out for me this evening and . . . well, I don't know when I'll be home. Some of the girls from her place are putting together a surprise party . . .'

'Sounds like fun!' Mark grimaced. What did girls who worked on Hamburg's Reeperbahn, the most notorious red-light district in Europe, consider a 'surprise'?

'I'm looking forward to it.' His voice did not suggest it. Perhaps poor old Harry was beginning to feel his years. 'I tell you what: why don't you call me on Sunday afternoon? I'm sure to be home by then.'

'I'll try.' Mark paused. That was the only time he did not want to be tied to a telephone. 'It will all depend on where I am. I may have to make it Sunday evening, after I've found somewhere to stay.'

'Fair enough. Don't forget.' Harry was relieved. 'Have you got a piece of paper handy? I'll give you the number.'

Mark wrote it down. 'I'll call you.'

'Thanks, lad. How's the weather? It's still pissing down here!'

'Not too bad.' He hesitated before adding more. Salzburg was the first name that had come into his mind, and he had no idea whether it was wet or dry. Harry would be unlikely to care, except that he had little to do with his time in the office. It would be typical of him to check the newspaper, if only out of goodwill. To end the conversation, he added, 'I'd better ring off now, before the money runs out.'

'All right, Mark. Enjoy yourself. Don't do anything I wouldn't!'

In view of Harry's plans for the weekend, that gave him a very free rein. 'I won't. Have a wonderful and memorable birthday party!'

Jack and Jill were already seated at their table when Mark entered the dining room. The young Englishman waved and pointed to an empty chair. His wife managed a wan smile.

'How was Lugano?'

'Super. It's much bigger than here, of course, but I liked it.'

'I'm told the English used to flock there at one time, before the pound devalued against the franc.'

Jill looked sullen. 'That probably explains it. I thought the whole place looked like Brighton: nothing but big hotels and expensive tearooms.'

Jack looked hurt. 'That's a bit unfair, darling. I thought you were enjoying yourself.'

'Did you find your miniature village?'

'Yes, after a while.' Jill sniffed, and he continued hastily, 'I didn't realize it was outside the town, and managed to get lost a couple of times. It was very interesting when we finally found it.'

His wife was contemptuous. 'It was nowhere near as nice as Bekonscot, if you have to look at that sort of thing. They hadn't planted any trees or grass, and the houses were set between concrete paths.' She eyed her husband accusingly. 'I broke the tip off one of my heels.'

Jack smiled bravely. It had obviously been a trying day. 'I did suggest walking shoes, darling.'

'Well, you should have warned me we were going to spend our honeymoon tramping in the heat, looking at a bunch of toy houses!'

'They were awfully well done.' He turned to Mark for support. 'They even had a model of the castle up the road at Bellinzona. I remember driving past it.'

Jill was not to be appeased. 'Toys!'

'How was your day?' Jack's voice was strained.

'Very pleasant, thank you. I found your shop with the maps. Otherwise, I had a lazy time, looking round the town.'

'Did you go up the hill to the church with the paintings?' When Mark looked blank, Jack explained, 'There's a lovely old church in the local style, overlooking the town, and anyone who's been cured of an illness makes a painting as a sort of thank-you offering, and hangs it up. The place is filled with them.'

Jill was patronizing. 'Catholics have such quaint customs, don't they? I'm sure half of them believe it was a miracle that they were cured. It was much more likely that penicillin did the trick, but they'll believe anything.'

For a moment, Mark was tempted to announce that he was a devout Catholic, if only to enjoy her reaction. Jack was nodding uncertainly, hoping to placate his wife, and Mark thought, 'If she didn't want me to join them for dinner, why the hell didn't she just say so?'

Jack poured some wine. 'What are you doing tomorrow?'

'I thought I'd walk over to Ascona.'

Jill spoke quickly. 'We did that yesterday. It was rather nice.'

Jack nodded. 'My parents took me there the first time we stayed, but they hated it. You see, they were there just after the war, when the place was deserted. They could hardly recognize it. There's a big car park all the way along the front, and my father talked about how it used to be completely empty, with old men sitting on wooden benches, playing chess under the trees.' He smiled. 'It was their honeymoon, too.'

Jill finally softened. 'You are sentimental, darling! Places always change. It's only natural.'

He kissed the tip of her nose. 'I suppose so. Do you think our kids will come here one day?'

Fortunately, the waiter arrived to take their orders before she could reply.

Throughout the meal, Jack was eager to propose an excursion together, and Jill's smile became tight-lipped. Mark found excuses. 'I'm afraid I'd prefer to do some walking, but I'm sure we'll run into each other, especially in the evenings. I need some exercise, after sitting around indoors all winter.'

'You're right. Perhaps we should be doing the same thing, darling.' He gave Jill's hand a squeeze.

'I haven't brought the right sort of clothes.' She extricated her hand and patted his. 'It's certainly not worth buying shoes here. The prices are ridiculous!'

The Arab had entered the dining room. As he passed their table, he smiled at Mark and nodded politely. Jack watched him. 'Friend of yours?'

'We shared a bench in the park this morning. He suggested I should try a walk up the Centovalli to the Italian border.'

Jack's face brightened. 'We were talking about the same trip. Why don't we drive you up to the head of the valley and have a bite of lunch somewhere, and you could do the walk back down. It's probably easier that way.'

'That's very kind of you, but I think I'll do it the hard way; otherwise, I won't be able to tell my friends what a virtuous hiker I've been.'

Jill was suddenly more friendly. 'You're quite right.' She smiled sweetly at her husband. 'Really, darling, I'm beginning to think you're getting bored with me already!'

# 6

Mark awoke early, seconds before the irritating high-pitched beeping of his pocket alarm clock. Heavy mist hung over Lake Maggiore. As he stood on the balcony, he was conscious of an uneasy silence, but then remembered it was Sunday morning and that even the industrious Swiss rested for a few hours longer than usual. He telephoned room service for breakfast, and showered and dressed slowly while he waited for it. There was no need to hurry; the cheerful Italian waiter who served his room always took his time.

He had spent a quiet, uneventful Saturday exploring Ascona, and had escaped from dining with Jack and Jill. They had spoken briefly in the lounge where coffee was served, but the honeymooners were patently engrossed with each other, sitting close together on a sofa and exchanging surreptitious caresses. Jack seemed blissfully content, and Jill was smugly back in command. She treated Mark to a warm smile when he excused himself early, claiming tiredness from the day's walking. Jack was too sleepily content to propose further excursions together.

By the time Mark finished breakfast, the sky was clearing, and the first grey outline of mountains had reappeared across the lake. Downstairs, he found the Arab standing in the hotel foyer. The man seemed to be waiting there for someone. He greeted Mark with a friendly nod.

'You are very early today.'

'Yes, I thought I would start walking before it becomes too warm.' Had the man been checking his movements?

'Which way will you go?'

'I haven't decided yet. I thought I might try the mountain road and look at some of the villages. They should be less crowded than the lakeshore.'

The man nodded. 'I will be travelling that way myself. Can I offer you a ride?'

'No, thank you. I'm looking for exercise.' Mark patted his waist, which was considerably thickened by the presence of the money belt. He wondered whether the Arab had noticed his sudden corpulence.

'Very well. I wish you a pleasant day.'

Mark walked through deserted town streets, climbing steadily in the direction of Solduno. The morning air was cool with a dewy freshness, and he lengthened his pace, pleasantly aware of a slight tension in the muscles of his calves. In the distance, a bell was chiming nine o'clock.

The road rose through the hills, until he found himself on a rocky ledge that followed the topographical lines on his map. To his right, flattened outcrops of granite marked the edge of a steep hillside. The valley to his left fell away precipitously towards a small, swiftly flowing stream, which the map identified as the River Melezza. The sun cut through the last of the mist, heating the atmosphere, and he removed his sweater, tying the arms around his waist. As though saluting the light and warmth, a chorus of insects came to life and, almost unconsciously, he slowed his pace to the rhythm of their repetitive sounds. Small lizards, their throats palpitating, posed immobile on the rock face, enjoying the heat, then scuttled into crevices on the surface as his shadow fell across them. He walked steadily, enjoying the exercise. There was no traffic on the highway, but he kept to the dusty footpaths that ran parallel with it, often dangerously close to the steep drop towards the river. The undergrowth was alive with tiny movements. The villages that he passed – Tegna, Verscio, Cavigliano – were little more than clusters of houses by the roadside, their streets empty and the windows of their houses closed and shuttered against the light. Compared with their cousins in French and German Switzerland, they were charmingly run down, shabby old stone structures, reminding him that this was the Ticino. It was a world far removed from the flashy villas and apartment buildings that ringed Lake Maggiore. An occasional new house, obviously belonging to some wealthy absentee owner, looked out of place with its plaster-coated walls painted a spotless, weatherproof white. He preferred the ramshackle farm cottages with their rust and cobwebs.

The upward slope of the road was gentle, but the gorge deepened until Mark found himself in a narrow pass between two mountain ranges. The river seemed to have dropped far below, to become a narrow ribbon of reflected sunlight, too distant for the rushing of its waters to be audible, and the hills above him were wild and uncultivated. He could not see the *Schmalspurbahn* which ran further up the mountainside, clinging to another topographical line, and he had not heard the sound of any trains. The valley had become a private domain, and the landscape basked in the heat. Mark looked at his watch and, finding that he was slightly ahead of schedule, sat against a rock for a few minutes, to smoke a cigarette. The undergrowth round him rustled as he disturbed its tiny inhabitants.

When he reached the larger village of Intragna, he searched for a bar or even a shop that might sell cold drinks, but it, too, was deserted. An old woman dressed in black and with a heavy scarf over her head, made her way slowly across the cobbled street. She saw Mark, and nodded politely before shuffling through an open doorway. He was tempted to call after her, to ask where he might find a café, but the door closed behind her stooped figure, and he returned to the main road, promising himself a long, cold beer when he reached his destination.

Just outside the village of Verscio, he heard a vehicle coming from the direction of Locarno. It was the first he had encountered all morning, and Mark turned to watch it. The car was an open red Mercedes sports model and, as it approached, the driver slowed down. The Arab was at the wheel.

'You have come very far. Aren't you hot?'

Mark grinned. 'Not bad. It's a lovely day for walking. I'm a little out of practice.'

'How far are you going?'

'Camedo, probably. The frontier's just beyond, and I haven't brought my passport, so I'll have to turn back.'

'I am going there also. It is where I have . . . business. You remember? Let me drive you the rest of the way.'

'No, thank you. I'm not in a hurry.' He was due to meet Stratta in less than an hour, and did not want company.

'But you have already walked a long distance. I am sure you have proved your stamina.'

'That's very kind of you, but I'm quite happy to keep going. We English enjoy punishing ourselves. It comes from living in a cold climate and believing that too much comfort is sinful!'

'I do not think I understand.' He seemed slightly irritated.

'I was joking.'

'Ah.' The Arab did not smile. 'There is a little café in Camedo. I would be pleased to buy you a drink. Come.' He leaned across the seat and opened the door.

Mark gently closed it again. 'Thank you very much, but I promised myself that I'd walk all the way to the head of the valley. Perhaps we can meet up this evening at the hotel.'

'I do not think so. Once my purchase is concluded, I will leave. I will have no reason to stay.'

'In that case, I may find you in Camedo when I get there. It's not far from here.'

'That is unlikely. I will wait for a short time until my client arrives.' The man's jaw was set in a stubborn line.

'Then I'm afraid we'll miss each other.' Mark smiled with an effort. 'I hope your meeting is successful.'

The Arab did not speak further, and pressed hard on the accelerator of his car, which leapt forward angrily, its tyres whining against the tarmac. The machine disappeared round a bend in the road as suddenly as it had arrived.

Mark waited until the dust settled again on the side of the road before moving. The man seemed curiously anxious for his company and unreasonably angry when he refused. He wondered who his client might be. Not, he hoped, a crooked Italian scientist with a briefcase full of computer information. He smiled, swinging into step. I'm getting paranoid! he thought. If he's got a date to meet Stratta, he wouldn't want me there. He's more probably planning to buy the place out with petro-dollars, and wants to show off! Christ, maybe he fancies me! It's an old Arab pastime!

He reached the head of the valley just before Camedo, and the road crossed a high bridge strung between steep hills that fell away sharply. Although Mark did not suffer from vertigo, he stayed towards the centre of the road, suddenly aware of the height. It was a long drop to the base of the valley, where the river had become a thin, sparkling line. As he turned the corner of the road, entering Borgnone, he was conscious of more human activity. A teenager passed him, riding a noisy motor scooter which left a vapour-trail of grey exhaust fumes; he heard children shouting in a field near the church; an old man in a straw hat was loading a small donkey cart with wood cuttings; a battered delivery van trundled past in the opposite direction. The Centovalli was coming to life, and Mark checked his watch yet again. It was just after one-thirty.

The café in Camedo was built on a flat ledge of land at the edge of the steep slope leading down to the railway line, and Mark could see the roof of the station at the bottom of the hill. The square on which the café faced was empty – a handful of houses – and the only sign of life was the mud-spattered motor-scooter that had passed him earlier. It had been propped against a low wall that marked the entrance to a small terrace at the back. There were a number of rusty metal chairs and tables, some of which were shaded by red umbrellas bearing the name of a popular beer. In a far corner, two old men, dressed almost uniformly in ancient brown suits with white shirts and black ties, sat in silence, watching their wine glasses, but Mark could also hear the sound of a jukebox coming from inside the café, and the occasional electronic ping of a slot-machine. There was a sudden burst of laughter, and he guessed that this was the central meeting-place for the younger men of the village.

Following Hyatt's suggestion, he chose a table under an umbrella and sat down, grateful to rest. Although he was on time, the walk had taken longer than he had calculated, and the exercise had made him tired and footsore. One of the old men looked up from his reverie and, seeing Mark, called in the direction of the café. After a moment, a young man wearing a dirty white apron over his jeans sauntered across the courtyard to take his order. Mark asked for a large beer and settled back comfortably. The brilliant sunshine was hot on his trouser-legs and he felt a sense of deep contentment. The hell with Hamburg, Harry, Hyatt and the whole bloody Department! He had just walked fourteen glorious miles up the Centovalli in Switzerland, and with a long cold beer to refresh him, it was a matter of total indifference to him whether the Italian showed up or not!

Twenty-five minutes later, he was less certain. There was still no sign of Stratta. The old men had departed, leaving Mark alone on the terrace and, as the minutes ticked slowly by, he felt a growing unease. How long should he wait? Hyatt had been very specific: two o'clock. It was nearly two-thirty. The jukebox had stopped playing in the café, and he wondered whether it would close for the afternoon. Unlikely. This wasn't an English pub, with licensing hours. He had planned to take the three o'clock train to Locarno, and had not bothered to check the timetable for a later departure. Much as he had enjoyed the walk, he was not anxious to make the return journey on foot. The waiter appeared in the doorway, and Mark ordered another beer. Where the hell was the man?

As if in reply to his question, he heard a car enter the square behind him, and waited expectantly without looking round. He heard it stop by the wall of the terrace, and its owner slammed the door shut. A tall man with red hair walked into view. He was wearing an open sports shirt and a pair of slacks, and he was carrying a leather shoulder-bag with a wide strap. It was extraordinary how Italian men could carry a handbag without looking effeminate. The man stopped close to Mark's table and stood for a moment, as though admiring the valley and the steep hillside opposite.

'*Dottore* Stratta?'

'*Si.*' The Italian turned slowly, removing a pair of heavy sunglasses. He smiled uncertainly, and Mark could see that he was trying to hide his nervousness.

'I believe we have an appointment.' Mark looked at his watch. 'I thought it was supposed to be at two o'clock.'

Stratta sat at the table, facing Mark. 'Ah, yes. You must forgive me for being a little late. The roads out of Milan were very busy, and I was delayed at the border.' He smiled uneasily. 'I think I interrupted the guard's lunch!'

The waiter arrived with Mark's beer, and looked questioningly at the new arrival.

'Can I offer you a drink?'

Stratta looked uncertain. 'No, I should really leave very soon . . . well, perhaps a glass of red wine.' He spoke in Italian to the boy, who strolled back inside the café. Stratta watched him. When he had gone, he turned back to Mark. 'Did you bring money?'

'Yes. It's in a belt . . . fifty thousand dollars. Do you want to count it?'

'No. I think I must trust you.' Stratta smiled, but his face was anxious. The fingers of his right hand were playing a silent tattoo on the table top.

Mark sat forward, slightly raising his shirt, and unbuckled the belt from his waist. It slipped free, and he coiled it on his lap. The Italian's eyes followed his movements. 'How about your papers?'

Stratta tapped the shoulder-bag, which he had hung on the back of his chair. 'They are all inside. I will leave the bag here when I go. Do you trust me also?'

Mark smiled. 'I have very little choice. I wouldn't understand what I was reading. I'm only a messenger.'

'That is what I expected.'

Mark glanced down at his lap, where the belt lay like a flattened snake. 'As it was explained to me, this represents a down payment.'

'*Si.*'

'In which case, it looks as though we're both supposed to trust each other.'

Stratta nodded, and seemed to relax. The waiter reappeared, carrying a tray bearing a single glass of dark red wine, filled to the brim. Some of it slopped over as he placed it on the table. In the square behind Mark, a car came to a halt with grinding gears and squeaky brakes. The waiter departed, and Stratta raised his glass with a slightly sardonic smile. He was about to speak, but hesitated, his eyes fixed on something behind Mark's shoulder. The smile vanished.

'Is anything the matter?'

'No.'

'You seem upset. What's wrong?'

'Nothing.' He shrugged his shoulders. 'A man was standing over there. For a moment, I thought he was watching me.'

'Where?' Mark turned in his chair, towards the square. There was nobody there.

'By the wall, behind you.'

'Did you recognize him?'

'No.' Stratta was ill at ease again. 'Perhaps I should leave soon.'

'I wouldn't worry too much about it. Strangers make people inquisitive in a small village.'

'Yes.' The Italian drank some of his wine. 'But I think I will go.'

'As you wish.' A thought occurred to Mark. 'Are you driving on to Locarno? I could ride with you some of the way.'

'No, I do not think so. I will go back the way I came.' Stratta was preoccupied.

'The border guards may be surprised. You only just came through.'

'It is not important. They are accustomed to Sunday drivers.' He looked at Mark closely. 'When will I receive the second payment?'

'I don't know. I'm only here to deliver the first. As I understand it, they want to look at the papers you give me, and provided they are satisfied, the rest of the money will be arranged via your bank in Lugano.'

'Yes, yes, that is what we agreed.' Stratta's fingers drummed audibly on the table.

'They didn't say how soon it would be, but I assume they will want a little time to check everything.'

'Very well. Give me the belt, please.' Stratta looked round to make sure the terrace was still empty.

Mark passed the money belt across the table, and the Italian grabbed it hastily, knocking his wine glass over. A pool of wine spread over the white metal surface. It looked like blood. Stratta edged the flap of the belt open, peering at its contents. He seemed satisfied with what he saw.

'There's still time to count it, if you wish.'

'No, that will not be necessary.' He stood, pushing his chair back so that it grated against the concrete. 'I must go.'

Mark remained seated. 'Are you still worried about the man who was watching you? If you like, we can leave together –'

'No, my car is parked where I can see it. Everything you need is in the . . .' His eyes slid in the direction of the shoulder-bag which he had left hanging on the back of his chair. 'Please tell your superior to arrange the second payment to Lugano as soon as possible. He has the details.' Stratta hesitated. 'He must be aware that I am taking a serious risk by bringing this to you.'

'I'll tell him.'

'I insist!' He looked round nervously.

'I've already explained: I'm simply here to deliver the . . . belt to you. What happens afterwards is none of my business.'

'But you will explain how urgent it is?'

'I'll pass it on.'

Stratta nodded and, without speaking further, walked rapidly to his car. Mark watched from his chair as the Italian raced the engine and let in the clutch with a jerk, making the vehicle lurch forward unsteadily. The Italian did not look back. The waiter appeared in the doorway, and Mark signalled to him, holding out a banknote. The boy moved quicker than usual, reaching into a back pocket for change.

Mark struggled. His Italian was almost non-existent. '*Il treno* . . .' He pointed to the roof of the station and held up three fingers. '*A tre ore?*'

The boy nodded, counting coins. '*Si, Signor*, three o'clock.' He looked pleased with himself. 'I speak English. I am well teached in the school.'

Mark looked at his watch. There was still plenty of time. As he stood, the boy handed him Stratta's shoulder-bag. It was heavier than he expected. He turned to leave, and the boy touched his arm.

'If you are going to walk to the station, sir, there is a quick way . . . there.' He pointed to a gap in the wall of the terrace. 'It is only a little path down the hill, but much quicker. The road for cars goes round a different way.'

'Thank you.' Mark placed a few coins on the table, which the boy scooped up.

'Thank you, *Signor*.' He bowed gravely. 'Bye-bye!'

The gap in the wall revealed a narrow, muddy footpath, trodden down by constant use, which curved down the steep slope of the hillside towards the station. Small stones in the earth made it slippery, and he descended cautiously, feeling his shoes sliding against the surface.

As he rounded a corner, a voice behind him spoke.

'That's far enough. Stay exactly where you are.'

Mark spun round, and his right foot slipped, making him throw his arms forward to maintain his balance.

'Don't try anything stupid. You'd better put your hands up.'

Jack Taylor was standing under the stone wall supporting the café terrace. Just behind him, Jill was leaning against the brickwork. Mark's glance travelled to the Smith and Wesson in Jack's hand.

'Don't move.' He edged his way down the slope, until he was standing on the path below Mark. The gun remained steady.

Mark stood very still, watching. 'What the hell's going – ?'

'Shut up!' He waited as Jill scrambled down the slope until she had reached the path a few feet above Mark. 'I told you to put your hands up.'

Mark raised his arms slowly. 'If you insist. You can see for yourself I'm not armed. What the hell do you want?'

Jack's voice was scornful. 'As if you didn't know!' He glanced past Mark. 'Move back, darling. Don't come any closer.'

'Look, this is ridiculous –'

'Stay where you are, and keep your arms where they are!' Jack stared at Mark. 'Well, Peter, if that's what your name is, it looks as though you've got something that belongs to us.'

'What are you talking about?'

'Don't be so bloody stupid! Just hand me Dr Stratta's pouch – gently! – and we'll be on our way.' He tried unsuccessfully to smile. 'If you do what you're told and don't try anything, we might even let you live!'

# 7

For a few seconds, the two men stared at each other. As Mark watched him, Jack seemed to become uneasy, and motioned with his gun.

'The pouch. Come on, don't waste my time.' His voice was tense.

Mark did not move. 'Why should I?'

'You'll save yourself a lot of trouble. If you don't hand it over, I'll have to . . . take it.' Jack's eyes flickered towards his wife, and Mark turned, his arms still raised, to look at her. Jill was clutching a straw basket, watching him, tight-lipped. When their eyes met, she took an unsteady step backwards. Jack continued, 'What I said about . . . well, we don't want more problems than necessary. Just hand over the documents and we'll let it go at that.' He grunted. 'It's more than your lot would probably do for me!'

Mark spoke quietly. 'Do you mind if I ask you something?' His voice was almost casual.

The question seemed to take Jack by surprise. 'What?'

'Were you expecting to meet the Italian too?' After a momentary hesitation, Jack nodded. 'I see. It looks as though one of us was being double-crossed.' Mark relaxed slightly, dividing his weight between his feet and digging his heels into the dry earth. He wondered whether the other man was as securely balanced on the treacherous slope. 'Unless, of course, you're just doing a little extempore hijacking of your own.'

'If there's any hijacking, it's you who's trying it. You're out of luck.' Jack scowled. 'You're going to have to report back to your bosses empty-handed: no papers, no money, no nothing! I wouldn't fancy being in your shoes when that happens!'

Mark shrugged, keeping his voice steady. 'I don't have much choice, do I? Anyway, I'm only a messenger-boy. As far as I'm concerned, it's just a job.'

Jack motioned impatiently. 'Let's get on with this.'

'I'm curious to know one thing. Did you guess what I was doing in Locarno?'

Jack appeared calmer. The gun in his hand was pointed lower, no longer aiming at Mark's heart. 'No, we didn't. It was a shock when we found you sitting up there on the terrace. We thought you were just on holiday. You fellows are well trained . . .' He looked past Mark to Jill, as if for confirmation.

'If it's of any interest, so are you. Under the circumstances, I don't understand why you were so eager for my company over the past few days.'

Jack again glanced at his wife. 'I thought you'd be good cover, if you must know.' Mark had the feeling that he was saying it for Jill's benefit. 'We're all supposed to be having a quiet holiday in Switzerland!'

Mark nodded, wondering how long he could play for time. 'But you even offered to drive me here. What would you have done when our mutual friend showed up?'

'That was the point. I offered to drive you here so that you could walk back down to Locarno. You would have been long gone by the time he got here. We weren't supposed to meet until three o'clock.'

'I see.' Mark was silent, trying to fit the pieces together. Hyatt had arranged his rendezvous with Stratta for two o'clock. He had been very specific. If Stratta had been on time, he would have been out of the way before Jack arrived. But did Hyatt know about Jack? He had intimated that there were other interested parties. If not, then the Italian had been negotiating with both of them, in case one of the deals fell through. That was a very dangerous game. In view of the Italian's nervousness, it seemed out of character.

'Look, we're wasting time.' The gun was raised again. 'Take that bag off your shoulder – slowly – and pass it to me.' The gun became very steady. 'Don't try to be a hero!'

In the square above them, a lorry coming from the Italian side was changing gears. For a moment, it sounded as though it might stop, but it continued down the hill. Mark looked up towards the road, where the vehicle was visible.

He turned again to Jack. 'You're taking a chance with that gun, aren't you? Suppose somebody sees you.'

'It's my risk.' He motioned with the gun. 'Don't push me. Give me the bag.'

Mark allowed the wide leather strap to slip from his shoulder so that it fell into his hand. The pouch dangled by his feet. 'Guns make a hell of a noise, especially in a quiet village.'

'So do lorries, and cars, and trains and God knows what else!' When Mark made no further move, Jack looked at his wife. 'Jill, turn on the tape.'

Mark turned to face the girl, swivelling his body. His feet were firmly planted on the dry earth. Stratta's shoulder-bag, gripped by the strap, swung heavily against his leg. Jill fumbled nervously in her basket and took out the tape-recorder, pushing a plastic button on its control panel. Nothing happened, and she muttered, 'Damn!' and pushed another button. Stravinsky's music suddenly blared, strangely tinny in the open air. It seemed shockingly loud.

'For God's sake, you'll wake the whole bloody neighbourhood!' Jack called to her angrily. 'Turn it down! The wheel on the left–' His attention was fixed on the tape-recorder as she struggled to find the volume control.

Using all his strength, Mark swung the pouch at Jack's hand. It struck him on the wrist, knocking the revolver from his grasp. Jack spun round to watch as the gun fell a few feet away, bouncing on tufts of grass. For a second, he was caught off-balance, and his feet started to slide uncontrollably. Mark took a pace forward and planted his foot against the man's ribs, kicking viciously with his heel. The man's arm flailed wildly as he fell backwards, unable to maintain his footing. He fell heavily and rolled several feet down the hillside.

Jill was standing frozen, her hands against her mouth. She had dropped the tape-recorder, which continued to play noisily. As Mark moved towards her, she gave a little yelp of fright. Her eyes were terrified and pleading, and he grasped her shoulders and threw her down the slope towards her husband, who was clumsily trying to get to his feet. Her body crashed into his, and they fell together, rolling and sliding downwards. For a moment, Mark watched them, thinking insanely, Jack fell down and broke his crown! Then he turned and scrambled up the path towards the café terrace.

His legs ached, his feet slipped against earth and pebbles, and he threw himself onto the long grass at the side of the path. With one hand still gripping the leather strap, it was harder to climb quickly, but his shoes were able to grip the surface. At one point, he fell forward, pulling at thick roots of grass as he dragged himself upward. He expected at any moment to hear the sharp crack of a gunshot and feel the searing pain where the bullet found its target. At the top of the hill, reaching out to the terrace wall to pull himself the last few feet, Mark looked back. Jill was standing, her face turned in his direction. Behind her, Jack was scrabbling on all fours, searching in the undergrowth for his gun.

Mark ran across the terrace and into the empty square, looking for somewhere to hide. In a shaded corner, near the entrance to the bar, Jack's baby Citroën was parked, but he could not risk the time to try to start it. For a moment, he hesitated, undecided, wondering which direction to choose. He was panting heavily, the sweat streaming down his face. In the back of his mind was the thought that he must find a way back to Locarno before they caught up with him. Alone, and without a gun, he was helpless.

The motor-scooter was still leaning against the wall, and he ran to it, grabbing the handlebars and pushing it towards the road. A bent and rusted key was in the lock, and he turned it, grateful to see a red bulb light up on the controls. It was an old machine with a kick-start, and he straddled it, pushing down with his foot on the rusty starter. The machine sputtered momentarily, then died, and he kicked again, twisting the accelerator on the handle. From somewhere behind, he heard an angry shout. Glancing back, he saw the waiter from the café running towards him. Mark gritted his teeth and kicked the starter again. The engine caught with a sudden, high-pitched roar. For a moment, he was unable to put the scooter into gear, and feverishly sought the controls, his hands slipping against the worn rubber handle grips. The gears meshed as the boy reached him, still shouting wildly, and Mark felt a pair of hands grab his shirt as he moved forward. In the gap at the side of the terrace, Jack's head appeared. Seconds later, he saw the man bring the gun level, resting his arm against the earth to take aim. Mark ducked his head and accelerated, letting the clutch out as quickly as he dared. He heard the gun explode, and a bullet struck the metal frame of the machine, making it shudder wildly and almost throwing him to the ground. Somehow, he managed to maintain his balance, and steered the scooter in an eccentric zigzag, its wheels skidding on the surface, using his feet to steady the machine as it tipped dangerously over. There was a second shot, and the bullet struck the road somewhere to his right.

As the machine came under control, Mark bent lower, desperately trying to coax it to move faster. He looked back for a second, to see Jack and Jill running towards their car. The waiter was lying in the road, where he had fallen. Mark faced the front again, to find that he was heading rapidly towards the edge of the road and the sudden drop beyond. He corrected the wheel too quickly, and the machine slid over beneath him, throwing him painfully to the ground. The engine stopped. Using brute force, he pulled the machine straight and kicked the starter again. The engine shuddered, but did not catch. Glancing back, Mark could see the Citroën starting to move, and again tried the starter. The engine fired, and he set the wheel straight, slowly accelerating as the wheels gripped the surface of the road. He risked one further backwards glance. The waiter was standing by the side of the road to let the Citroën pass. It was gaining on him rapidly.

Mark settled forward, concentrating on the road and gently urging the machine on. It barely responded. At about thirty miles an hour, it seemed to have reached maximum speed, and his arms ached as the loose steering forced him to correct and adjust in order to stay upright. He reached the bridge and aimed down the centre, hoping there would be no oncoming traffic. Over the noise of the motor, he could not hear the Citroën, but he was certain that it was closing on him with every second, and could not risk another backward glance. Jack had complained that his car would not go more than fifty miles an hour, but that gave him more speed than the scooter, making it a matter of minutes before he caught up. There was a chance that Mark could risk one of the narrow footpaths down into the valley, too difficult for the car to negotiate, but he was not in full control of the machine and the paths were steep and slippery. Even then, he could be trapped lower down, with perhaps no escape route.

At the far end of the bridge, he slowed almost to a halt and looked round. The Citroën was approaching, and accelerating towards him as the road straightened. Mark moved off, manoeuvring the corner and guided the scooter through a series of bends where the highway clung to the steep slope of the mountainside. The machine was sluggish, fighting against him as he urged it round the corners. The sweat had dried on his face and back, and his arms trembled with the constant vibration. He realized that he was gripping the steering too hard and tried to relax, but lost control again. He no longer dared to look back, concentrating on the road, his eyes searching for a possible escape path into the hills that might give him a moment's respite.

The village of Borgnone seemed to flash past before he could decide whether to turn off the main road and seek refuge among the houses, and he started a long downward slope, feeling the scooter gathering speed. There was a sharp corner about seventy yards ahead, and he checked the brakes, which gripped intermittently, causing the machine to shudder. It reduced his speed sufficiently to manage the bend in the road, which fell away sharply where the mountainside became a steep drop. Mark steered towards the centre and, as he rounded the corner, a huge shape loomed into view. It was a donkey cart, overloaded with branches and wood cuttings. The old, straw-hatted man was walking next to his animal, leading it by a short rein. The cart was top-heavy, its contents spilling out over its sides, so that it appeared to occupy most of the road, and Mark swerved wildly to avoid it. The scooter's wheels slithered on the tarmac, and it overturned. Mark steered to the left, unable to control the machine, until he crashed into a clump of bushes growing at the foot of the hillside. The scooter came to a sudden halt as its front wheel struck a rock, and Mark was thrown into the grass verge. He lay for a moment, regaining his senses. The soft ground had broken his fall. Looking up, he saw the old man, an anxious expression on his face, coming towards him, still leading the donkey cart as he crossed the centre of the road. Mark was already scrambling to his feet as the man approached. In a moment, the car would arrive.

It all happened in seconds. The donkey cart was in the centre of the road, partially blocking it in both directions. As Mark stood, the old man hurried forward, calling to him. He could not understand what the man was saying, but the look of concern on his face needed no translation. At that moment, the Citroën rounded the corner, travelling fast, its body leaning outward from its chassis. Mark had a momentary glimpse of Jack's face, pale and suddenly horrified with the realization that the road was blocked. There was a scream of brakes and tyres as he tried to stop, and the car began to slide. It moved sideways, slithering forwards as the Englishman spun the wheel in a wild effort to regain control, then straightened at the last moment, passing the cart on the right side. The wheels crashed through a painted wooden barrier, and the Citroën mounted the bank of the road. Carried onward by its weight, the car rose over the sharp edge of the escarpment. For a moment, it seemed to come to a rest, motionless. Mark saw Jill's mouth open in a silent scream. Then the vehicle tipped lazily over the side of the hill and dropped out of sight.

The old man had stopped, astonished, and as the car disappeared, he crossed himself, muttering under his breath. Mark ran past him to the broken barrier, standing on the edge. The car was still upright and seemed to be half falling, half riding down the slope towards an outcrop of rocks. It looked as though Jack was steering it, but the vehicle hit the rocks and somersaulted high on its back, turning and twisting in the air like a demented creature. Each time it struck the ground, there was a grinding crash, and jagged pieces of metal were thrown clear. It continued down the mountainside, catapulted further by each impact and crushed into a shapeless mass, until it reached the rocky basin through which the river flowed. For a few seconds, it was still. Then a sudden explosion enveloped what remained of its broken carcass in a mass of flames. The sound reached Mark's ears long after he saw it, and he stepped back from the ledge.

The old man had led his donkey cart off the highway to a patch of grass on the opposite side. He stood with his hand on the animal's neck, as though comforting it.

Mark walked over to him. *'Io telèfono.'* He mimed holding a telephone to his ear. *'Polizìa.'* He could not remember the world for 'help', but raised his hand. *'Te reste. Reste. Capische?'*

*'Si, signor.'* The old man nodded once and lowered his head. He had removed his straw hat, revealing silver hair. His fingers picked at the torn strands of the hat, and Mark suspected that the man feared he would be accused of causing the accident.

*'Reste là.* OK?' He indicated the spot where the car had crashed through the barrier. *'Non e possibile . . . Io . . .'* Mark shrugged helplessly to explain that he could not communicate further, and the old man nodded again, then turned to comfort his donkey.

The motor-scooter did not appear to be damaged. There was a strong smell of petrol where it lay on its side, but the front wheel was still intact. Mark slung the shoulder-bag across his back and pushed the machine on to the tarmac. He used sign language to indicate to the old man that he would continue down to the next village.

'Io telèfono. OK?'

The man watched him with watery eyes, saying nothing, and Mark walked the scooter across the road. The vehicle was still warm and started immediately. He drove slowly, steering cautiously. When he turned to look back, the old man had not moved.

He drove steadily, letting the machine carry him at a gentle pace through the valley. Several cars heading in the opposite direction passed him, but he ignored them. With luck, there would be time to abandon the scooter and take one of the smaller paths into Locarno before the old man could make himself understood. From time to time, he glanced over his shoulder, wobbling slightly as he shifted balance, but no one approached from behind. The journey seemed endlessly slow, even though familiar landmarks from the morning's walk came into view sooner than he expected them to. It had taken much longer to pass them on the way up.

He left the scooter propped against a wall in Solduno and continued on foot. There were a number of streets connecting the village – more accurately, a suburb – to Locarno, allowing him to avoid the main road. As he started downhill, Mark thought he heard the sound of police sirens, and caught a glimpse of distant vehicles with flashing blue lights travelling at high speed up the highway in the direction of the Centovalli. Word must have spread sooner than he hoped. All that remained was for him to leave Switzerland before any investigation developed. Even so, at the very worst, he would be accused of stealing an ancient motor-scooter. The old man with the donkey cart had simply witnessed a road accident.

The air had cooled considerably, and gathering clouds suggested a break in the weather. They provided an excuse to put on his sweater again. His shirt was sweat-stained and dirty, torn at the back when the waiter had tried to stop him. It made him feel conspicuous, and the sweater helped to change and improve his appearance.

He wondered whether the mysterious Arab would be back at the hotel. What did the man want? He was the only witness from Locarno who could associate Mark with Camedo and, from what he had said, was unlikely to return. That left only one identifiable item: Dr Stratta's shoulder-bag.

Mark was walking down a narrow lane which separated the gardens of several large villas. From its appearance, it had been built quite recently, to accommodate the new developments that had sprouted around the town. He paused for a moment, to inspect the contents of the pouch. Inside, there were two large files containing sheets of xeroxed paper. They had been carefully wrapped in a white plastic carrier bag. Mark removed them, and pushed the shoulder-bag deep into a clump of bushes at the side of the road. It would be weeks before it was discovered.

The concierge at the Park Hotel presented Mark with his keys with his usual ceremonial gesture. He was a large, cheerful German, proud of his linguistic abilities. 'Good evening, Mr Williams. I hope you have enjoyed your day, *ja*?'

'Yes, thank you. I took a walk in the hills.'

'Ah, that is very good. I think perhaps it will rain tomorrow.' He frowned at the thought. Rain was bad for tourist business. 'A moment, please.' He produced a small piece of hotel notepaper. 'Mr Taylor left a message for you. He requests that you meet him and Mrs Taylor for dinner this evening.'

'Thank you.' Mark hoped that his face remained impassive. 'I'll be leaving in the morning, by the way. Is there a train to Zurich? I want to take a flight from there to London at midday.' He would have preferred to leave sooner, but it was too late to make any connections.

'Of course, sir, but you have to change at Bellinzona. The train goes through the Kloten airport.'

'Very good. I'll check the times after dinner.'

'At your service!' He was the sort of concierge who always liked to have the last word.

In his room, Mark telephoned Harry Price, but there was no reply. He let the phone ring for a long time. Presumably, the surprise birthday party had carried over the whole weekend. For a man of Harry's age, that took stamina!

In the early hours of the morning, long after all the guests had retired for the night, Mark climbed round the partition separating his balcony from Jack and Jill's. The door to their bedroom had been left unlocked, and the bedside light was still burning from when the maid had turned down the covers. Searching systematically, he worked his way through cupboards and drawers, looking for evidence that might be a key to their background. Their clothes were mostly new and bore the names of English shops, and there was nothing amid their possessions to suggest they had been anything more than they pretended. There was a sad collection of souvenirs: match books from restaurants in France and Switzerland; a couple of printed guides to historic buildings; cardboard beer mats from a café in Zug; miniature shampoo and bubble-bath containers from hotels where they had stayed. In one of the empty suitcases stored in the front closet, he found a few pitiful scraps of confetti. It was only when he saw the tiny petals of coloured papers that Mark permitted himself to pause and consider the day's events. He closed his eyes. A honeymoon couple!

But they were not. He had to hang on to that fact. They had been in Camedo to meet Dr Stratta, just as he had, and Jack had been prepared to kill him, if necessary, for Stratta's papers.

Lying on his bed a few minutes later, Mark lit a cigarette. He was very tired and his limbs ached, but his mind would not let him sleep. Who the hell were they, and who had sent them?

London, 1976

# 8

Following routine procedure, Mark telephoned the London house from Heathrow, while he was waiting for his luggage to arrive. The operator connected him with Alex Beaumont.

'Aren't you supposed to be in Hamburg? What are you doing here, Mark?' Beaumont was attached to Head Office and, as such, considered himself senior to field men. He was also Eton and Oxford, with a First in Classics, which made him feel superior to everyone else.

'None of your business, Alex. Just tell the man on the front door that I'm on my way in.'

'That isn't exactly how it works, Mark.' Beaumont's voice was cool. 'You're expected to have a specific reason for entry before you're granted admission.' He spoke precisely, enjoying his momentary authority as duty officer.

'Don't be so bloody silly!' He had always disliked the man. 'Just tell the guard on the front desk to expect me in about half an hour.' His luggage had already arrived.

'Not until you clear yourself properly.' Alex always did everything by the book. Mark had heard that his original intention had been to join the Diplomatic Service and, even though his father was a reasonably senior ex-Guards officer, he had failed to pass the necessary entrance examinations. Spending a few years in the Department was supposed to offer an entrée via the back door. In Beaumont's case, it had not worked. 'Who are you coming to see?'

Mark took a deep breath. Until he was cleared, the guard would not let him pass. 'I'm here to see the old man, if you must know. He asked me to report to him personally.' It seemed odd to refer to Hyatt as an old man, but the title accompanied the job. Whoever originally established the Department had an obvious nostalgia for his military years. When Beaumont did not reply, Mark asked, 'Are you still there?'

'Yes.' His supercilious manner had gone. 'I think you'd better come in.'

'I intend to. What's the matter?'

'Quite a lot.' Beaumont was silent again.

'Such as?'

'Just come in. It's not the sort of thing I want to discuss on the phone. Did you say half an hour?'

'Give or take. It depends on the traffic.'

'Very well. Ask for me when you arrive, and –'

'I don't want to see you, Alex. I've already explained –'

'I'd be grateful if you'd stop by my office first, nevertheless. You'll understand why when we've talked.' He hung up before Mark could reply.

Although several years younger than Mark, Alexis Beaumont looked much older. He was small, pink-faced and plump, with thinning brown hair and the beginning of a premature middle-age spread, which he did his best to conceal beneath expensively tailored suits. Mark had always thought that he looked like the school swot twenty years on; the one who only became Deputy Senior Prefect and bullied the junior boys for minor transgressions that others ignored. Perhaps that, too, reflected a nostalgia for past times. Somebody had told him that Alex had a penchant for teenage boys.

When Mark entered Beaumont's office, deliberately ignoring the printed plastic sign requesting him to knock first, he found the man standing by the window, his hands clasped behind his back, staring at the small patch of untidy garden at the back of the house. He had the impression that Beaumont had taken up the position as soon as the front desk had telephoned to say that Mark was on his way up. With sunlight behind him, shining directly into Mark's eyes, he probably felt it gave him a slight physical advantage. No doubt he read lengthy American executive manuals devoted to the subject.

'Hello, Alex. What's all the fuss?'

'Come in, Mark. Please sit. I'd still like to know what you're doing in London.' He seemed to have regained some of his sense of superiority, but he looked troubled.

'I've already told you, and I'm also on holiday. I've been away for the past four or five days.'

'Oh. I thought you were here about . . .' Beaumont was pensive. 'I suppose you haven't heard.'

'Heard?'

'About Harry Price.'

'Harry? What about him?'

'He died last Friday.'

'Good God!' Mark sat in a chair before the desk, and Alex occupied the black leather seat facing him. He folded his plump hands together, letting them lie on the polished surface. Unlike his face, they were pale and lifeless.

'What happened?'

'I'm sorry to have to break the news, Mark. Harry had an accident on Friday evening. It appears that he tripped on the stairs to his flat and fell down them.' When Mark said nothing, Alex continued, 'I'm rather sorry to add that it looks as though he had been drinking at the time, although that could be an unfair assumption. His . . . er . . . good lady had the presence of mind to phone here. It seems that Harry listed me as his next of kin, and had given the woman this number to call in case of an emergency.'

'Was she with him when it happened?'

'No.' Beaumont flicked some dust from the polished surface of the empty desk. 'He was supposed to meet her that evening, and when he didn't show up after an hour or so, she went round to pick him up and found him at the bottom of the staircase. She called a doctor immediately, but Harry was already dead. The fall broke his back.'

'And he'd been drinking?'

'Apparently. Why do you ask in that way?'

Mark shrugged. 'Because people who are very drunk usually sustain a fall better than when they're sober.'

'I suppose so. It must depend on the way they land.' Beaumont hesitated. 'I was rather touched that he used my name for next of kin. Poor man. He only had a couple of years to go before he retired.'

'Yes, I know.'

'It must be a shock for you. I'd offer you a drink, but I'm afraid I don't keep anything in the office. Would you like a cup of tea? One of the girls could rustle up –'

'No. It's all right. Poor sod!'

'I don't think you should speak like that, Mark. Harry was a fine man . . .'

'Yes, of course. I didn't mean it that way. To be perfectly honest, we weren't very close. I hadn't been in Hamburg long, so we didn't know each other very well. He did go out of his way to make me feel at home. Poor old Harry!'

'Quite. When you called, I thought you'd probably come here to discuss the situation in the Hamburg office.'

'No. I haven't been there since last Thursday. As a matter of fact, I spoke to Harry around midday on Friday. I made a routine call in.'

'I see. I think you should try to go back as soon as possible, Mark. With you away and Harry . . . there's nobody there.'

'The place won't fall apart for a couple of days. Let's face it, Alex, we could close it up tomorrow and nobody would notice the difference. I'll go back when I've finished my business here.'

'I understand.' Alex shrugged helplessly. 'Everything seems to have turned upside-down at the same time.' He watched Mark for a moment. 'I wonder if you'd mind telling me why you want to see the DG?'

'Sorry, Alex. It's a private matter between Hyatt and me. Those were his instructions, by the way; not mine.'

Beaumont was silent for a moment. He seemed to be avoiding Mark's eyes. 'I think you should tell me about it, nevertheless.'

'No. What's got into you, Alex? Why all the mystery on the phone, and why the hell are you questioning me about my business with Hyatt? I'm hardly going to discuss it with you.'

'I suppose not.'

'Then what are you playing at?'

Alex looked directly at Mark. 'Richard Hyatt is dead.'

'What?'

'He died last Saturday.' Beaumont was enjoying the drama, although he maintained a suitably dignified expression. 'It was a heart attack. It seems he hadn't been well for some time, but he wouldn't tell anyone about it. He was down at his cottage in Sussex for the weekend – it's somewhere near Arundel. A friend looked in on Saturday night and found him lying on the living room floor. He called the local GP, who confirmed that Hyatt had been ill for a long time. It seems the doctor had been treating him for months, and had expected something like this to happen. Hyatt had sworn him to secrecy about it.' Beaumont looked up. 'What's the matter?'

'Nothing. It's a shock. That's all.'

'I wasn't aware that you knew Hyatt.'

'We met on a couple of occasions.' It seemed to Mark that Beaumont was sitting very still, his hands flat on the desk.

'I see. Well, I'm sure you can understand that all hell's broken loose around here. First, there was the news of poor old Harry Price, and now this. If you have anything for Hyatt, I think you'd better hand it over to me. I'll look after it.'

Mark hesitated. 'No. We were just going to talk.'

'Are you sure you're all right? You look rather pale.'

'I'm fine. I didn't get much sleep last night.'

'Oh. Well, everyone's down in Sussex for the funeral this afternoon –'

'This afternoon? Isn't that rather quick?'

'Not really. It was an open-and-shut case, so to speak. The doctor didn't even seem very surprised when he was called in. According to him, Hyatt had been living on borrowed time for the past six months. He didn't have any family, so there was no one to inform.' Beaumont paused. 'I think it was also felt that we should avoid undue publicity. As you know, we don't broadcast the name of the Director General more than absolutely necessary, although I'm sure our . . . opposite numbers across the way are perfectly aware of who he is.'

'Yes.' Mark lit a cigarette. He wanted time to think.

'So everything's going to be at sixes and sevens for the next few weeks, until the office is reorganized. It's bound to involve all sorts of reshuffling.'

'I suppose so.' Cigarette smoke caught in his throat, and he coughed.

Beaumont pursed his lips and opened a drawer in his desk. He produced an ashtray, which he slid towards Mark, and as if to emphasize his disapproval, walked to the window and opened it. 'Until a new DG is named, I assume we'll all have to take on extra responsibilities.' He frowned. 'Unless, of course, they decide to bring in some total outsider to replace him.'

It occurred to Mark that Beaumont's preoccupation with departmental reorganization was prompted by personal aspirations which could include some sort of internal promotion for himself. No wonder he was so curious to know about Mark's involvement with Hyatt before he revealed that the man was dead! 'Is anyone inside the Department likely to get the job, Alex? Knowing the way Whitehall works, I'd be surprised.'

Alex lowered his voice. 'I don't have a lot to go on, but H. W.'s name has been mentioned.'

'Willis?' The disbelief in Mark's voice made Beaumont look up in surprise.

'He's brilliant, and he knows our operation better than anyone else. I must say I've always admired him –'

'You're joking!'

'Not at all. You know, Mark, if you don't mind a word of friendly advice, your running battle with H. W. has become common knowledge around the building. You would probably do yourself a favour by sorting out your differences with him.'

'I'd do myself an even bigger favour by getting out altogether. Where is Willis?'

'At the funeral, of course. He and Hyatt were very close, you know.'

'No. I didn't know.' Mark was thoughtful.

'Oh yes. Dick Hyatt was a sort of protégé of H. W.'s in the old days. When he was promoted all the way up the ladder, even over H. W.'s head, he never complained, which I thought was rather generous of him. On the contrary, he was very proud of it. I'm sure Hyatt was grateful. It's my guess that if he had anything to do with nominating a successor, he would have put in a good word for H. W.'

'I see. On the other hand, his death was very unexpected.'

'Not by him, it appears.'

'You're probably right.' Mark stubbed out his cigarette. 'I would have thought you'd be at the funeral too, Alex.' He would like to have added, 'It's not like you to miss a promotional opportunity like that!'

Beaumont returned to his desk. 'I wanted to go, but somebody has to mind the shop. The work goes on, you know. Excuse me a moment.' He lifted the telephone receiver and dialled an internal number. When there was a reply, he said, 'This is Beaumont. Is there any word yet? Oh. Very well. Call me as soon as you hear anything. I'll remain here until you do.' He replaced the phone slowly.

Mark sat back in his chair, watching Beaumont and debating whether to tell him what had happened in Switzerland. The DG had explained his reasons for secrecy, but they no longer applied, and without Hyatt to verify his story, the whole mission suddenly seemed far-fetched. At least he had the papers safely stored at the bottom of his suitcase. Who should he give them to? Willis? Beaumont's theory that he was next in line was worrying. Was it really true that Hyatt and Willis were old friends? Shit!

Beaumont was still staring at the telephone, as though willing it to ring. He seemed to have ignored Mark for the moment, and was lost in thought. 'What's the matter, Alex? Still more problems?'

Beaumont's eyes flickered. Head Office information was restricted, and a field agent was not, in his view, senior enough to be included. 'It's nothing, I hope. I'm waiting for a rather important call.'

'Is that why you couldn't go to Sussex?'

The sympathy in Mark's voice seemed to strike a responsive chord, and Beaumont relaxed. 'Yes, as a matter of fact, it is.' He smiled wanly, with more than a suggestion of self-pity. 'They say bad news travels in threes, but I hope it's just a stupid superstition.'

'What's wrong?'

'Nothing very drastic. We sent one of the younger men on a simple errand, and he hasn't reported in. He's nearly twenty-four hours late.' He looked at his watch, as though to confirm the statement.

'Serious?'

'It shouldn't be. It was an easy enough job. I said we shouldn't have let him . . .' Beaumont left the sentence unfinished, conscious that as a desk man, hopefully soon to be promoted, he should not be gossiping with the field staff.

'Anyone I know?' Beaumont's eyebrows were raised in surprise, which irritated Mark. 'Oh, come on, Alex! I do normally work out of London. I've been in Hamburg less than a month and, from what I've heard, I'm about to be shipped back. You don't have to play games with me! Who's missing?'

Beaumont sighed. 'A young fellow from the Manchester office, so you wouldn't know him. He only started down here a couple of weeks ago. It was some sort of promotion for him, not that he's proving very worthy of it. He was due for a holiday, and we asked him to do a quick pick-up at the same time. I can't understand what's the matter with him. These new kids have no sense of responsibility when it comes to normal office routine. He was told to call in as soon as he picked up the material yesterday afternoon. Bloody irresponsible!' He glared at the silent telephone.

Mark kept his voice very calm. 'What's his name?'

'Taylor. Jack Taylor. Seems nice enough. I can't think how he could be so damn lackadaisical. Bloody nuisance! I should have been in Sussex.'

Mark's fists were clenched, but he held them on his lap, under the desk. With an effort, he kept his voice impersonal. 'Perhaps he's not near a phone.'

'In Switzerland?' Beaumont laughed. 'My dear fellow, you can pick up a phone and dial direct practically anywhere in the world. I told you: it was a simple job. The trouble is that he's off on his honeymoon at the moment, and because he was heading for southern Switzerland, we thought we'd save on the travel budget. He's probably so enthralled with the joys of married bliss that he's forgotten all about us. It wouldn't surprise me to learn that he forgot to keep the bloody appointment! I hate amateur arrangements!'

'Why amateur?' Mark busied himself with lighting another cigarette.

'Because if you're sending somebody on a job, no matter how simple or uncomplicated it is, you don't allow him to combine it with any kind of personal arrangements. It's unprofessional. They should have chosen someone else, or told him to postpone his bloody honeymoon!' His face took on a pained expression. 'Do you have to smoke those damn things all the time? You've only just put one out.'

'I'm sorry.' Mark ground the cigarette in the ashtray. He hoped his hands were not trembling.

Beaumont sighed philosophically. 'I suppose I'm making a fuss about nothing. He'll probably call in the next hour or so, full of apologies and all sorts of excuses. They always do! Frankly, for the sake of an air ticket, they should have done it the right way, but they're always carrying on about the cost of running the bloody office.' Beaumont walked to the window again, opening it further. 'I'm really disappointed. I would like to have been at the funeral today.'

'I thought they were keeping it rather quiet.'

'Well, just the people who were close to him. I like to think I should have been included.' He looked round. 'You know, you really do look awful, Mark. Are you sure you're not ill?'

'Yes.' Mark grinned weakly. 'I celebrated a little too much last night, and I'm paying the price.'

Beaumont looked disapproving for a moment. Then his expression changed. 'Look, I know your meeting was supposed to be with Hyatt, but under the circumstances . . .' He left the sentence unfinished. 'I'm rather curious to know what it is you were supposed to discuss with him.'

Mark shrugged. 'My future in the Department.'

'Oh?' Beaumont was suddenly wary.

'It's not what you're thinking, Alex. I was sent to Hamburg because I told Willis I wanted to quit. Hyatt asked me to take a few days off, and then come in for a talk. I think he was planning a little fatherly advice.'

'I see.' Alex was more friendly. 'Well, it certainly makes sense although, as I said before, you'd be better off burying the hatchet with Willis. You're sure you haven't anything else for him?' Beaumont's gaze was steady.

'Positive. As for Willis, I'd sooner bury a hatchet in him!'

'Have it your own way. What do you want to do? I can give you H. W.'s number in Sussex, if you want to talk to him.'

Mark was silent for a moment. He needed time to think, and he could not do that inside the London house. What the hell had Hyatt dragged him into, and why? At length, he looked up. 'I think I'd better go back to Hamburg straight away. With Harry gone, there's nobody there except Kurt. He's a local employee of Harry's, but I don't think he's aware of the real purpose of the office.' He looked at his watch. 'I can still make an afternoon flight.'

Beaumont nodded. 'It's probably the best thing to do. Would you like me to call a minicab?'

'Don't worry. I'll pick up a taxi outside.'

'I'm sorry to break all this bad news at one time.' Alex smiled. 'The ancient Greeks had a nasty habit of running a sword through messengers with bad tidings. I'm glad you spared me that particular discomfort! Shall I tell Willis you were here?'

'No. If it's all the same to you, Alex, I'd prefer to keep this visit confidential. Do you mind?'

Beaumont shrugged. 'Why should I?'

'Because I'd like to think over your advice before I confront Willis officially. Maybe it is time to make peace, in which case I'd prefer him to think I reached the decision in Hamburg, without any outside prompting.'

'Good man.'

'I'll phone in a couple of days, when I've had a chance to sort things out.'

Beaumont looked smugly conspiratorial. 'As far as I'm concerned, you were never here.'

There was an hour and a half to kill before the Hamburg flight, and Mark found a quiet corner in the departures lounge.

What the hell did he do next? It was a bad dream. He was trapped in the middle of a maze, and every path he took led back to the centre again. Who was going to believe him? Willis? He would want proof of some sort. But Willis was attending the funeral of the only man who could verify Mark's story. Then the questioning would begin. Knowing the sort of moral coward Beaumont was, what was he going to say when the pressure started to build? Mark had been to visit him, had learned about Jack Taylor's failure to call, and had said nothing. Why? Why was Mark holding the papers Jack Taylor had been sent to collect? Who sent him? Could he prove that he had ever met Richard Hyatt, and what was all this nonsense about a 'borrowed' house in a suburb of Hamburg? Did Harry Price know about the meeting? Had Mark told him about it? But Harry Price was dead.

Mark lit a cigarette. Had that really been an accident, or had somebody pushed Harry down the stairs? If so, who? For a moment, Mark felt a sort of panic: take the next flight out – to any destination – and start running. But where? And, in God's name, why? He had done nothing wrong! Hyatt had sent him and Jack Taylor had tried to stop him.

He walked over to the bar and ordered a brandy. 'Slow down, for Christ's sake,' he thought, 'and think it through, step by step. Richard Hyatt came to Hamburg and met you in secret, adding that Harry was not to be told about it. Why not? Think about that later. He gave you a simple assignment: go to Switzerland with fifty thousand dollars and give them to a bent Italian in exchange for two files of scientific papers. A simple job! Beaumont used the same description. But Jack Taylor from your own Department was in Locarno on the same damned assignment! Hyatt must have known about it. Why was he hijacking his own property? To produce his famous trump card for the final hand? That's bullshit!' Mark drank the brandy quickly, and returned to his corner seat.

Hyatt had been specific: the meeting with Stratta was two o'clock in Camedo. 'Did he know Jack's meeting was arranged for three? If the Italian had been on time, you would both have been gone before Jack arrived.' It made no sense! 'Unless . . . unless Hyatt was going into business for himself, and selling to another buyer.' Mark sat forward. At their meeting, Hyatt had said something about outlasting the Whitehall boys longer than they expected. 'Start again from a different angle. Suppose Hyatt is working for the other side. For money? It's unlikely. Wait! Suppose he was always working for the other side. Jesus! Try the story again. Hyatt knew Jack Taylor was meeting Stratta at three, so he called the Italian and rearranged the meeting for two o'clock with you or, at least, with Peter Williams. You even supplied him with a suitable alias; one the Department didn't know about!' Mark sat back. 'All right, you collect the papers and hand them over to Hyatt. What happens next? Sooner or later, Jack Taylor is going to come home, saying that Stratta reneged. At the same time, you're about to be transferred back to London. Unless Hyatt was planning some sort of disappearing act, what was he going to do when you and Jack met one another and started to compare notes? How was he going to keep you quiet?'

Then Mark remembered what had happened to Harry Price. He spoke aloud. 'It wasn't an accident!' Hyatt had to make certain that Price was out of the picture. He had to be sure that Mark had not said anything to Harry, even accidentally. Besides, if Jack's story ever reached Harry, it was conceivable that he might put two and two together: that somebody had intercepted Stratta at the time that Mark had been away on an unexpected and unexplained holiday. Mark hesitated. It was impossible! But Harry Price was dead.

'Go forward one more step. What would have happened if you had delivered the papers to Hyatt?' Mark was very still. 'He'd have no alternative. The moment I handed him those papers, I was signing my own death warrant. He couldn't afford to have me around!' Mark closed his eyes. Only one factor had saved him. Tricky Dicky had not foreseen a heart attack.

A small girl was standing in front of Mark. She was clutching a worn rag doll. 'Did you know you're talking to yourself?' Her voice was accusing.

He looked up, and smiled at her. 'I'm sorry. I didn't know I was.'

'It's quite all right.' She hugged the doll. 'I often talk to Lucinda.'

'What does she say?'

The child was contemptuous. 'That's silly. Dolls can't talk!'

He watched the child walk back to her mother. Calm voices over the loudspeakers announced flight departures, and the electronically controlled information board clattered as new listings were displayed. The Hamburg plane had not yet been called.

Mark closed his eyes and concentrated again. They would never believe him. The whole story was too far-fetched. Hyatt was dead. Why should they accept the idea that the Director General had masterminded the plan? It was much more logical to assume that Mark had changed sides and had set himself up as the double-agent. There was no one left to disprove it. For a moment, he tried to dispel the image of the Citroën hurtling down the mountainside. How long would it take before the news reached London? A tragic road accident: two lives lost, and everything destroyed by the fire.

'The fire!' That was the answer. Everything was destroyed! The only people who knew that he had been to Locarno were dead. No, that was not entirely correct. The hotel staff, the Arab property dealer, the few strangers to whom he had spoken knew an Englishman called Peter Williams had been there on a walking holiday. A waiter in Camedo would remember a tall man who had stolen his motor-scooter. Presumably, the Swiss police would eventually find it and return it to him. That only left Stratta, but who the hell was he going to tell? And, when the charred remains of the Citroën had been identified and the information relayed back to London, the Department would assume that Stratta's papers had been lost in the blaze. They might even contact the Italian again, asking for duplicates. It would be interesting to see his reaction!

He took a taxi directly from Hamburg airport to the office. It was quite late, and the building was empty. The window of Kurt's basement flat was dark. Mark let himself in with a pass key. He unpacked his case quickly, removing the carrier-bag containing Stratta's files.

The only piece of official equipment that London had thoughtfully installed in the office was a shredding machine. He remembered teasing Harry about it shortly after he arrived in Hamburg. What the hell did they have that was worth destroying? Harry had been offended at the time, and had muttered something about maintaining strict security. It had occurred to Mark that the machine made Harry feel like an active member of the organization.

The equipment hummed softly when he switched it on. Placing the carrier-bag at the base, Mark fed the documents into the vent at the top, and thin strands of paper, about a quarter of an inch wide, spewed into the plastic container. It took about five minutes to destroy everything. As an afterthought, he added the Peter Williams passport.

On his way down the street, Mark passed a rubbish bin and dropped the carrier-bag into it. He felt light-headed. It was as though the past five days of his life had been eliminated.

San Francisco, 1986

# 9

Mark spotted Ernie Sullivan sitting towards the centre of the broad expanse of Ghirardelli Square. The ex-CIA man's eyes were closed, and his bony frame was stretched across a wooden bench. A few yards away from him, musicians in open-necked shirts were performing an eighteenth-century woodwind quintet, the music as clear and sparkling as the morning air. Farther away, a young girl was playing unaccompanied Bach on a flute, and her sound occasionally blended with that of the quintet. Ernie might have been their contemporary, dressed in a red plaid shirt and a pair of faded blue jeans, but his shock of white hair revealed his age.

The square was one of San Francisco's most popular tourist attractions. It was not so much a formal square as an open park facing the sea and bordered by an old wood-constructed chocolate factory, from which it took its name, that had been converted into colourful boutiques and restaurants.

There was a cool breeze coming off the water, counterbalanced by brilliant sunshine which seemed to intensify each detail of the scene with the power of a theatrical spotlight. As Mark approached, he wondered whether Ernie might be asleep, but the American looked up with a grin and glanced at his wristwatch.

'I like a man who's punctual.'

'Hello, Ernie.'

Sullivan stood. He was almost as tall as Mark, and straight-backed as a soldier. For a moment, he took Mark's hand in a firm grip, then engulfed him in a bear hug. 'It's good to see you again, son. Hell, you must have an awful ugly-looking picture stored away somewhere in your attic. You've not changed in ten years!' The gravelly voice was warm.

'Neither have you.' Ernie's leathery face was ageless, and the lines at the corners of his mouth and eyes suggested that he was a man accustomed to smiling frequently.

'I feel pretty good. Life's quiet, and all I have to think about is my health. That's become an old American tradition. Besides, I've got a whole herd of grandchildren now. They keep me on my toes.'

'I was sorry to hear about Martha.'

'Yeah.' Ernie looked across the crowded square, filled with sightseers and strollers, some of whom had stopped to listen to the musicians. 'I was thinking about her while I was waiting here for you. She used to like to drive here on a Sunday and listen to the kids playing music or do a little window-shopping. I miss those days most.'

'You must.'

Ernie turned towards the sea, half closing his eyes against the bright light. 'I guess that's what immortality's about: being remembered.' He was silent for a moment, then seemed to brush the thought aside. 'When did you get in?'

'Yesterday, I think.' Mark smiled. 'I was on a flight from Tokyo and arrived before I started, so to speak, crossing date-lines and time zones and God knows what else. I found a motel down by Fisherman's Wharf and slept round the clock, but I still don't know whether I'm supposed to be awake or asleep at the moment.'

'You sure move around.' Ernie chuckled. 'What are you doing these days: selling refrigerators to Eskimos?'

'Almost the same thing. I manage classical musicians. One of my young pianists was making his Japanese debut, so I went along for the ride.'

'Musicians?' The American nodded slowly. 'I guess that must be a good kind of life. Martha would have approved. Do you want to walk a little or sit here in the sun?'

'Let's walk. After all those hours in a plane, I can use the exercise. Air travel may be quick, but the wear and tear is hell.'

'OK.' Ernie pointed beyond an expanse of grass towards a promenade. 'We can stroll by the water, or make a tour of the stores. One of my daughter's kids loves the kite shop, and there's a fancy clock store that sells all kinds of crazy timepieces that need a book of instructions before you can tell the hour or the minute. I'm darned if I can make head or tail of most of them!'

'There's a clock like that on the Kurfürstendamm in Berlin, with flashing bulbs and colours. The first time I saw it, I thought it was a sort of traffic light!'

Ernie grunted. 'I'll stick with my old Timex. We'll go down by the water. It's a little breezy, but not so many people get under your feet.'

They walked towards the bay, and Mark looked round. 'San Francisco is lovely, Ernie. I'd forgotten. It must be the most beautiful city in America.'

'Son, it's the only beautiful city we have. We make fine buildings and lousy cities. I guess Washington's OK, if you don't mind the artificiality of it, and New York's as impressive as ever, but it lost its soul in among all that concrete.' He paused to glance back, taking in the city. 'This place is like Venice: it lives up to all its clichés. I guess it's all those hills and whiteness that make it so special. First time I saw it, I was on a troopship, heading for the Pacific, and I swore I'd settle here one day. It took me another thirty years, but I finally made it. Are you still living in London?'

'No. I moved to Geneva when I left the Department. I've been there ever since.'

'That's a long time.' Ernie did not speak for a while. 'You didn't mention a wife or kids, son.'

Mark's voice was impersonal. 'There was someone, for a long time. She died.' He seldom thought about her anymore, but the pain of her memory, recalled with a start, had never ceased.

'That's too bad.' Sullivan walked in silence. When he spoke again, his voice was soft. 'You're still young, Mark. There's time.'

'I hope so.' Mark kept his voice light.

'Listen, how long are you going to be here? I'd like to have you up to the house. Hell, I bet you never even saw a real redwood face to face! Photographs don't do them justice. Come and see some genuine country for a few days.'

'I'd love to stay, Ernie, but I can't. I must be back in Geneva. My office is too small to run itself without me, and musicians are more demanding than grandchildren.'

'Is that so?' Ernie paused for a moment, and Mark suspected that they had been walking too fast. The American was the kind of man who would never concede to his age. 'I always thought those guys wandered around with their heads in the clouds, thinking great thoughts about Life and Death and Beethoven.'

Mark laughed. 'Some of them do, I hope. That's why they have managers like me to worry about programmes and fees and flights and hotel bookings. I ought to take a plane this evening.'

'That's too bad, but I guess I should feel honoured. Maybe next time?'

'Definitely next time.'

Ernie smiled. 'In which case, you'd better tell me why you're here. If you want the goddam truth, I've been busting my gut waiting to ask you ever since you phoned! What the Sam Hill's going on? I haven't thought about Richard Hyatt in a donkey's age, and then you call out of the blue, dropping his name like it was yesterday. Didn't he die some time back in the seventies?'

'Yes, as far as I know.'

Sullivan looked puzzled. 'As far as you know?' When Mark did not reply, he asked, 'Why the sudden interest?'

Mark hesitated. 'Because, two nights ago in Tokyo, a dying man begged me to get a message to the Department in London, telling them to warn Richard Hyatt that he was in danger.' Sullivan had stopped walking, and was staring at Mark, his face expressionless. 'He said I must tell Quentin Sharpe – I don't think you'd know him; he's after your time – to warn Hyatt in Dresden –'

'Hold on! You're going too fast for me. Richard Hyatt in Dresden? That's East Germany, isn't it?' Mark nodded. 'Who was this dying man, and what the hell's Richard Hyatt doing in Dresden? He's dead! Jesus, Mark, you're talking in riddles!'

They began walking again. 'I'd better try to start from the beginning.' He slowed his pace, and Sullivan moved closer, his shoulder brushing against Mark's. On the flight from Tokyo, he had mentally prepared his story many times, and he now recounted it carefully, as though he had memorized it, trying to include every fragment. Sullivan did not interrupt. Occasionally he looked up, raising his bushy eyebrows in a silent question, waiting for Mark to clarify a detail.

When Mark had finished, the American continued to walk, his head bowed, without speaking. At length, he spoke softly. 'This guy Bailey, you're sure it was he?'

'Yes. We'd met on several occasions in the past few years.'

Sullivan's eyes narrowed. 'I thought you quit long ago.'

'I did, but our paths crossed occasionally.'

'How come?'

'It's hard to explain, Ernie. There have been a few times when

'. . . circumstances have brought me into contact with the Department again.' A shadow crossed Mark's face. 'It wasn't by choice, I can assure you. I didn't leave on the best of terms.'

'I heard something like that.'

'Really? Who from?'

Sullivan shrugged. 'I don't recall. All I remember was asking after you one time and getting one of those cool stiff upper lip answers you Britishers are so expert at. I figured out the rest for myself.'

'You were right.'

'But you stayed in touch nonetheless?'

'No. They stayed in touch with me – several times!'

'How do you mean?'

'I found myself dragged back into their dirty games, against my will, if you must know. It's a long and complicated story.'

'OK.' Ernie was silent. If he had further questions on the subject, he did not pursue them. At length, he said, 'But you're sure the man who died was Bailey?'

'Yes. He was only a few feet away from me. It was dark, but I saw him clearly enough before they started shooting at me. After that, I was too busy running for my life.'

Ernie was silent again, as though absorbing the information. 'But when you looked for him later, he'd disappeared.' It was a statement rather than a question.

Mark nodded. 'Whoever fired at me must have taken the body away while I was inside the hotel, asking for help. I couldn't prove I'd ever seen him. The police thought I'd been drinking, but you have to believe me: I didn't imagine what happened!'

Something in Mark's voice made Sullivan pause. His voice was gentle. 'I believe you, son.'

'Thank you. That's why I called you.'

'Why me?' Ernie had stopped walking, and was watching Mark's face.

'There were several reasons. I suppose the first was that I had to travel back from Tokyo to Switzerland, and San Francisco was on the way. That's why I telephoned.'

'OK.' Sullivan did not seem convinced.

'That wasn't all. You see, I've only told you half the story, Ernie. There's a lot more to come.'

'Oh.' The American glanced round. 'In that case, I guess I'd like to sit a while. I don't walk as far as I used to.' He indicated an empty bench, facing the water. When they were seated, Ernie smiled wryly. 'I have the sneaky feeling I'll need to be sitting for the next part!'

'You could be right. You see, the real reason for my being here involves you very slightly.'

'Me?'

Mark nodded. 'According to Hyatt, he once paid me a visit because you had recommended me to him.'

'Oh?'

'I was on a posting to Hamburg at the time. Do you remember doing that?'

Sullivan shook his head slowly. 'Not really.' He closed his eyes for a moment. 'Hell, yes, I remember. I asked Hyatt to give you my best the next time he saw you.' He grinned. 'I may even have thrown in some crap about you being a pretty smart operator – something like that. Come to think about it, I guess that must have been the last time I saw him. The news of his death came through a few weeks later.'

'Yes, that would fit.' Mark lit a cigarette, cupping his hands over the flame to protect it from the breeze. He inhaled slowly.

Ernie's voice was soft. 'If I didn't know you better, son, I'd say you were playing for time. What's on your mind?'

'Before I tell you, Ernie, I'd like to ask you something. You may not want to tell me, but I'll ask anyway.'

'I'll let you know, son. I've been out of the service for a long time now, so I guess there's very little restricted information that would affect either of us. Go ahead.'

'How important was Hyatt, as far as your operations were concerned?'

Sullivan did not reply immediately. At length, he said, 'Very important.'

'Why?'

The American stared out to sea. 'There had to be someone who could act as a go-between, someone we could trust when it came to high security operations. Despite all the sophisticated communications systems, there are times when you don't want to put things in writing, so you opt for a man who'll keep it all stored away in his head. We chose Hyatt. He had the right credentials, and he was senior to any man in Washington.'

'I see.'

'We were working pretty closely in those days. I guess they

were a good time. As head of your service, Hyatt was automatically a key figure in our operations, especially involving anything in Europe. I'm not saying we told him everything, but he was better informed than anyone else from your side of the ocean. We were always pretty cautious about how much we should give out.'

'Mistrust?'

'Yes and no. When it comes to national security, there has to be a cut-off point. Who else was there? We never really trusted the French, and the Germans made us nervous. It was too easy for them to move from East to West and back. They all spoke the same language. I guess language was always the basis of our special relationship. At least we all spoke English. When somebody finally writes it down in the history books, I hope they take into account that Americans are lousy linguists! So, let's put in this way: Richard Hyatt knew just about as much as we were prepared to give out at any one time, certainly more than anyone else.' He looked at Mark curiously. 'Does that answer your question? We're talking about a hell of a long time ago.'

'I think so.'

'What does that mean?'

'It means that if Bailey was telling the truth, Hyatt is alive and well and living in East Germany.'

'That's a very big if. As far as we know, Hyatt died of a heart attack about ten years ago. Your people confirmed it.'

'Yes.'

'In which case, this guy Bailey either got it wrong, or was deliberately fooling you –'

'A dying man doesn't do that, Ernie.'

'If you say so. Mark, I'm not disbelieving you, but you're the only one who saw him die.' When Mark was silent, Ernie shrugged gently. 'Could there be two Richard Hyatts?'

'No. That's an even wilder coincidence.'

'Either way, the story doesn't make sense. We're talking about ten years ago, Mark. Why do you want to know how important Hyatt was?'

Mark ground his cigarette underfoot. He turned to face Ernie, staring into the other man's eyes. 'Because I'm reasonably certain that, at the time he died, Richard Hyatt was working for the other side.'

Ernie spoke slowly. 'How certain is that?'

'About as sure as I can be. It was one of the reasons I left the Department.' His gaze did not leave Ernie's face.

The American shook his head. 'That's a pretty strange statement, son. Who else knows about this?'

'No one. I couldn't tell anyone until now. You're the first, Ernie.'

'For Christ's sake, why?'

Mark sighed. 'Because nobody would have believed me, and because I was in the middle of a situation where they would have thought that I, not Hyatt, had gone over to the other side. I only realized what was happening after he was dead, and by that time it was too late.' Mark lit another cigarette, conscious that his hands were trembling. 'At that moment, I was more concerned with self-preservation than with setting any records straight. Anyway, Hyatt was already dead, and I had no way of proving what I knew. Anything I could have said or done would have made me appear guiltier than ever. You have to believe me, Ernie. The only thing I could do was keep my mouth shut.'

'What happened?'

Mark threw the cigarette aside and stared out to sea. 'Not long after you last saw Hyatt, he came to Hamburg and asked me to meet him. I was sharing the office there with Harry Price.'

'I seem to remember him.'

Mark nodded. 'More than likely. He'd been around for a long time. Richard Hyatt met me in secret, in a house he said he'd borrowed from a friend. When I think about it now, he made very certain that Price didn't know about our meeting, and asked me not to tell him. He phoned me a few minutes after Harry went to lunch. I think he was watching the office, and waited for Harry to leave before he called.'

'OK.' Ernie's reply scarcely concealed his impatience.

'I'm sorry. I don't mean to string it out. I'm still putting all the pieces together. It was a long time ago. When I met Hyatt, he gave me a simple assignment. I had to meet an Italian electronics expert who had some valuable documents for sale. They involved developments in computer technology. You have to remember that this was the mid-'seventies, when we were all changing over to machines.'

'I remember.'

Mark lit another cigarette. 'The pick-up involved meeting in a small Swiss mountain village just across the border from Italy. I was pleased to get out of Hamburg at the time. It was a difficult period for me. To be honest, I was preparing to chuck it in.'

Sullivan nodded slowly. 'I guess we all had moments of doubt somewhere along the way. Don't assume you were the only one. Keep going.'

'I mention it because the Department knew I was angry, unhappy – I don't know what. If you're an agent and start to feel that way, you're regarded as an increased risk. That's why they sent me to Hamburg.' Mark leaned forward, his hands resting on his knees. 'I made the exchange –'

'Exchange?'

'Money. A down-payment on the documents. The rest was to follow later into a Swiss bank account. It was as simple as Hyatt predicted.' He paused.

'Except?'

'Except that somebody else was there, expecting to make the same deal. If the Italian hadn't arrived late, the other man and I would never have met.'

'But you did.' Mark nodded. 'What then?'

'He tried to take the papers from me – with a gun. I managed to get away, and he came after me in his car. It's a very mountainous area.' Mark hesitated and, for a moment, recalled Jill's terrified face as the little Citroën tipped over the edge of the precipice. 'His car went over the side of a hill.' He could not bring himself to mention her presence.

After a long silence, Ernie spoke. 'There must have been more to it than that.'

Mark looked at him. 'There was. The man who tried to stop me was one of ours.'

'Are you sure?'

'Positive. He'd been sent there by the Department on the same job. Hyatt must have known about it.' He looked down, to find that he was gripping his knees tightly.

'When did you find out?'

'When I reached London.' Words came more easily, and he told the rest of the story quickly, describing his meeting with Alex Beaumont and the news of Hyatt's death and Harry's accident.

Sullivan was watching him carefully. 'What did you do?'

'What the hell could I do, Ernie? Hyatt was dead. I'd caused the death of the man officially sent to collect the papers. I couldn't prove that Hyatt had also assigned me and, to make matters worse, I was already on the Department's shit list. They could only have reached one conclusion: that it was I and not Hyatt who had changed sides. And if they needed further evidence, I had the papers. Who was going to believe my story?'

Sullivan frowned. 'Are you sure the man who sent you was Hyatt?'

'Certain. It was Tricky Dicky himself. I'd seen his picture several times, and I checked the files back in Hamburg. I can only assume now that he wanted those papers as a housewarming present for his new employers.' Mark paused again. 'I'm also reasonably sure that Harry's death wasn't an accident.'

'Why is that?'

'It was too convenient. Harry was supposed to have fallen down some stairs when he was drunk. I believe Hyatt was tying up loose ends. He had to be certain I hadn't let anything slip in Hamburg. Perhaps he was afraid Harry might mention my absence at the time of the switch.'

'That's a long shot, but you could be right. Hyatt was a real smart operator, one of the best I ever met.'

'I was supposed to report to him and no one else when I got to London. He'd given me a bunch of rather phoney reasons for keeping quiet about the job.' Mark hesitated again. 'If I'm right about all this, I would have been the next on the list after Harry. If Hyatt was really playing a double game, he couldn't afford to have me around.' His eyes met Ernie's. 'The only thing he hadn't anticipated was a heart attack. It probably saved my life.'

'What did you do?'

Mark stared at the water. 'I kept my mouth shut and got out, as fast as I could. I'm not very proud of it. My only concern was self-preservation. Nobody was going to believe me, and I didn't fancy spending the next twenty years of my life doing time for treason. I'd covered my tracks well enough, but I couldn't risk anything. The only danger was that the Italian could identify me, but I hoped the Department would assume their man and the papers were lost in the car crash.' He paused. 'It caught fire when it hit the bottom of the hill.'

For a moment, Ernie said nothing. Then he asked, 'What happened to the papers?'

'I destroyed them. There was nothing else I could do. A few months later, I resigned from the Department and, with a little help, moved to Geneva.' He looked at Sullivan. 'You're the only person who knows any of this, Ernie.'

The American placed an arm around Mark's shoulder. 'That's a hell of a story to live with all these years, son. I guess I'm flattered to be the one that finally hears it. If it makes you feel better, I'll add that it won't go any further.'

'Thank you. It's strange, but I feel better for telling you. The damned thing's haunted me for a long time.'

'Yeah.' Ernie looked slightly embarrassed. 'Give me one of those cigarettes, will you. I gave up smoking years ago, but this is kind of a special occasion.'

Mark held the lighter for the American. He was grateful to find that his hand was steady. 'Now, it appears that Hyatt has suddenly risen from the dead, Ernie, and I'm supposed to call London and tell them about it. What the hell do I do?'

Sullivan frowned at the glowing tip of his cigarette. 'Is London going to believe you?'

'I don't know. Probably not. Christ! I couldn't even persuade the Japanese a few minutes after Bailey died!'

'That's what I was thinking.'

'But I watched him die, Ernie! Whether they believe me or not, I saw it!'

There was a gentle smile on Ernie's face. 'I guess that was always your problem, Mark. You had too much conscience!' He hunched his shoulders. 'Let's move on. The breeze off the water is chilling me.'

They walked back towards the square at a leisurely pace. Small white clouds, moving rapidly across the blue of the sky, momentarily hid the sun, and the air felt cold. 'Do I call Quentin Sharpe?'

Sullivan stopped for a moment. 'Maybe. Just how important is this to you, son?'

'I don't know. I do know I don't want to get involved again. That was another life, and it ended a long time ago. At the same time . . .' He left the sentence unfinished.

'At the same time, you saw a man in Tokyo die, and you can't walk away from it.' Mark nodded. 'Then call London. You don't have to speak to this Sharpe fellow if you don't want to.'

'I tried to call him from Tokyo, but they said he was on holiday.'

'Fine.' Ernie's voice was calm. 'So pass on the message. Find someone to talk to, tell him what Bailey told you, and leave it at that. Listen, it's not your problem any more. They can make of it whatever they want, and if they need to know more, they'll come find you.' His voice softened. 'Go back to living your own life, Mark.'

'You make it sound very easy.'

'Maybe it's easier than you think. Look, it all happened a long time ago. The whole world's changed since then, and so have you. You don't owe them. Hell, they probably have inventions in Silicon Valley that your Italian genius never even imagined.' Ernie moved closer. 'I watched your face when you were talking, Mark. You don't have to tell me what was on your mind. It was all written there, plain as day. You'd be crazy to get yourself involved again.'

'Then why call at all?'

'Because you won't be clear inside your head until you do. You saw this guy Bailey. Use a telephone. Forget about Hyatt, and whether he's alive or dead. Just tell them what they need to know, and hang up. You're out of it, and if you have any horse sense, you'll stay out of it.'

'You're right, Ernie. Maybe I'm relieved because you're telling me what I wanted to hear.'

'Could be. You've been living with your memories for a long time, Mark.' Ernie halted for a moment, and Mark sensed that he had become very still. His voice remained casual. 'Has anyone contacted you since Tokyo?'

'No. As far as Tokyo was concerned, I was just another Westerner who drank too much sake!'

'I wouldn't be so sure.'

'Why do you say that?'

Ernie resumed walking slowly, hardly turning his head. 'Because there's a fellow over there in the square who seems very interested in taking our photographs.'

'Where?'

Ernie shrugged very slightly. 'I'd sooner not point. Can you see a man in blue jeans with a white rollneck shirt? He's carrying a fancy camera with a long telephoto lens.' Sullivan's head did not move. 'I'd put him at about two o'clock from the wind players.'

Mark centred his attention on the woodwind quintet. A little behind them, to the right, a man in a white shirt was fiddling with a camera slung from his neck. 'I've got him.'

'Well,' Ernie's voice remained calm, and his drawl had become slightly exaggerated, 'I noticed him taking pictures when you arrived. It seemed to me at the time that we must be getting in his way. I guess that makes it just a little too coincidental that he's still shooting in the same direction, with us in the middle of each shot.'

'Are you sure?'

Ernie grinned. 'I may be old, Mark, but I'm not that dumb! I wouldn't look straight at him if I were you, son. That's a pretty long lens on his camera. If he looks through it and sees you watching him, he'll know you're on to him.'

Mark turned to face Sullivan. 'I'll see if I can get a little closer.'

'Why don't you do that.' Ernie was smiling broadly. He was enjoying himself.

'In a moment, I'll say goodbye and move off.' Ernie nodded. 'I'll find you in a few minutes by the kite shop, if I'm not . . . delayed.'

Ernie continued to smile. 'I'm with you. You can't miss the shop. Good luck!'

They shook hands, and Mark turned away, walking swiftly in the direction of the square. From the corner of his eye, he could see the photographer look up. The man stood, uncertain, for a moment, then walked away at a brisk pace. Mark quickened his step, unwilling to run, but the man was heading into the building housing the shops and restaurants. As he entered, he turned for a moment, looking directly towards Mark. They were still far apart, and Mark was unable to make out the man's features. He increased his pace, but the photographer had already entered the building and was lost from sight. Mark broke into a run, but he knew he was too late. There were several exits on the far side of the shopping concourse, which bordered on a busy street.

By the time he reached the street, there was no sign of the man. Mark glanced in either direction, and his attention was caught by a dark car accelerating away from a parking space. It seemed to be moving faster than the rest of the traffic. Several blocks away, it turned a corner, its tyres skidding on the tarmac, and disappeared from view.

Berlin, 1986

# 10

Konstantin Steigel was pacing restlessly by the reception desk at the Kempinski Hotel, his hands locked behind his back and his tall frame leaning forward. Despite the warm weather, he was dressed in a dark suit with a slightly old-fashioned cut, and his silver tonsure of close-cropped hair seemed to gleam in the subdued lighting. As Mark entered the foyer, he saw the old conductor consult his watch, peering myopically through the glasses perched on the end of his nose. He seemed ill at ease.

'Hello, maestro.'

'Ah, Mark, my dear, I was hoping you would arrive soon.' His face relaxed, but his bony hand had a remarkably firm grip. 'Thank you for coming to Berlin so promptly.'

'I always enjoy being here, and you said it was very urgent when you called this morning.'

'Yes, I believe it is, but I hope I have not disorganized your office too much with my anxieties.'

'Not really.' Mark smiled. Konstantin lived in a world where any anomalous deviation from his musical routine took on critical proportions. On this occasion, he had not even been prepared to discuss the 'crisis' on the telephone. 'I came back from Japan a couple of weeks ago, so there's been enough time for me to catch up with all the accumulated paperwork. Is Heidi with you?'

'Yes, yes.' Konstantin gestured impatiently. He seldom travelled anywhere without his cheerful, ageless wife, who had acted as confidante, secretary, assistant, adviser, dresser and handmaiden for nearly half a century. 'As a matter of fact, she is resting upstairs at the moment. Otherwise, I would suggest that we go immediately to the room.' For a moment, he looked dismayed. 'Perhaps you would like to check in before we talk?'

Despite his autocratic lifestyle, Steigel still possessed an old-world courtesy that was endearing.

'I can do it later.' Mark nodded to the concierge, who had recognized him and was bowing ostentatiously. A moment later, a bellboy, summoned with an imperious click of the fingers, relieved him of his suitcase.

'Good.' Steigel glanced towards the elevators with a frown, as though willing Heidi to appear. Then he grasped Mark's forearm and steered him towards one of the hotel's spacious lounges. 'Come, we will find a quiet corner to sit and talk. I would prefer to have absolute privacy, but thank God this place has enough room to allow us to speak undisturbed. Shall I order coffee?'

'No, thank you. I had to kill time this afternoon, changing planes at Frankfurt, and drank too many cups in the departure lounge.'

Steigel selected two heavy leather armchairs in an alcove, and settled himself. Moments later, an obese German businessman with a copy of *Der Spiegel* tucked under his arm approached the third chair in the group, but the conductor fixed the man with the same icy stare that had quelled orchestras, and he retreated, selecting a sofa in the middle of the room.

Konstantin sat forward, resting his elbows on his knees, his fingertips touching. 'It is very good of you to come so quickly, Mark. I had hoped we might talk in the privacy of my room, but Heidi . . .' He gave an irritated frown, leaving the sentence unfinished.

'I shouldn't imagine we'll be disturbed here.' The lounge was almost empty.

'I hope not.' He lowered his voice. 'What I have to tell you is extremely confidential.' Steigel looked around, to reassure himself that no one was within earshot. A waiter hovered nearby, his eyebrows raised inquiringly, and the conductor waved him away.

'Perhaps we'd better get down to business. I must admit you've had me guessing all the way from Geneva.'

'Very well.' Steigel took a deep breath. 'Tell me, Mark, how much do you know about the music of Gustav Mahler?' His eyes gleamed, and Mark could sense his suppressed excitement.

The question took him slightly by surprise. Mark had half-expected some unreleased item of news in the endless chess game of musical politics. On the flight from Frankfurt, he had wondered whether Konstantin had been offered the directorship of one of the more prestigious orchestras. It had happened quite frequently in the past. He could even believe that the old conductor had finally decided to retire. The man was approaching eighty, and had aged noticeably in the past few years. Mark could not really imagine a music world without Konstantin Steigel on the podium, but the years were passing. Certainly, a momentous decision such as that would have prompted the dramatic summons to Berlin.

Aware that Steigel was watching him intently, Mark said, 'Mahler? I must have heard most of his music over the years.' He shrugged. 'The symphonies are played to death these days. I think I prefer the song cycles. They seem less self-indulgent. He's forced to tailor his music to the words, instead of wandering off into all those additional pages.'

There was a satisfied smile on Steigel's face, and Mark felt a growing exasperation. Had the old man really dragged him halfway across Europe just to discuss Mahler? He wondered whether the management of the Berlin *Festwochen* had invited Konstantin to conduct a cycle of the composer's music. That could easily have been arranged with a phone call or a telex!

The conductor was nodding amiably. 'You probably assume that you have heard all of Mahler's music at one time or another, my dear Mark, but I can assure you that you have not.'

'Really?'

'I am certain. You see, it is only because he was recently discovered by the general public that there is such a fascination for him.' He shrugged. 'That, together with a certain neurotic element that seems to strike a responsive chord with present-day concert-goers. To me, it is astonishing to think that Mahler died seventy-five years ago but was hardly performed for the next thirty or forty years. Of course, a handful of us continued to perform his music: Bruno Walter, Klemperer, and myself, but he remained little more than a musician's musician. Audiences didn't want to know. When I tried to programme his symphonies in London, I was met with a blank refusal.'

'I suppose so.' Mark could feel a growing irritation as Konstantin settled into one of his favourite lectures.

The conductor shrugged irritably. 'Then, along came young Bernstein and Haitink and one or two others.' He glowered. 'You would think they had discovered Mahler all by themselves!'

'They certainly helped to re-establish him.'

Konstantin sighed. 'I suppose they did. We should at least be grateful to them for that.'

Mark lit a cigarette. 'Perhaps you should tell me why you've asked me to come to Berlin.'

'Yes.' Once again, Konstantin looked round to make certain that they were not overheard. Then he leaned towards Mark, lowering his voice. 'You said a moment ago that you had probably heard all of Gustav Mahler's music. I am prepared to wager that you have not!' His voice contained an element of excitement that made Mark look up.

'Why do you say that?'

'Because we know that he left behind a number of unpublished manuscripts that have never been found. There is a youthful Nordic Symphony, which you can read about in all the textbooks, and which he is supposed to have destroyed himself.' Steigel drew in his breath, enjoying the drama. 'But there was more – much more. You know, the late Deryck Cooke, the man who edited the Tenth Symphony – and that's a masterpiece, by the way – he told me that he had held the unpublished scores of two complete symphonies in his own hands!'

'Really? When?'

'In 1938, on a visit to Dresden. Imagine, Mark: to have held two unpublished scores by Mahler!'

'What happened to them?'

'They were lost, destroyed when the British and the Americans flattened Dresden towards the end of the war with their thousand-bomber raids. Can you imagine such an appalling deed?' It was clear that, in Steigel's opinion, the systematic destruction of Dresden had been the blackest moment of twentieth-century musical history. 'And for what? To destroy the morale of a people who already knew that they had been defeated. It was unforgivable!'

Mark nodded. He had read Kurt Vonnegut and was about to say so, but Steigel's expression silenced him.

'They were not destroyed, Mark.' His voice had reduced to a whisper. 'They were stored away in a deep cellar in an old house in the suburbs of the city. Nobody knew they were there.'

'Why not?'

'The owner died – he was killed in the war – and the house

changed hands several times. Presumably, it finally became the property of the State.'

'And the scores?'

Once again, the light seemed to glint on the conductor's glasses. 'The scores lay there through the years, packed away in a wooden case. That was until a few months ago. You see, the building was to be demolished, to make space for a new development of workers' flats.' When Mark did not reply, the conductor settled back in his chair, satisfied that he had an attentive audience.

'What happened next?'

'Some workmen were checking the premises before the wrecking machines arrived. I would imagine they were scavenging in search of possible antiques or anything of minor value. Being employed by a totalitarian regime makes petty thieves of everyone.' He grunted. 'They probably hoped to find a few bottles of wine abandoned in the cellar.' He paused, like a good story-teller. 'So, one of the men found the case, and took it for firewood. He was about to throw the papers away, when he noticed that they were covered with musical annotations, so he spirited them away and took them home.'

'And?'

Konstantin shrugged. 'He didn't know what to do next. He couldn't read music, and he hadn't the faintest idea what he had found. Perhaps he had heard stories about valuable discoveries: that little Mozart symphony that showed up a few years ago, and those very dubious Bach chorales that the Americans found in their own museum. Do you remember how they tried to auction them off to the record companies? Anyway, he did nothing. The man just kept quiet for a few weeks, and made a few cautious inquiries. Finally, he took the scores to a teacher in the local academy, begging him first not to tell the authorities what he had found. The teacher recognized the signature and even the writing. It's interesting, you know, but the notation of music is as individual as handwriting. There are some fascinating books on the subject. My favourite is by Emanuel Winternitz, who used to be at the Metropolitan Museum in New York. Did you know, for example, that Beethoven drew notes in a reverse circular motion when he composed fast pieces? One can see the excitement he felt as he put them down, but what a mess he made! Of course, the musicians who earned a living as copyists had the clearest hand.

Bizet, for example, and Delibes. Their scores are elegantly set down.' For a moment, Konstantin was lost in thought. There were times when his lifelong love-affair with music gave him a slightly professorial air.

Mark waited patiently. At length, he said, 'What happened next?'

Konstantin was disturbed from his reverie. 'What?'

'The teacher at the academy.' Mark smiled, but felt a pang of sadness. The conductor was growing old, and his concentration seemed to wander. It was only when he stepped on to a podium, ready to guide an orchestra through a complicated score he had committed to memory, that he fought back the years.

'Ach, yes.' Konstantin leaned forward to place his hand over Mark's. 'You must forgive me if I ramble. My memories sometimes intrude upon my thoughts. The teacher is a man called Karl Wolpert. He wanted to keep the music. He even offered to buy it, but the workman became suspicious, afraid that he might not receive a fair price for his discovery.' He shrugged. 'The problem is that you cannot keep a secret such as that for very long, especially if you want to make a profit from it. Apparently, they argued for a long time, and eventually decided that their best approach would be to offer the music for sale.'

'How?'

'Obviously, they couldn't do that in the East. The authorities would simply take it away in the name of the State. Fortunately, for us, Karl has a brother living here in West Berlin. He and his parents managed to cross the border many years ago, before they built the wall. Only Karl remained behind. I do not know all the family details, but it would seem that he wanted to stay there. He was an idealistic young man at the time, and believed the new Germany should be rebuilt along the democratic lines outlined by their Russian allies.'

'Then why didn't he take the music to the authorities?'

Steigel shook his head slowly. 'Idealism doesn't last forever, my dear Mark, especially when you do not have enough to eat, or sufficient clothing for the winter months. Karl was a very young man when he decided to stay in the East. Later, it was too late to change his mind. He discussed the idea with the workman, and they agreed to contact his brother, who came to see me.' He paused again. 'That was not so easy for them. Karl and his brother do not like each other. When they finally talked, he agreed very reluctantly to make contact. Karl had two demands: that the scores should be sold in the West, and that I should be offered them first. The price is not very high; quite insignificant by our standards.'

'Why did Karl specifically ask for you?' Mark regretted the question as soon as he had asked it.

Steigel stared at him for a moment. 'I have a certain reputation when it comes to Mahler, Mark. I thought you were aware of that.'

'Yes, of course.'

'Are you asking me why they wanted me to have the score when they could have sent it to von Karajan, or Solti, or Bernstein, or some of the more glamorous interpreters of his music?'

Mark could feel himself blushing. 'Not really.'

'They would attract greater publicity, I suppose, but I believe Karl thinks I would be more faithful to the original score. I have made a lifetime study of Mahler's music. I would have thought an Englishman like you, with your quaint Victorian tradition of art for art's sake, would have approved of such a decision.'

'I do. It simply occurred to me that the Berlin Philharmonic or the Chicago Symphony might have offered greater publicity, if not a better price.'

'I am sure they do, but Karl wanted the first reading to be mine. You forget, Mark, that he is a musician and, even if some of the fervour has been replaced by need, an idealist.' Steigel became businesslike. 'Anyway, the others will have their opportunity. I will also make sure that orchestral parts are properly prepared under my supervision. We will rent them out for a suitable fee, which I propose to share with Karl and the workman.' He smiled. 'I have the feeling that the rentals may provide a better pension for Heidi than all those record royalties I have been promised.'

'I hadn't thought of that.'

Steigel's smile grew broader. 'That is because you English have a deep-rooted suspicion that there is something vaguely distasteful about making money from serious music.' He grunted. 'I recommend the correspondence between Beethoven and his publishers, especially the part where he complains about the paltry fee he received for his Ninth Symphony!'

'What arrangements have you made so far?'

Steigel lowered his voice slightly. 'They are rather complicated,

Mark. That is why I asked you to come to Berlin. You see, it will involve removing the scores from East Berlin without arousing suspicion. I am a somewhat familiar figure in musical circles, despite your hesitation over my suitability as curator of these scores.'

'I didn't mean to suggest –'

Steigel again placed his hand over Mark's. 'It's no matter, my dear. I suppose, if I am honest with you, that I asked the same question myself. I was very touched that Karl Wolpert thought of me first.'

'He was right.' Konstantin smiled his forgiveness. 'What would you like me to do?'

The conductor placed his fingertips together, resuming his 'schoolmaster' posture. 'Unfortunately, Karl's brother will offer no help. He is some sort of minor bureaucrat, and kept telling me that he could not be involved in any kind of scandal between East and West Berlin. I didn't believe him. There is some sort of old hatred, dating back to the past. He made the original contact with me, passed the message, and bowed out. 'I have therefore made arrangements for us – you, Heidi and myself, and a third party whom I haven't mentioned yet – to go across to East Berlin tomorrow. Heidi and I will travel separately, to make a visit as tourists. The hotel has looked after the details for me.' He sighed. 'You know, I have not been there for many years. What you call East Berlin used to be the centre of the town. It was a wonderful, exciting city before that ugly little corporal took over.'

'Have you not been there since before the war?'

'No, Mark. There was never a reason. I prefer to remember it as it was.'

'You must be anxious to see it again.'

Steigel shook his head sadly. 'No. It is always dangerous to go back to a place you have not seen for so many years. I would like to see the Pergamon Museum one more time. I am told it has not changed, but I doubt whether I will recognize very much else.'

'The Unter den Linden looks much the same, I suppose, with the University and the Opera House. Beyond the Dom, you won't recognize anything. There's a huge Alexanderplatz, in the best Soviet tradition. It's impressive, but not very inspiring.' Steigel nodded sombrely. 'If you feel this way, why go at all?'

'Because I have to see the scores. I will be carrying a fairly large amount of money on me, in dollars, but I am not prepared to pay them over until I have satisfied myself that the music is genuine.'

Mark sat forward. 'Maestro, are you certain that you want to get yourself involved in something like this? There are very strict currency laws in the East. If they were to suspect –'

Steigel raised his hand. 'Who is going to suspect an elderly gentleman and his wife on a sightseeing tour of Berlin's most famous art treasures? Don't worry, my dear. I have thought it all out very carefully.'

'What exactly are you planning to do?'

'Karl will be waiting for me in the museum. There is an exquisite blue ceramic Babylonian arch in one of the halls, decorated with a frieze of animals. Surely you have seen it?'

Mark shook his head. 'I haven't been to East Berlin. I've seen lots of photographs of it, and I've often seen it from the air, when the plane comes into Tegel from the right direction.' It was only a half-truth. He had once been in the city, travelling with false papers, but that had been a mission for the Department, and there had been no time to visit museums.

Steigel beamed. 'You will enjoy it. The Pergamon is one of the most spectacular museums in the world. When you first enter, and see that magnificent temple from which it takes its name, you will be spellbound! Karl will meet me by the Babylonian arch. We will leave the museum together, and he will drive me to his house.' There was excitement in his voice. 'If I am satisfied that the scores are genuine, I will give him the money, and he will drive us back to the centre of the town. That is where I will meet you and your companion.' He looked at Mark closely. 'What is the matter?'

'I'm sorry, maestro, but I don't like the plan.'

'Why not?'

'Because you have no guarantee that this isn't some kind of elaborate confidence trick. You're proposing to go with Heidi into East Berlin to meet some character whom you don't know, who *says* he has some rare Mahler scores. Furthermore, you'll be carrying a large amount of illegal money with you. How do you know this isn't some sort of trap?'

Konstantin smiled. 'I have not told him I would bring money. I am there only to verify the music. If I am satisfied with what I find, I will offer to pay him on the spot, and take the scores with me. He does not know that.'

Mark shook his head. 'You're taking too many risks. Why

doesn't he make a xerox of one or two pages for you to look at before you go? That way, there is no danger that –'

'Mark, there is no danger!' Steigel's voice was irritated. 'I am not as foolish as you think! I can tell the man is genuine. Besides, I'm not interested in xeroxes. I want to hold those scores in my own hands! I have waited more than fifty years for this moment. You have no reason to believe it is a trick.'

'Then at least leave the money behind. You can go back the following day. Better still, let me do it for you. What you're suggesting leaves you completely unprotected.' Steigel hesitated before replying, and Mark continued, 'After fifty years, an extra day isn't going to make any difference. Let me come with you to the house. As your manager –'

'No! It is important that we don't travel together, simply because you are my manager.'

'Why?'

Steigel looked uneasy. 'People talk. Now, as far as I know, only Karl and this workman – and Karl's brother – know about this, but there is always the danger that one of them may let something slip. Maybe one of the other builders' men saw the man take the music. In a police state, one cannot take chances. It is because you are my manager, Mark, that I do not want to arouse any suspicion. That is why I am travelling with Heidi. If they see you with me, people could suspect that we are there on musical business.'

'But that's an even better idea. Listen, let me call the *Intendant* of the Opera and tell him that you would be interested in conducting a new production. He'd jump at the opportunity. That way, we could make a perfectly normal business visit to East Berlin, you could make contact with Karl, and I'd have a reason to be there with you. It would reduce the risk considerably.'

Konstantin nodded slowly. 'You are right, but we do not have enough time.'

'Why not?'

'Because Karl lives in Dresden. He only has a permit to remain in Berlin for a few days. You seem to forget that the city is forbidden to him, too, and that East Germans are not allowed to travel freely.'

'Then let's wait until he goes back to Dresden. I'll contact the manager of the *Staatskapelle* with the same proposal.'

Steigel shook his head. 'No. I have already made up my mind. I want to see those scores as soon as possible.'

'It would only take a few days to arrange –'

The old conductor smiled sadly. 'At my age, Mark, a few days can sometimes seem like an eternity! You are being too cautious. I tell you, there is nothing to fear.'

'Then at least leave the money behind, and we'll arrange the exchange a couple of days later. You'll see the scores, but you won't risk anything more.'

Konstantin was silent, his head bowed as though deep in thought. At length, he said, 'Very well.'

'I'll go over the following day, if you like, and take the money with me.'

'I'd prefer you to come tomorrow, as planned. You see, my intention is to meet you there, hand the scores over to you and return with Heidi. In that way, no one would associate you with Karl Wolpert, which is important. It is still possible that he will let me take some of the music immediately, so that I can study it. I warned him already that I could not necessarily verify it on the spot, although I know very well what to expect. It could be that an early score would have certain differences . . . I don't know what I will find. You know, Mahler had the habit of substituting movements from one symphony to another. I have to accept the possibility that all Karl has to offer is music that Mahler reworked at a later date. It will be historically interesting, but no great discovery.'

'Then you have all the more reason to be cautious.'

'Yes, I suppose so.' Steigel looked disappointed, and Mark regretted that he had undermined the old man's hopes. 'But if Karl allows me to take some pages of the music to study, I will pass them to you, as I had originally planned. Will you come tomorrow?'

'Yes, of course. What exactly would you like me to do?'

The old man's mood brightened immediately. 'I have not yet mentioned the fourth person involved. Karl has a sister, Sigrid, who now lives in Munich. She is driving to Berlin today, and I have arranged that we will all meet here at the hotel a little later this evening. Sigrid will drive you to East Berlin tomorrow afternoon, through Checkpoint Charlie. She knows the city quite well and, unlike Berliners, she is allowed to go there without special permission.'

'How does she feel about Karl?'

'I am not sure. I do not have the feeling that there is the same antipathy between them. She certainly mentioned that she had stayed in touch with her brother over the years.'

'Where will we meet?'

'It seems there is a little square with an open-air café on the Unter den Linden, directly opposite the Tomb of the Unknown Soldier. It is a very popular place, always crowded, and she warned me that one usually has to queue for a few minutes before finding a table.' He smiled briefly. 'One always has to queue in Eastern Europe! We have arranged to meet at the café, and whoever arrives first will take a table. If Karl has given me some of the music, I will pass it to you to bring back across the border. If not . . .' He shrugged. It seemed to Mark that Konstantin suddenly looked very old. He had settled back in his chair, his watery eyes staring vacantly, lost in thought.

'Does Heidi know about all this?'

'Of course. I have discussed everything with her.'

'What does she have to say about it?'

Konstantin focused his attention again, a slightly puzzled expression on his face. 'Heidi? She does not say anything about it. She leaves such decisions to me.'

# 11

The attractive young woman, whom Mark had noticed as she entered the lounge, walked quickly towards the alcove where he was sitting with Konstantin. She was pretty, with shoulder-length brown hair framing a face almost devoid of make-up. Two violet lines emphasized her large, grey-blue eyes. She did not wear any lipstick. She was quite small, and he might have used the adjective petite, but her full breasts and narrow waist belied such a description.

'*Herr Doktor* Steigel?' Her voice was low pitched.

'*Ja?*' Konstantin looked up suspiciously. He was accustomed to impromptu approaches by journalists and concert-goers, and did not always welcome them. After a concert, however, when an eager student had a serious question, he would devote time and energy discussing it.

'I am Sigrid Wolpert.'

'Oh.' The conductor slowly rose to his feet, and seemed to tower over her. 'Please forgive me.' He bowed graciously. 'I had not expected such a charming young lady.'

She smiled easily. 'I am not sure whether I should accept that as a compliment.'

Steigel looked earnest. 'It was most certainly intended. Please sit down. This is my friend, Mr Holland.' She nodded in Mark's direction. 'May I order you something to drink?'

'Thank you. A coffee.'

While Konstantin searched for the missing waiter, Mark said, 'Did you have a pleasant drive?'

She pulled a humorous face, and Mark had the impression that she reacted quickly and with self-assurance, like a polished actress. 'There is not much one can do on such a journey. The autobahn has no permitted exits, so it is a matter of pointing the car in one direction and counting the kilometres. Billy Joel kept me company.'

Konstantin looked round. 'Who is he?'

'A singer.'

'I hope you did not discuss the reason for your visit with him. I thought I had emphasized the need for complete discretion in this matter.'

She laughed. 'No, I mean that I played a tape of his music.'

The conductor looked relieved. 'Ah. I do not think I know him. Is he a tenor?'

Mark smiled. 'He sings popular songs, maestro.' Steigel grunted ominously. 'He's very good.' Sigrid's eye caught his, and she smiled gratefully.

'If you say so, Mark. I have never understood this generation's fascination for primitive rhythms and mindless doggerel. When you said music, I assumed you meant music.'

Sigrid laughed charmingly. 'Some of the doggerel isn't so mindless. I like the other music, too. I brought a tape of *Die Zauberflöte* with me, but it made me drowsy.'

'Who conducted?'

'Karl Böhm.'

Steigel frowned. 'Then I'm not surprised. Where is that waiter?' The unfortunate man arrived, and Konstantin snapped his order. Then he turned to Mark. 'I have taken the liberty of booking four seats for the Berlin Philharmonic tomorrow night. May I assume that you and Miss Wolpert will join us?' He stared at

Sigrid for a moment. 'Unless, of course, it will put you to sleep.'

'I would love to go, and I promise to stay wide-awake.'

Her smile was so engaging that Konstantin, almost against his will, was won over. 'Very well. It is all arranged. There will be plenty of time after we return, even allowing for delays at that stupid border. What ridiculous conditions politicians impose on us!' He brushed aside more than a decade of international tension. 'It is only a guest conductor, a young Scandinavian who interests me, but it will be interesting to see what he makes of the Bruckner Ninth.' He chuckled. 'The last time I heard them play Bruckner for a visitor, they ignored his efforts completely, and played it the way they had been trained. Occasionally, the poor fellow managed to keep up with them!'

Sigrid looked shocked. Mark suspected that she over-reacted slightly for the conductor's benefit. 'But that's awful!'

Konstantin shrugged happily. 'Perhaps. You have to remember, my dear, that – good manners notwithstanding – the Philharmonic is the finest orchestra in the world. There is a kind of magnificent arrogance in their excellence. I do not know of any other group of musicians who perform with that special mixture of warmth and virtuosity. They are unique.'

'It must be a frightening experience for a young conductor.'

'Either frightening or exhilarating, depending on what you are made of. If you like fast cars, for example, would it not be your ambition to drive a . . . a . . .' He searched for a suitable name. 'A Bugatti?' Mark and Sigrid exchanged amused glances. 'No, the Philharmonic certainly separates the men from the boys. That is why I am interested to see how this young Swede manages them.'

'May I ask you about him afterwards?'

'Yes, my dear.' Konstantin smiled benignly. 'But you must not expect me to tell you the truth. Musicians are not always so generous in their estimation of other musicians. I am told the young man is very handsome.'

'I hope I am old enough not to be swayed by that.' Her voice was firm, but her expression softened the blow.

'I am glad to hear it.' Steigel was enjoying himself. He looked at her for a moment. 'Is everything arranged for tomorrow?'

Once again, her mood changed, and she became serious. 'Yes. I spoke to Karl yesterday. He will be waiting for you in the museum at one o'clock. Will that be convenient? The apartment where he is staying is only a short drive away.'

'It should be time enough to begin with. How much time I need depends on what he has to show me.'

'I understand there is quite a large amount of music.'

'Then I hope we will have enough time.'

'Good. If you are satisfied with what you see, you will bring it to us – Mr Holland and me – at the open-air café on the Unter den Linden.'

Mark leaned forward. 'Will your brother permit maestro Steigel to take the music without paying for it?'

She seemed surprised. 'Yes. Why do you ask?'

Mark looked at Steigel. 'I had assumed he would not allow us to take it without a payment.'

She smiled. 'My brother is very anxious for the maestro to have the scores. I thought he had already made that clear to you.'

'But what guarantee will he have?'

Her gaze was steady. 'He does not ask for guarantees. His greatest concern is that the scores should find their way into the right hands.' Her smile returned. 'Besides, we have arranged that the maestro will hand the scores over to me at the café. I am Karl's sister, and I will bring the music into West Berlin. I have no reason to mistrust you.'

'All right.'

'If you are satisfied with what you find, you will pay me the sum that Karl has requested, and I will arrange for the money to be paid to him. If not . . .' she shrugged, 'I suppose I will have to see if there is another buyer. To be honest, I have not even thought about such a situation.'

Steigel was silent for a long time, as though lost in thought. When he finally spoke, his voice was low. 'You must forgive me, Miss Wolpert. I did not realize that your brother had such a high regard for my work, or that he placed such faith in me.' Sigrid watched him curiously. 'You see, my dear, I overlooked the fact that Karl is a man of conscience. Before you arrived, Mark and I discussed the situation. I had decided to take Karl's money with me tomorrow, and pay him immediately. Mark thought this was unwise.'

'He is right. You are not permitted to take a large sum of Western currency into East Berlin without telling the border control. They would want to know what you need it for. It would be very dangerous for Karl –'

'Yes, I know that.' He paused. 'It was not my intention to declare the money. I thought I would just make the payment –'

'But there is no need. Don't you trust us?'

'Yes, I do. In my excitement, I was afraid that Karl would not let me take the scores without paying for them. I did not want to wait.' He sighed. 'I suppose I am a foolish old man.'

Sigrid nodded kindly. 'I think I understand, but you are making complications where they do not exist. It is really a much simpler arrangement than you or Mr Holland suspect. In East Berlin, you will have enough time to study the scores briefly. Provided you are satisfied with what you see, we will bring them back here in my car. Then you can examine them at your leisure, to satisfy yourself that they are completely genuine. You will pay me Karl's price, in dollars, and they will be yours. That is all.'

Steigel spoke slowly. 'Thank you.' He glanced towards Mark. 'We should learn to trust people more openly. I suppose it is a disease of our time that we always suspect a catch somewhere.' When Mark did not reply, he looked at his watch. 'If you will both forgive me, I will leave you for a moment, and go to my wife. She was feeling a little tired today. I would like to make sure she has everything she needs.'

'Of course.'

He rose to his feet. 'I was hoping we might all dine together. If Heidi is up to it, we will.'

Mark and Sigrid watched in silence as he made his way slowly across the lounge. She smiled. 'He is not quite as fierce as I thought he would be.'

'He's not fierce at all, but don't tell him I told you. The famous Steigel outbursts of temper are reserved for orchestras who have forgotten what discipline means.'

'I see.' She seemed slightly self-conscious to find herself alone with Mark. 'I like him.'

'So do I. I suppose that's why I was being over-cautious about the plan. It was I who suggested that your brother wouldn't hand over the music until he had been paid.'

'It is understandable.' She glanced towards the foyer. 'I am glad Karl chose maestro Steigel to have the scores.'

'It means a great deal to him. He knew about their existence and has dreamed of finding them for half a century. I suppose he hoped that, by some miracle, they survived the bombing of Dresden.'

'It appears they have.'

'What if Steigel is not convinced by what he finds?'

She shrugged. 'Then he will have wasted a day in East Berlin, you will have made an unnecessary trip from Switzerland, and I will drive back to Munich.' Her eyes were fixed on Mark's face. 'I am not an expert, Mr Holland. Otherwise, I would verify the music for myself. Karl is a musicologist. I trust him.'

'I thought he was a teacher at the local academy.'

She smiled sadly. 'He has to earn a living. You do not always have the opportunity to follow your true calling in the People's Republic! So, if Karl's discovery is what we believe it to be, it would be unwise for him to be seen in my company. Once the news is announced, questions will be asked. Where was the music found? Who found it? How did it come to be in West Berlin? If this happens after I visit Karl, people will put . . . how does one say? . . . two and two together. That is why it is better for Herr Steigel to meet him privately. I will only act as a courier.'

'What about your other brother, here in Berlin?'

'Franz? He is a rabbit: an ambitious rabbit, but scared of his own shadow! When he told me about it, all he would say was that he didn't want to get mixed up in any trouble. He is always that way.'

'Even when the news is announced?'

'All the more so. He pretends not to have a brother living in the East, in case it casts any suspicion on his lousy little government job. Here in Germany, we're always having minor scandals when some tin-pot politician discovers his secretary or his assistant has been planted in his office by the East Germans. Most of them are quite paranoid about it. When the news is announced, Franz will do everything in his power to dissociate himself from it.'

'Konstantin gave me the impression that your brother doesn't approve of Karl.'

'I think it would be more accurate to say that they hate one another. I was surprised that Franz even passed Karl's message to Herr Steigel, especially as there was nothing in it for him.'

'Why is there such bad feeling between them?'

Her face was sombre for a moment. 'My brothers are much older than I am. I was always the baby of the family. When we left East Berlin, and Karl said he wanted to stay behind, Franz never forgave him. I was only a little girl at the time, but I remember them shouting at each other while our parents sat in the room, watching them in silence. I don't know why my father did not say anything. Perhaps he was afraid that Karl would denounce him, as if he would do such a thing! I was very frightened. They nearly came to blows, and my mother took me next door and put me to bed. I could still hear their voices through the wall. The next day, we left. Karl kissed me goodbye, and said, "One day you will understand all this," or something like that. I did not really know what has happening, but I remember being very sad. I loved Karl. He was always my favourite. Later, when I grew up, I understood better, but I never hated Karl for his decision. Now, I suppose I feel sorry for him.'

'Do you think he'll ever try to leave?'

'Maybe. It's not so easy to do, and he has a wife and family to think about. That's why he wants to sell the scores. I would like to see my family reunited. It might even persuade Franz to forget the past.' She smiled suddenly. 'I should not be troubling you with my personal problems.'

Mark returned her smile. 'I'm glad you did.'

Steigel rejoined them a few minutes later. 'You will have to forgive me if I postpone our dinner together. Heidi is still very tired, and I think she would prefer to have a little food sent up to our room.' He seemed preoccupied. 'I worry about her, you know. She tires very easily.'

'Then she should rest. You should have an early night too, maestro. You're going to have a busy day tomorrow.'

Steigel stood straighter. 'There is nothing the matter with me, my dear. I am as fit as I ever was. I just don't want to see Heidi over-exert herself. If she still feels tired in the morning, I will arrange to go alone.' He shook Mark's hand. 'If we miss each other in the morning, I will see you tomorrow at four o'clock, in the café opposite the Tomb of the Unknown Soldier.' He looked exhausted.

'Very good. I'll be there a few minutes before four. Are you sure you will have no difficulty in finding it?'

'Of course not!' For a moment, a spark returned to his eyes. 'I may be old, but I am not yet senile. The hotel has arranged a car and a chauffeur. I am sure he will know the place.' He bowed to Sigrid, and with a wave of his hand returned towards the foyer.

Sigrid giggled. 'Are you sure he only reserves fireworks for contrary orchestras?'

'Mostly. He hates to be reminded about his age. You speak excellent English, by the way. It makes me ashamed of my German.'

She shrugged. 'I had an English boyfriend for a long time. It's supposed to be the best way to learn a language.'

'I notice you used the past tense.'

She smiled. 'He went back to London. How old is Herr Steigel?'

'Nearly eighty. He relies absolutely on Heidi. She's looked after him for years.'

'You make him sound a little selfish.'

'Not really. She enjoys it, and he depends on her for everything. If anything happened to her, he would be completely lost.'

'You're very fond of him, aren't you?'

'Yes. He's a great conductor.'

She laughed, and shook her head. 'Oh, you Englishmen!'

It made Mark smile. 'What does that mean?'

'Just that you're always so afraid to express your emotions openly, especially to a stranger like me. My friend was the same. You hate to let people see when you care about someone.'

'Not always.'

Her voice softened. 'I think that would be interesting to see. You smoke a lot of cigarettes.'

'Bad habit.'

'Yes, and it keeps you occupied when you do not want people to know what you are thinking.'

'Perhaps.' Her directness was appealing. 'What do you do in Munich?'

'I'm a freelance.' She laughed. 'It means I do all kinds of work. I am available, for a fee. Oh, that doesn't sound very good, does it? Officially, I am in public relations. I used to work for the Bavarian radio, but it is a very bureaucratic organization. It is like your BBC, but not as big. After a while, I was tired of living in a pigeon-hole. A few years ago, I borrowed some money, and set up a little office of my own.' She searched in her handbag. 'I think I have a business card somewhere, but I'm always losing them.'

'Do you have many clients?'

'Yes, but they change from month to month. People call me when they want to make a promotion for a few weeks. I know all the press, and it's very interesting.' She smiled. 'I don't charge much, and I work very hard. That's probably the best definition of a freelance! My busiest time is during the Festival. There is always someone looking for a little extra push. I even present a few concerts myself.'

'Really? Who do you present?'

She laughed again. 'Whoever asks me. It's not so easy to find a manager in Germany, and I know how to promote a concert and persuade a few critics to attend. Most of the permanent managers can't be bothered, and somebody has to do the work. Do you ever come to Munich?'

'I haven't been there for a long time.'

'Perhaps I can persuade you to come. I am presenting a young Israeli cellist next month. He's very good. It would be nice to tell him I've asked an important manager from Switzerland to come and hear him'

'Not very important.'

'Well, important enough to represent a very famous conductor. If my cellist is as good as I think he is, you might even be prepared to recommend him. Would you come?'

Mark found that he was smiling. 'I might.'

'You won't regret it. I promise.'

'All right. Shall we have dinner?'

'Yes, please. I have not eaten since this morning. But not here. It's too grand for me.'

'The Kempinski Eck isn't. It's a sort of café overlooking the street.'

'I know, but I'd rather walk in the town for a while. You forget that I'm from Munich. I feel like a country cousin, here to see the sights when I'm in Berlin. It's very exciting. Munich is a village compared with this.'

'I think of it as a big town.'

'It is, but Berlin is so much more . . . alive! There's nowhere else like it in Germany. There's always something happening here – in the theatre, in the cabarets, in the art world, everywhere! I love the way it never stops, twenty-four hours a day. Munich is all very well, if you like Bavarian charm and *gemütlichkeit*, but Berlin has real character!' She pointed vaguely towards the foyer. 'There's always something happening on the Ku'damm. It's like Broadway in New York.'

'Have you ever been to New York?'

'No.'

'Well, I won't spoil your illusions of Broadway, but I know what you mean. Berlin is an exciting town.'

'There's nowhere else like it. It was always that way, long before they put up the wall that's supposed to make everyone neurotic.' She grinned. 'You know, we Germans are supposed to be a very serious race: very disciplined, very conscientious. People in Berlin are not like that. They are like . . .' she frowned, searching for the word, and her expression was charming, '. . . like quicksilver. They're very funny, and very cynical. They have a special humour of their own. I think Americans would call it "laid back".'

'Maybe it's because there are so many Americans here. If you drive to Dahlem, you'll see those endless blocks of army apartments.'

She shook her head. 'No, it was always that way, long before the Americans occupied us.'

'And are you an exception?'

She winked. 'You forget that I'm from here. Berlin is in my blood. I'm coming home!'

'In that case, I'll let you choose the restaurant.'

She stood. 'I must change first. I want to take a bath after all that driving. It's still quite early. When should I be ready?' Her eyes seemed to sparkle.

'Whenever you like. I have to call my office for a few minutes. Eight o'clock? It's only –'

'Make it seven-thirty.' She laughed. 'I want to walk up and down and see everything that's going on.' As Mark stood, she moved towards him. 'I have a small confession to make. I hope you won't mind what I have to say.'

'Oh?'

'I'm rather glad your conductor and his wife decided not to have dinner with us tonight. Is that very ungrateful of me?'

'No. To be honest, I was about to say the same thing.'

'I don't believe you.'

Mark smiled. 'Well, think it, anyway.'

She smiled happily. 'That I am prepared to believe. You forget that I know how Englishmen behave!'

'I'd better watch my step.'

'No, you'll just smoke another cigarette.' She grinned. 'I'll be watching!'

'In that case, I'll give it up for the evening, just to confuse you.'

'Good.' She took his hand to say goodbye, then as if on impulse raised her cheek towards his, to receive a farewell kiss. 'I will be in the foyer at seven-thirty, scrubbed clean!'

He watched her walk briskly across the lounge, conscious of a faint perfume and the warmth of her cheek where it had rested against his.

# 12

Sigrid chose an Italian restaurant called Ciao, about a block from the Adenauerplatz, after a walk that had taken them most of the length of the Kurfürstendamm. Mark had been there before. An Italian conductor with a natural instinct to seek out the best traditional dishes had taken him some years earlier. He decided not to tell Sigrid. It was a warm, sultry evening, and the waiter found them a table outside, where they could watch the endless stream of pedestrians and the steady flow of traffic.

She sighed, nursing a Campari and soda. 'I don't know why I live in Munich when I love this place so much. You know, if you wait long enough, you can see the whole of Berlin pass your table.'

Mark smiled. 'That's because it seems to be the only street in Berlin. There's nowhere else to go.'

'Don't be cynical! Berliners like to look at their town. They still talk to each other. All the English want to do is go home and watch their television sets. Clive said so.'

'You could be right. What did he do in Munich?'

'He worked in an art gallery. He was on a year's exchange from London. I met him when the gallery had an exhibition of avant-garde painters and I provided a composer who played electronic tapes to accompany the pictures.'

'Were they good?'

Her gesture was theatrical. 'Who can tell? The best I can say is that the noises were as unintelligible as the canvases, which seemed to satisfy the customers. They were quite horrible, but Clive thought I was terribly clever!'

'What about the rest of your family? Do they live in Munich?'

She shook her head. 'My mother lives outside Frankfurt in one of those apartment towns they built in the forest. My father died a long time ago. He knew the area because my mother and Karl lived in a village a little farther south during the war. They went back to Berlin in 1946, and Franz and I were born there. So, when it was time to leave again, we went back to Frankfurt, and my father worked for a bank. I suppose I grew up there, but in my heart I belong to Berlin. I was born in 1955.' She smiled, half-closing her eyes. 'Are you calculating my age?'

'Not really, but it would seem you're thirty-one.'

'I don't believe you. Men always want to know how old a woman is, even when they pretend they don't. How old are you?'

'Forty-six.'

She put her head to one side. 'That's not so bad.'

'How do you mean?'

Sigrid laughed. 'To find the ideal woman in your life, you are supposed to divide your age by half and add seven years.' She frowned, pretending to calculate, then smiled. 'I'm a year too old for you.'

'On the other hand, you were exactly the right age two years ago.'

'I didn't think of that. What a shame we didn't meet then.' She paused. 'I hope you do not mind if I flirt with you a little.'

'I'm very flattered.'

'You must blame Berlin. Whenever I am here, I feel released from the heavy, serious business of being a German. In Munich, I would be much more correct, more proper.' She blew out her cheeks, like a heavy brass player. 'This town always has that light-headed effect on me.'

'Too bad. I hoped it might be mutual attraction.'

'Well,' she ran a narrow index finger round the rim of the glass, 'I think I also wanted to see if I could dislodge your English calmness enough to make you take a cigarette. You haven't smoked one all evening.'

'That's because I've had my hands full, dragging you away from all the sights.' It had taken them more than an hour to reach the restaurant, with constant delays as Sigrid had pulled at Mark's arm to lead him towards each new diversion: a pavement artist who had created an enormous, ugly religious picture with coloured chalks; a white-faced mime, emulating Marcel Marceau for an enthusiastic crowd of spectators; a shop window displaying electronic jewellery which winked and glittered in the dark;

restaurants boasting menus that offered culinary delicacies from every corner of the globe. The similarity to New York was evident. Sigrid had clung to Mark's arm, steering him along the busy pavement and pulling him towards each new distraction with the delight of a child. Standing very close, her head touching his shoulder and her full breast pressed tightly against the crook of his arm, she shared each discovery with the intimacy of a lover, and he found himself responding, enjoying her pleasure. He had resisted the temptation to smoke for fear that it would diminish her closeness.

Sigrid stared at her drink. 'I think maybe it is also because I am a little keyed-up about tomorrow.'

'Are you worried about it?'

'Not for myself. I am afraid for Karl. I do not want anything to happen to him. If the authorities were to learn about what he is doing, it would be very serious.'

'Would you prefer me to arrange a different plan? I think I could persuade Konstantin to make alternative arrangements.'

'No, it is too late to do anything else in the time we have. Perhaps I worry too much. Nobody is going to watch us. East Berlin has changed in the past few years. They are not as suspicious as they used to be.'

Mark nodded. 'I can remember when visitors were made to feel distinctly unwelcome. I once walked through Checkpoint Charlie, a few years ago. Apart from the officials who shouted at me and refused to understand a word of English, it was an unpleasant experience to see a guard with a machine-gun following my progress through the gate.'

'Then you can imagine what it was like for me as a German.' She swallowed the rest of her Campari. 'That was before the East German government realized it was losing millions of dollars in Western currency by not encouraging tourism. Now, they're only too eager to see us and get their hands on our money, even if the guards are still a little surly.'

Mark watched her face. 'But you're uneasy?'

'Perhaps a little. The thought of smuggling, even if it is only some sheets of music, makes me apprehensive. Poor Karl! He must be suffering agony.'

Mark placed his hand over hers, and she gripped it tightly for a moment. 'We're probably both worrying unnecessarily. When it comes down to it, I doubt whether the East Germans care that much either way about the music. It's not as though we're stealing state secrets.'

'Yes.' Her hand held his. 'I'm being foolish. Thank you for understanding.' Their waiter had arrived at the table. 'Let's order our food. I'm starving. I haven't eaten anything since I left Munich. Do you mind that I chose an Italian restaurant?'

Mark smiled. 'Of course not.'

'I shouldn't really eat it, but I adore pasta. Clive always called it "instant hips".'

'That wasn't very gallant of him.'

She shrugged. 'He was a very fashionable young man, but he hated it when I said he was trying to be trendy. He used to quote Oscar Wilde at me, saying I could resist everything except temptation.'

'Then I hope you remembered to add that the best things in life are illegal, immoral or fattening.'

She laughed. 'That would have given me too much freedom!'

'He was very important to you, wasn't he?'

'Clive?' Sigrid's eyes met his. 'I thought so, at the time. Later, I realized it was just a very strong physical attraction. It's sometimes easy to confuse lust with love.' She looked away. 'I think I learned a lot from my time with him.'

'Including excellent English.'

She giggled. 'I haven't used any of the naughty words yet!'

'I'll try not to be too shocked.'

'You won't be.' The waiter shuffled, and she stretched sensuously. 'I am going to eat a plate of pasta, and I would like to drink a lot of Italian wine, so that I can relax and enjoy myself. Why don't you order the food and smoke one of your horrible cigarettes? I know you want to, and I won't make you feel guilty. It will be a treaty between us: wine and pasta for me, and tobacco for you!'

Despite her promise, Sigrid ate sparingly, and the slightly rough Italian wine blended with the food and the warm evening air. Towards the end of the meal, she smiled. 'You surprise me.'

'Why is that?'

'We have talked all evening, and I have told you about my childhood and the years I spent in college, but you have never once mentioned the war or the Nazis. Clive always said that the English were preoccupied with them. He said that your television programmes are still full of war films and documentaries. Are you being terribly discreet with me?'

Mark lit a cigarette. For a moment, he remembered his first visit to Berlin, when he had stood, looking up at the golden angel on the *Siegesaule* on the Strasse des 17 Juni. In the distance, the Brandenburg Gate marked the end of the Unter den Linden and the Eastern zone, and the long, straight avenue passed close to the old Reichstag. He had wondered then whether the ghosts of all those goose-stepping uniformed figures still marched in gloomy silence. It had seemed impossible to be in that part of Berlin without being reminded of that era. Later, he had visited West Berlin frequently, when the world had become involved in a new form of war and the German 'enemy' had been replaced by another threat. Despite her family's flight from the Eastern zone, Sigrid was too young to understand how easily the sides changed and made new alliances.

She was watching him, and Mark smiled. 'That all finished a long time ago. As far as I'm concerned, it's ancient history – before my time. Besides, you seem to forget that I don't live in England. They don't show things like that on Swiss television, as far as I know. I seldom see it.'

'I forgot. You see, as a German, I still need to explain my family history, because the shadow of that time still lies over us.' She smiled sadly. 'My father was a cook in the Luftwaffe – not a very glamorous occupation. He served on the Russian front for a while . . .'

Mark placed his hand over hers. 'It's not very important. As I said before, it's ancient history.'

'Yes.' She was silent for a while. 'You live in a very special world, don't you, among your musicians?'

'I suppose so. Yours is not so very different.'

'No. It is almost . . . enclosed, away from the real world.'

'Perhaps that's why we chose it.'

'Yes.' She was lost in thought. 'I think maybe that is why I worry about tomorrow. It brings me back too close to reality.'

'Are you still concerned?'

'No.' She stretched. 'But I am suddenly very tired. It has been a long day for me. Do you think we could have the luxury of a taxi back to the Kempinski? I don't think I could walk any more.'

'Not even to see your favourite sights?'

'They will be there again tomorrow night. After the concert, when Herr Steigel and his wife have gone to bed, I will take you for a drive in my car. There is much more to see than the Ku'damm.'

Mark smiled. 'I believe you.' Perhaps, one day, he would know her well enough to show her the spot on the wall where he had broken clear, leading a young East German to safety, and the open stretch of land where the machine-guns had opened fire on him. He lit another cigarette. The wine had made him sentimental.

At the door of her room, Sigrid reached up to place her hands on Mark's shoulders. 'Thank you. This evening has been very special for me. It is strange. I find it difficult to believe that I met you only a few hours ago.'

He kissed her gently. Her lips parted slightly, and her arms encircled his waist, holding him tightly. For a moment, the tip of her tongue explored his mouth before she pulled her head back and smiled. Her voice was breathless. 'I like the way you taste: Italian food and wine – and cigarettes!'

'I was about to say the same thing!'

'Or, anyway, think it.' She raised her face again, and kissed him briefly. 'You will save tomorrow night for me? It will be a sort of . . . celebration.' Before Mark could reply, she turned and unlocked the door of her room. She paused for a moment, then placed her hand on his cheek. 'I will call in the morning.'

'I'll wait for you. Sleep well.'

Before switching out the light in his room, Mark stared at the telephone next to the bed. He waited a long time, then raised the receiver and dialled a number. It rang briefly until someone replied.

'London Arts.' The line crackled slightly.

'Can you connect me to Quentin Sharpe, please?'

'Who's calling?'

'My name is Mark Holland.'

'Just a moment.' After about a minute, the voice returned. 'I'm sorry, but Mr Sharpe can't be reached. Would you like to talk to anyone else?'

'No, I don't think so. I phoned and left a message for him some time ago, but he didn't call back. I wondered whether my first message ever reached him.'

'When did you call?'

'About two weeks ago.'

'In that case, I'm sure it was passed on to him. Did you ask him to call you?'

'No, not exactly, but I was almost certain he would want to call back. I'm surprised he didn't.'

'I see.' The voice was impersonal. 'Perhaps he didn't think it was necessary. I'm afraid I can't really help you. Do you want him to call you?'

'No, I don't think so.'

'Very good.' If the man at the other end was curious, he did not indicate it. 'Would you like to leave another message?'

'Yes.' Mark hesitated. 'Would you tell him that I'm going into East Berlin tomorrow. I'll be there for the day, on private business.'

'Right. Where are you calling from?'

'The Kempinski Hotel, in West Berlin.'

'I'll just write that down, Mr Holland.' There was a slight pause. 'Anything else?'

'No, not really, except . . .' The other man did not interrupt. 'I expect to return by six o'clock tomorrow evening . . .'

'Yes?'

'I wonder if he might call me here at seven. If he isn't free, perhaps he could ask one of his assistants to call.'

'All right.'

'I'll definitely be here by seven. In fact, I'll make a point of it.'

'Then why don't you call us?'

'Yes, I suppose I could do that. In fact, if I don't call by seven at the latest, would you be sure to let him know?'

Mark thought that he detected the slightest hesitation before the man replied. His voice, however, remained briskly efficient. 'Very good, Mr Holland. I'll make sure your message is passed to Mr Sharpe some time during the day tomorrow.'

'Do you expect him in the office?'

'I'm afraid I wouldn't know. I am the night operator. Your message has been noted.'

'And someone will tell Quentin?'

There was a trace of impatience. 'Yes.'

'Then you'll hear from me by seven o'clock, Berlin time.'

Mark hung up, and lay on his back, staring at the ceiling. He was not quite sure why he had called London. Quentin was hardly likely to be interested in a rediscovered Mahler score, no matter where it came from, but at least he would be aware that Mark was crossing into East Berlin. Why the hell hadn't he called back two weeks ago? Mark had followed Ernie Sullivan's advice, reporting Bailey's death and his barely whispered message. Even on that occasion, the man who had received the information had made no comment. For all the emotion he had displayed, Mark might have been calling in a cricket score. But surely, Quentin should have called back, asking for more details! There had been nothing – no response – and with each day, the incident had faded into the background, like a slightly unreal dream.

For a moment, Mark sat up. 'I didn't imagine it, for Christ's sake, and I wasn't drunk! Who the hell was taking my picture in San Francisco, or did I imagine that, too? Why didn't Quentin call back?'

He reached across the table to light a cigarette, but the packet was empty. There was another in his suitcase, across the room, but he lay back again, unwilling to move, and closed his eyes. The wine had made him drowsy, and he switched off the light. The image of Sigrid floated before him, and he could still taste her mouth against his, and the gentle pressure of her body as she had pulled herself close. He looked forward to seeing her again.

The insistent ringing of the telephone awakened him.

'Mark?' Sigrid's voice had the same breathless quality.

'Yes.' He answered slowly. A ray of sunlight through a parting in the curtains shone in his eyes, blinding him.

'Oh. I think I woke you. I'm sorry.'

'It doesn't matter. What time is it?'

'Nine o'clock. I didn't mean to disturb you.'

'I should have been awake by now. I think I must have drunk too much wine. Are you up!'

She laughed. 'I have been up for hours! I couldn't sleep, so I took my car and drove to the lake. Have you been there?'

'Yes.'

'Oh Mark, it was so beautiful! You would never believe you were still in Berlin. There was fog on the water – very mysterious and strange and romantic – but the sun came out and burned it away. I sat on the beach under some trees, and watched it disappear. I wish you had been there.'

'I do, too.'

'Really?' She sounded pleased. 'Perhaps we can do that tomorrow.' Her voice softened. 'I think I would like that.'

'Have you had breakfast?'

'Hours ago! I found a little café overlooking the water, and drank litres of coffee and ate hot rolls and butter. They were delicious, and I don't care what they did to my hips!'

'If you give me about twenty minutes, you can have some more.'

'No, but I will watch you.'

'It's not a very appetizing sight.

'Perhaps.' Her voice became softer. 'I think a man sometimes looks his best when he first wakes in the morning: like a small boy, with sleep in his eyes and his hair all tousled.'

'I'm afraid I would disappoint you. I look more like the wild man of Borneo, and distinctly unfriendly.'

She hesitated before replying. 'Maybe.'

'Anyway, I'd better shower and shave before I make a public appearance. I don't want to frighten the natives. Half an hour?'

'You said twenty minutes.'


After breakfast, they walked again on the Kurfürstendamm, and Sigrid led the way, heading towards the Europa Centre with its familiar rotating Mercedes sign.

'Where are we going?'

'I want to look at Ka De We. You know it, of course.' Her hand held his.

'I don't think so. What is it?'

'It's the finest department store in the town, like Harrods in London. I thought you said you knew Berlin.'

'I don't often have time to look at shops. In fact, when I think about it, I seem to spend most of my stays here commuting between the hotel and the Philharmonic.' In the old days, he had sweated out hours of waiting in a scruffy little apartment near Templehof. The Department had discouraged being too visible in the centre of the city.

'Ka De We isn't a shop. It's an experience! You cannot come to Berlin without a quick look. It has the most amazing food department in the world, with everything you could imagine.'

Mark smiled. 'I'm beginning to sympathize with Clive. You have a positive preoccupation with things to eat!'

'Wait until you see it. It is unbelievable!' Her eyes closed for a moment in joyful anticipation. 'The smell of all those hundreds of varieties of sausages! I'm amazed you don't know it.'

'I don't think it was in the last guidebook I saw. When do you want to go over to East Berlin?'

Her mood changed quickly, but she smiled. 'I thought we should leave about one o'clock. It's not very busy then, and we will have plenty of time, unless you want to go sooner?'

'No. Steigel doesn't expect us until four.'

'It's such a beautiful day. I thought maybe we could stroll in the Tiergarten or go to the zoo.'

'Whichever you like.'

She stopped walking. 'I'm sorry. I'm a little jumpy. I'm still nervous about our plan, so I am putting off the moment until it is absolutely necessary. Do you mind?'

Mark held her hand tighter. 'No. Let's enjoy ourselves. I've no desire to spend more time over there than necessary. You'd better show me this fantastic display of food before the supplies run out.'


They collected Sigrid's car a few minutes before one. It was a red Audi with Munich number plates. She drove the powerful vehicle smoothly, concentrating her attention on the busy traffic, but Mark was conscious of her tenseness. At a traffic light on the Potsdamerstrasse, she swore under her breath. 'I always forget where that damn road turns off to Checkpoint Charlie. It's so badly signposted.'

'Try that one, over there.'

Quite suddenly, they were approaching the wall and a stretch of open ground that looked like no-man's land. The road wound round a corner, and a hoarding warned them that they were leaving the American sector. Moments later, they drove past the Allied post, whose guards ignored them, and were confronted by a series of metal barriers painted with red and white stripes. A queue of cars was waiting. Beyond them, an open-ended shed with translucent plastic roofing marked the frontier. Looking up, Mark noticed a catwalk on which two armed guards were standing. Checkpoint Charlie had changed since he had last visited it. In the past, there had been no overhead cover, and the East Germans had set up a series of roadblocks: low, overlapping walls that required a driver to follow a zigzag course. Few pedestrians now used this particular entry point. It was quite a long walk from the centre of the city, and the U-Bahn station at Friedrichstrasse provided quicker access to the main sights.

The cars moved forward slowly, until they found themselves at the head of the queue. Mark looked at Sigrid and smiled. 'All right?'

'Yes. I don't know why I'm making such a fuss. I hope I don't look as guilty as I feel.' She was tight-lipped.

'There's no reason why you should. You haven't done anything illegal.'

There was a hut running the length of the right-hand side, through which pedestrians passed. From a window hung with vertical plastic slats, a hand emerged, beckoning to Sigrid to continue along the driving lane. She let out the clutch clumsily, and the car shuddered. The disembodied hand remained in position, and Mark opened his window. 'I think he wants our passports.'

Sigrid fumbled in her handbag. After a moment, she handed him a West German passport, and Mark added his own. He was aware that they were being scrutinized from behind the slats. Sigrid, slightly pale, stared straight ahead. The car in front of them had moved forward to the next striped barrier, and the driver emerged and walked over to another window.

'What's the next step?'

'That's where we pay: five marks for a day visa, and we also have to buy a minimum of twenty-five German marks. They don't refund them on the way back, so you either spend the money or leave it behind. Sometimes they don't ask for it.' Talking seemed to help, and she relaxed, settling back in her seat. 'It's very quiet today. We've only been waiting for about ten minutes.'

At length, their passports were returned. They waited until the barrier was raised and the car in front of them moved forward to the final exit, where yet another guard examined papers. Looking across the yard, they saw vehicles returning to the West standing in line for inspection. All doors were opened, and engines were inspected. There were mirrors mounted on trolleys, and a uniformed guard placed one of these under the first car in the line. It was a Mini with English number plates. Mark watched the examination.

'I doubt whether anyone would get through, hanging under the chassis of that!'

Sigrid's voice was contemptuous. 'The border guards wouldn't know that. They're not trained to think!' She seemed to have regained her confidence, but she did not smile.

Sigrid drove to the next barrier. 'We pay at that window.'

Mark opened his door. 'I'll look after it.'

'I'd better come with you. If one of us waits behind, it makes them suspicious.'

At the window, a uniformed woman took the passports and stared at Mark. 'You give me thirty marks.' Her English was heavily accented.

She slowly counted out brightly coloured scraps of paper money that looked as though they had been printed that morning. Sigrid took his place at the window, and he returned to her car, pocketing his passport. He sat, watching Sigrid through the windscreen. She was a very attractive woman. Her warmth and sudden changes of mood were curiously appealing. It was hard to believe that he had met her less than twenty-four hours ago. There had been moments when they shared a kind of intimacy that only lovers exchanged. He wondered, almost impersonally, whether they would make love. Sometimes, it felt as though they already had.

Sigrid was leaning forward, replying to a question from the woman in the booth. Her face had the earnest expression that travellers reserve for official inquiries. The woman behind the window asked something else, and Sigrid spoke again, talking rapidly. She seemed nervous.

Mark half-opened the door of the car, uncertain whether he should offer to help her. As he did so, the door was suddenly pushed shut against his arm, throwing him back into the seat. A guard had moved forward, and was leaning with his back to the window, blocking the view. Mark was about to speak to him, when he was aware of movement in the back of the car. He turned, but his vision was impeded by the head-rest attached to the top of the seat. At that moment, he felt the cold metal of the barrel of a revolver on his cheek. It pressed against his skin, gently compelling him to face forward. He glanced up at the rear-view mirror, but it had been tipped upward, preventing him from seeing who was there. The owner of the gun had not spoken.

Mark edged forward to look through the windscreen. The gun stayed close to his head. Another guard was now standing next to Sigrid, and was holding her arm. She tried to turn towards Mark, but the man tightened his hold, making her face the booth. Before Mark could speak, a third man, dressed in a dark leather overcoat, opened the other door of the car and sat in the driver's seat. He started the engine.

The pressure of the gun barrel on Mark's face increased slightly. Lying flat against his cheek, it forced him to turn his head sideways, so that he found himself staring at the greatcoat of the guard posted by his side window.

Behind him, a voice spoke. 'Good afternoon, Mr Holland. Welcome to the German Democratic Republic.' It was only slightly accented. 'Please do not move.'

It had all happened in a few seconds. The man in the driver's seat revved the engine. Ahead of them, the barrier was raised, and he let in the clutch slowly, so that the vehicle moved forward smoothly. The man guarding Sigrid now held her close to the wall of the hut. She struggled against his grip, twisting round to look at Mark for an instant, and their eyes met. Her face was terrified.

# 13

'Where are we going?' It seemed to Mark that his voice sounded remarkably calm.

The pressure of the gun against his cheek was reduced for a moment and a hand reached out to push down the safety lock on his door. The driver accelerated through the last barrier, and the heavy car moved swiftly over the uneven road. At the first corner, it skidded on the surface. The driver over-corrected, apparently unaccustomed to power steering. Mark was conscious of a strong smell of body odour.

The man behind him spoke quietly. 'I hope you are not going to act the outraged citizen or the hero, Mr Holland. I can assure you that neither gesture would make any difference.' Like so many Germans, his accent was slightly American.

'At least tell me where we're going.'

'Not far.' By the sound of his voice and the absence of the gun, he had moved back in his seat. Perhaps the speed at which they were travelling had thrown him back.

'What about Sigrid – Miss Wolpert? This is her car you've stolen.'

'It is not stolen, and it will be returned to her. Miss Wolpert will be looked after. I expect she will join you later.'

The car turned right on the Unter den Linden and slowed to a less conspicuous speed. Mark turned to speak to his captor, but the side of his forehead encountered the barrel of the gun again. Gentle pressure made him face forward.

'Why are you doing this?' They passed a large hotel on the right. Its terrace was filled with tourists eating lunch in the warm sunlight. 'What do you want?'

'It will be explained later, Mr Holland. I have been asked simply to collect you from the frontier. I suggest you reserve your questions for when we arrive.'

'Where?'

'We will be there shortly.'

The car continued down the broad avenue with its heavy, square-cut blocks of grey buildings. There were only a few reminders of its more elegant past: the ornate façade of the Opera House, and the ancient walls of the University. To the front, the magnificent Dom cathedral grew larger. Beyond, the ever-present television tower that had become East Berlin's focal point reached up into the pale blue of the sky. Looking again to his right, Mark saw the busy open-air café where he was supposed to meet Konstantin Steigel. How the hell would he explain his absence? He would have to deal with that later. Sunshine glinted on the glass and concrete of the Palace of the Republic, and the busy Karl Liebnechtstrasse, with its show stores and cafés, was filled with tourists and sightseers. The huge Alexanderplatz looked empty. Mark glanced at the driver, who stared fixedly at the road. The man was sweating under his leather overcoat, and the smell of his body seemed to fill the enclosed space of the car.

'I'd like to make a formal request to see an official British representative.' The man in the back chuckled, and Mark's voice grew irritable. 'Yes, I'm perfectly aware that it's pointless to ask, but I'll go through the ritual anyway. Later, you can always deny that I said it.'

'Come, Mr Holland, there's no need to make such a fuss. Nothing has happened to you.'

'You mean I should allow myself to be abducted at gunpoint without saying a bloody thing?'

'Nobody's abducting you. I was asked to collect you from the checkpoint.'

'With a gun and a stolen car?'

The man laughed pleasantly. 'The gun is for your protection, and the car has been temporarily borrowed. It will be returned.' His voice hardened. 'Don't waste time with idle formalities. You are not a diplomat, Mr Holland, and even if you were, you should know that it makes very little difference to us. Just sit quietly. Nobody has harmed you.'

They were leaving the centre of the town, and the carefully constructed showplaces were now replaced by rows of dour-looking apartment buildings, many of them brown with age and disrepair. This was the real East Berlin. The area surrounding the Alexanderplatz was for tourists. Bearing slightly to the left, the driver steered the car up the slope of a steep hill. It was unexpected. Berlin seemed to lie in the centre of a flat plain with almost no variation. The only exception Mark knew was the great artificial mound created from the rubble of the war. The driver accelerated past lines of run-down houses whose drab architecture scarcely seemed to change.

After another turn, they joined busy traffic on the Schönhauser Allee. Running alongside, in the centre of the road, the concrete pylons of the elevated S-Bahn flicked past with monotonous regularity. The dirty little shops along the street appeared to be closed. A queue was waiting patiently outside a kiosk with a chipped plaster ice-cream cone attached to its roof. The car pulled to the centre lane at a traffic light, and turned left into Gleimstrasse. On the corner, a faded sign advertised the Venezia restaurant. There was another queue standing in its doorway.

After thirty yards, the car stopped in front of a four-storey building whose cement-block front was barely covered with peeling brown paint. At the end of the street, about a hundred yards away, a section of the Berlin wall was visible. The driver said nothing, his hands on the steering-wheel, his eyes facing to the front. Sweat glistened on his forehead. The man in the back said, 'Out here, please.' He opened his own door quickly.

When Mark stepped out, to confront his abductor for the first time, he wondered whether the surprise showed on his face. The owner of the revolver was a handsome young man with long blond hair, dressed in a lightweight grey suit whose sleeves had been rolled up to his elbows. His pink shirt was open-necked and, at first glance, Mark might have mistaken him for a Scandinavian. His clothes were certainly not East German. The revolver was still in his hand, but he held it casually, pointed towards the ground.

The young man followed the direction of Mark's eyes and pocketed the gun, smiling self-deprecatingly. 'I'm sorry about that. I don't think there's any need to be dramatic.' Looking in the direction of the wall, he added, 'It's a little too far to think about making a break. Besides, the ground is mined.' He nodded towards the front door of the building. 'In there, please.'

They passed through a shadowy hall with a linoleum-covered floor, and Mark recognized the stale aroma of cigarette smoke and disinfectant that seemed to permeate government buildings everywhere in Eastern Europe.

The young man led the way up a wooden staircase without bothering to see whether Mark was following. He moved gracefully, two stairs at a time, like an athlete. At the first floor, he opened a door and stood to one side.

'Wait here, please.' His courtesy was exaggerated.

The room was empty, except for a single wooden chair placed in the centre. There were no windows. As soon as Mark entered, the young man smiled and, with a casual wave, stepped outside. The door closed, and a key turned in the lock.

For a moment, Mark stood facing the door. Then he turned to inspect the room. It had been painted a uniform white, and from the light of a bare bulb hanging from the ceiling, he saw that a heavy board had been screwed over the window frame. There were no tell-tale recesses disguising hidden cameras or microphones, and the wooden floorboards had been sanded to a smooth finish. The room was hospital clean. He glanced at his watch. One-forty. Then he sat in the chair, facing the door and lit a cigarette. The room seemed very silent, and he could not hear any sounds coming from outside. There was nothing to do except wait. What the hell did they want, and what had happened to Sigrid? Why? He fought back a mounting sense of panic.

The young man returned about an hour later. Mark had smoked three cigarettes, stubbing them underfoot with deliberate disregard for the carefully swept floor. He saw the man glance down, but he made no comment.

'I'm sorry to have kept you waiting, Mr Holland, but we arrived at an inconvenient moment.' He grinned. 'This is the lunch-hour.'

'How long do you expect to hold me here?'

'I could not say. If anything, that will depend on you. Besides, I think you are being unduly sensitive. It seems to me your English police have a very appropriate expression. Don't they call it assisting with their inquiries?'

'It doesn't usually involve kidnapping at gunpoint.'

The man shrugged, still smiling. 'We still have a lot to learn from you. Will you come this way?'

He led Mark across a landing to a door opposite, standing aside politely to let him enter first. The room was not unlike the first, but had been furnished with a plain wooden table and chair. Two filing cabinets stood in a corner. Once again, the windows had been boarded over. The white walls were bare.

Seated behind the table was a small, round-faced man wearing thick glasses. It was hard to guess his age – late-forties, probably – but his dark hair was receding rapidly to reveal a pink forehead which, combined with fleshy jowls, helped to create the rotund impression. The man looked up from a file of papers he had been reading, and stared at Mark irritably, as though his arrival was an unnecessary disturbance.

'Why are you here?' His tone was unfriendly, and the question was snapped.

'You tell me.' Mark stepped forward until he towered over the man. 'I'd like to know what the hell's going on –'

The man cut across the rest of Mark's prepared speech, staring up into his eyes. 'Don't waste my time. What are you doing in the Democratic Republic? Who are you trying to contact?'

Mark paused for a moment. The question took him by surprise. Surely the police were not concerned with Karl Wolpert and his musical discovery. 'Contact? Nobody. I came over today to look at East Berlin. Check for yourself. I asked for a tourist visa, and –'

The young man behind him hit him brutally in the kidneys with a rubber truncheon. The sudden flash of pain was sickening, and Mark stumbled forward into the table, reaching out with his hands to steady himself. A second blow landed on his shoulder-blade, hard enough to swing his body round, and he felt his legs buckle. The surface of the table seemed to rush up towards his face, and he turned his head as he fell, protecting himself with an outstretched arm. The shoulder that had been struck felt as if it was paralysed. He lay for a moment, staring up at the unpainted surface of the makeshift desk. The wooden legs of the table and the trousers of his interrogator appeared in grotesque perspective, like an axonometric drawing on an architect's plan. A moment later, hands grasped his collar and pulled him to his feet. The young man was very strong. Mark found himself standing in front of the table again.

The interrogator's expression had not changed. 'You are being very stupid. It will achieve nothing for you expect a great deal of . . . discomfort. I asked you a question. Who are you trying to contact?'

Mark waited until the worst of the pain had passed. 'You've made some sort of mistake. I'm not here to contact anyone.'

The truncheon struck again, carefully aimed at the other side of his back, and Mark gasped, throwing back his head. He closed his eyes, gritting his teeth, waiting for the next blow, but none came. For a moment, he thought he would vomit, and doubled forward, his hands clamped over his mouth.

The man behind the desk watched him impassively. Looking past Mark's shoulder, he nodded slightly to the other man. 'This is pointless. Nothing will be gained by trying to hide the truth. If you don't tell us what we want to know now, you'll tell us in a few hours' time. Save yourself a beating.' He waited. 'Well?' Mark shook his head silently, his eyes closed. He was not sure whether he could speak. The man closed the file he had been reading, and eyed Mark disapprovingly. 'I find violence distasteful, Herr Holland. There is a limit to the amount of punishment a human body can withstand. I am told that a heavyweight boxer sustains enough damage to the walls of his stomach and the intestine behind it to warrant surgical treatment after a fight.' He watched Mark's face. 'It would be quite easy to reproduce the same effects, Herr Holland, and you are hardly in the same physical condition as a professional fighter.'

Mark's voice was hoarse. It sounded strangely unfamiliar to him. 'I don't know what you want me to tell you.'

The man shrugged. 'Very well. You'd better go and rest for a while. It may refresh your memory. We will talk again later. Perhaps, when you have had a chance to reconsider the situation, you will remember the instructions your Mr Quentin Sharpe gave you.'

The haziness faded suddenly, and Mark eyed the man warily. 'Quentin Sharpe? What the hell has he got to do with this?'

The man's expression did not change. 'That's what we want you to tell us. Have you anything to say?'

'No. There is nothing! I don't work for –'

He could not finish the sentence before the truncheon struck him again, close to the base of his skull. For a moment, everything went black and his senses reeled. Mark fell backwards, aware that he was only semi-conscious, but once again the young man caught him as he toppled, holding him on his feet. Mark felt himself being shaken, his head lolling from side to side, until the waves of nausea receded, to be replaced by sharp pain.

His interrogator watched him with an expression of distaste. 'We will talk later, then, when you have had a chance to think about it.' He nodded briskly, to indicate that the interview was over, then re-opened the file he had been reading. He did not look up again.

The young man led Mark through the door, supporting him with one hand. He was deceptively powerful. At the head of the staircase, he paused. 'Can you manage down there?' He chuckled agreeably. 'I wouldn't want you to fall and hurt yourself!'

'Give me a moment.' Blinding shafts of pain made it difficult to speak.

'Of course. Hold on to that rail.'

Mark breathed deeply. His body ached with each breath, but his senses were returning. Moving cautiously, he limped down the stairs, gripping the wooden handrail. At one point, his foot slipped and he started to fall, but the young man reached down and held him by the collar until he regained his balance. His progress down the staircase was painfully slow.

At the foot of the stairs, the young man took Mark's arm and led him to the back of the building. A door opened into a small, empty cell. Unlike the rooms on the first floor, its walls were unplastered bricks, and the floor was cement. A bright light shone from a recess in the ceiling, protected by wire netting.

The young man pushed Mark gently into the room. 'This place isn't quite as fancy as the last one. Give me your watch.' Mark handed it to him and he examined it approvingly. 'Nice! That must be one of the advantages of living in Switzerland. Now your shoes and socks, please.' He smiled amiably. 'We don't want you trying to walk out of here.'

The cement felt cold and slightly damp. The young man placed the shoes and socks outside the door of the cell. He stood in the doorway, still smiling. 'OK. Now the rest of your clothing.' Mark hesitated, and he added, 'Don't force me to do it for you.'

Mark undressed slowly. When he reached his underwear, he paused, but the young man glanced at him and said, 'Those, too.' He gathered the pile of clothes carefully and carried them outside, where he dropped them in a heap on the floor. Then he returned to the doorway, leaning casually against it. 'I'll be back later. Don't take too long, Mr Holland. This room is very cold at night.' He slammed the door shut.

Mark could not estimate how long he waited. For a while, he tried to count off the seconds, but pain and nausea distracted him, and he paced across the cell blindly, fighting to remain conscious, his arms outstretched to prevent himself from falling against the rough brick surface.

Why did the man upstairs ask him about Quentin Sharpe, and what were the instructions he was supposed to have been given? He had not spoken to Quentin for God knows how long. Even when he had called him, the bastard had not been there. As time passed, he became confused, unable to focus his thoughts. His memory seemed to be playing tricks. Why had he called Quentin? Then he remembered Bailey and the darkened street outside the Okura Hotel. Had he imagined that? There had been no Bailey when they had looked for the body. What had Bailey said? It had been a message about someone. What was his name? He could remember the man's face, but not his name. Hyatt. That was it! But that was impossible. Hyatt had been dead for years. Bailey must have got it wrong. Maybe he gave another name, which sounded similar. It couldn't have been Hyatt. Mark stood still. Why did the man upstairs talk about Quentin? Another wave of nausea engulfed him, and he doubled over, fighting against it. The cell was becoming increasingly cold, but there was sweat running down his face and body. He wiped a hand across his forehead. It slid across the clammy surface of his skin.

For a moment, he lost consciousness. He awoke to find himself on his knees, his head bowed, as though praying. He was shivering violently. As he rose to his feet, the shooting pains in his shoulders and kidneys were so sharp that he fell forward, supporting himself with his hands. The cement on the floor was uneven, and his skin was grazed and bleeding. He lay, face down, forcing himself to relax and willing himself to sleep, but the shivering returned, and movement sent needles of pain through his flesh where it rubbed against the harsh surface. With some effort, he slowly rose to his feet, leaning against the wall, and resumed walking. He tried to concentrate his mind, but the faces and the names became a blur.

When the young man returned, Mark was sitting on the floor, his back against the wall, shaking uncontrollably. The movement of his body against the bricks tore at the skin of the shoulder-blades, but he was hardly conscious of it.

'It's time for another talk, Mr Holland.' His voice was cheerful, and he reached down and pulled Mark to his feet.

The effort of standing seemed to exhaust Mark's strength. He did not trust himself to speak.

The young man looked solicitous. 'You're having a bad time. I warned you that it would get cold in here.' He examined Mark carefully and smiled. 'I like your body. You've looked after it well.' His eyes travelled down. 'You're very attractive. I prefer tall men.'

Mark clenched his fist and swung it at the man's jaw, but he laughed and stepped back. He watched contemptuously as Mark lost his balance and fell heavily. Then he reached down and pulled him roughly to his feet again.

'Come along.' His voice was impersonal. 'They want you upstairs.' His voice softened. 'I was only being friendly.' He walked at Mark's side, holding him up. At the staircase, he used his enormous strength to lift Mark the short distance to the first landing.

Through half-closed eyes, Mark searched for a window, to see whether it was still day, but there was none. He could not tell how long he had spent in the cell. He vaguely remembered an appointment to meet Konstantin Steigel.

'What time is it?'

The man chuckled. 'Still early. Don't worry about it. If you take my advice, you'll tell my colleagues what they want to know.'

'I don't know what they want to know!'

'That's up to you. They'll ask the questions. All you have to do is answer them, or I'll be forced to punish you. You don't want that, do you?'

When they entered the interrogation room, there was a new person seated behind the table. An attractive young woman with short, dark hair, confronted him. Her eyes travelled slowly over Mark's body, and when he placed his hands over his groin, she seemed vaguely amused.

Her manner was friendly. 'I have a number of questions to ask you. I hope you're feeling more . . . co-operative.' She spoke without a trace of accent, and Mark had the impression that she might be English.

'I don't know what you want.' His voice was hoarse. The sudden warmth of the room, after the cell, helped to revive his senses.

'You'd better let me worry about that. Now, who sent you to East Berlin?'

He hesitated, conscious of the young man standing behind him. 'Nobody. I came here as a tourist.'

She shook her head slowly. 'That's not the right answer.'

The blow to his good shoulder followed a moment later, and he allowed himself to fall. It may have been his imagination, but the force with which the young man struck him did not seem as strong. He lay on the wooden floorboards, thinking inconsequentially that they were less uncomfortable than the cement floor of the cell.

Her voice seemed distant. 'Get up, Mr Holland.' He lay still, and the young man grasped his arms and pulled him to his feet, holding him erect.

The woman stared dispassionately. 'You might just as well answer. A single blow, aimed at the right place, will break an arm or a leg. Why suffer? You have nothing to prove. In the end, you'll tell us what we want to know. How much punishment you take is up to you. Shall we start again?'

'I don't know what to tell you.' Dizziness was returning, and he leaned forward, placing a hand on the table to steady himself.

'All right.' She smiled, and placed her hand over his. 'Who did you hope to meet?'

Mark closed his eyes against the next onslaught of pain. 'Konstantin. Konstantin Steigel.'

Her voice was soft. 'Tell me.'

'We were supposed to meet at the café on the Unter den Linden, opposite the Tomb of the Unknown Soldier.'

'Go on.'

'The scores.' Mark opened his eyes. 'Konstantin will give me the scores. He's been searching for them for years. They're valuable. I'm supposed to take them back to the Kempinski for him. He's too well-known. That's why I had to meet him.'

Her voice remained soft, but her eyes were cold. 'I'm not interested in your cover story, Mr Holland. I want the truth. Tell me why you're really here.'

'But it is the truth! I have to meet Konstantin. He's waiting for me. You must let me see him. He's old, and he won't understand what's happening.'

The woman stood, facing him. She was tall, and she leaned across the desk so that her face was close to Mark's. 'Stop this nonsense! Look, we know you were sent here by Quentin Sharpe. We've been watching you for weeks. Why did you visit Mr Sullivan in San Francisco? How does he fit into the plan? Who are you trying to protect? You're not fooling anybody, Mr Holland. We even know that you reported in to Sharpe last night. Your calls have been monitored since you arrived in the city. Do you think we don't know? Who are you trying to reach?' She took a hypodermic syringe from a pocket of her jacket.

Mark stared at her, uncomprehending. 'Konstantin. I have to meet Konstantin. He had the Mahler scores, and –'

He heard the swish of the blackjack as it descended on his neck. For a moment, there was agonizing pain. The floor seemed to tip beneath his feet and, almost with relief, he lost consciousness.

He awoke to find himself lying on his back, shaking feverishly. The floor was cold, but his body was covered with sweat. His shoulders and back felt as though they were on fire, and his groans were punctuated by the involuntary movements of his torso. Above him, a bright light shone through wire netting. He was back in the cell. He closed his eyes for a moment, but it made his head spin.

Slowly, Mark forced his body to stop shivering, as he breathed steadily and pressed the palms of his hands against the floor. It required every effort of concentration. After a few minutes, he rolled over on his side, turning cautiously and waiting until he regained his equilibrium in the new position. Some of the pain had receded, and he found that by taking shallow breaths, the bruises on his ribs and shoulders ached less. He rested on his side. A wall was nearby and, inching slowly upwards, he worked his back round until he was leaning against it. The effort tired him, but he could feel his faculties returning.

The door of the cell opened slowly, and the young man looked in. 'I see you're awake. That's good.' Mark did not reply, and the young man continued, 'I thought you might enjoy a little company. Just a moment.' He disappeared from view.

Mark remained immobile, his head turned towards the door. He found it hard to focus his eyes.

When the young man returned, he was smiling. 'I've brought you a little playmate.'

The young woman was naked. Her arms were crossed over her breasts, and her hands were pressed tightly to her face. She was sobbing. There were bruises and ugly red welts on her forearms, her ribs and her buttocks.

The young man dragged her into the room, and she crouched in a corner like a trapped animal, bent low behind her knees, her hands still covering her face.

The man laughed quietly. 'Have fun!' He slammed the door shut.

Mark had not moved. He turned his head slowly to watch the woman. He had recognized her as soon as she had been brought in. It was Sigrid.

# 14

They spoke in whispers. Mark had not yet moved. He did not trust his body to respond.

'Sigrid?'

She looked up. 'Mark! Oh my God!' Her eyes were red-rimmed and swollen. 'Why have they done this?'

'I don't know.'

'Are you badly hurt?'

'I don't think so. That little blond bastard worked me over, but he avoided doing any permanent damage. I think they pumped drugs into me, but I can't remember. I'm still very fuzzy.' He spoke with difficulty. 'I can't think properly. You?'

She closed her eyes, as though to erase the memory. 'Oh Mark, they hurt me! They . . .' Tears ran down her cheeks and she buried her face in her hands again.

Mark was silent. The effort of talking seemed to have exhausted him, and he lay back against the wall, watching Sigrid helplessly. At length, he said, 'They're probably listening to us.'

'Why? I have nothing to tell them. We haven't done anything. They kept asking me questions, and when I couldn't tell them anything, they . . .' Once again, her voice trailed into silence.

'It was the same for me. I don't know what they want.'

'Are they going to . . . to kill us?'

'I don't know. I don't think so. They seem to think that I . . .' He hesitated.

'Yes?'

'That I have information that's important.'

Sigrid looked puzzled. 'What information?'

'I don't know. If I did, I would tell them.'

She crawled painfully towards him. 'I'm frightened.'

He opened his arms, and she lay against him, burying her face against his chest. Her body felt soft and warm, comforting him against the coldness of the cell. For a while, she did not move, but he could feel her tremble as her tears returned.

'What are we going to do?' Her breath felt moist against his skin.

'Wait.' He pressed his cheek closer, feeling the softness of her hair. 'There's nothing else we can do.'

'Did you tell them about Karl?'

'No, I don't think so. I told them I had arranged to meet Konstantin. I think I mentioned the music, but it didn't seem to mean anything to them.' Mark frowned. 'I can't remember!'

'What shall we do?' She repeated the question, but he knew that she did not expect him to answer.

'Try to rest. They'll come back in a while.' He felt her grow tense. 'This is a kind of softening-up technique.'

'I don't think I can stand any more.'

'If there's anything you know – even about Karl – you'd better tell them. They'll drag it out of you eventually. It's useless to fight them.'

'But I don't know anything!'

'Neither do I. Let's try to rest.' Still holding Sigrid, Mark swivelled his body so that he was lying on his side, his back to the wall. She rested her head on his outstretched arm, twining a leg over his so that she could hold herself closer to him, and their bodies were pressed together. He was conscious of her perfume and the slightly viscid contact of her bare skin. Almost instinctively, his free hand cradled her breast, and he felt the nipple harden against his own.

Her voice was soft, and she spoke haltingly. 'I thought, when we were together, that we might perhaps . . . find ourselves . . . in this way. It seemed we were very . . .'

His hand caressed her smooth skin. 'I felt the same.'

'But not like this! Not like this!' She began to cry quietly.

'Try to rest.' He spoke soothingly, holding her closer. Her presence gave him strength. The fiery rawness of his skin seemed to ease, and his body subsided into a dull ache.

He wavered on the brink of consciousness. He did not notice when the door of the cell was opened, and looked up to find the young man standing over them, his hands on his hips. He had changed his clothes, and now wore a white T-shirt and slacks. The tight-fitting shirt emphasized his muscular frame.

The man grinned. 'How charming! The babies in the wood? Come, it's time for another little talk.'

Hearing his voice, Sigrid started, rolling away from Mark. She folded her arms over her exposed body and shuffled to a corner, where she curled herself into a foetal position.

The young man eyed her contemptuously. 'It's all right, Miss Wolpert. I've come for Mr Holland. There's no need to be afraid.' His eyes were cold. 'Your turn will come later.' Sigrid buried her face in her hands, whimpering softly, and he turned his attention to Mark. 'Come.'

Mark tried to rise to his feet. He had lost the circulation in the arm on which Sigrid had lain, and his body seemed unwilling to react. The young man reached down and dragged him to his feet.

'Give me your hands.' The man led him out of the cell, walking backwards. When they reached the stairs, he transferred his grip to Mark's forearms and, climbing one step at a time, half-lifted him up the staircase. The effort was exhausting, and Mark again found that sweat was pouring from his face and body.

The man pulled a face. 'God, you smell like an animal!' There was a towel hanging on the banister, and he handed it to Mark. 'Wipe yourself down.' The material was coarse, and chafed Mark's skin, but the movement helped to revive him. The young man stood back, arms folded. 'You'd better keep it. Wrap it round yourself, for God's sake!' He smirked. 'Have you no shame?'

Both interrogators were seated behind the makeshift desk when Mark entered the room. The man spoke first.

'Have you anything further to say?' Mark was silent. 'We are prepared to wait, but the longer you refuse to co-operate, the more unpleasant it will be for you.'

'I don't know what you want me to tell you.' Mark's voice was low, but he was able to articulate the words and his mind felt clearer. Perhaps the effort of climbing the stairs had diluted the effect of the drugs.

'Very well. Start from the beginning.'

Mark took a deep breath. 'I received a call this morning – yesterday morning. I don't know what day this is. It was from the conductor, Konstantin Steigel. He had been offered some rare Mahler scores that had been found in an old house in Dresden. He wanted to buy them illegally, and asked me to accompany him to East Berlin. He was going to pay for the music and give it to me to bring back to the West.' He spoke in a monotone, his eyes fixed on a point on the wall above his interrogator's head.

The man waved his hand impatiently. 'I know all about that! We don't care about music by some Jew-boy composer!' He thumped the table suddenly with his clenched fist. The sound was startling. 'Now you will tell us the real reason you are here.'

Mark looked at him. 'That is why I am here.'

The woman took over. 'Why did you call Quentin Sharpe?'

Mark hesitated. 'I'm not sure.'

'That's not good enough!'

'It's the truth. Look, I used to work for the Department –'

'Used to?' She showed mock surprise. 'We are much better informed than you think, Mr Holland. Are you trying to suggest that you don't work for them now?'

'Yes. I stopped a long time ago. You must know that. If you keep records on me, you'll be aware that I quit ten years ago and moved to Geneva.'

'That isn't significant.'

'It was for me.'

'But you called Sharpe?' She watched Mark's face.

'Yes.'

'Why?'

172

'I told you, I don't know. I was worried about coming into East Berlin, so I left a message for Quentin. I asked the man on Reception to tell him that I would be back by seven. If you know that I called, you'll know what I said.' The woman nodded. 'I said I would call again when I returned.'

'Why?'

'So that they would know I was back.'

The interrogators exchanged a glance, and the man spoke. 'This is not logical. You expect us to believe that you no longer work for Sharpe, that you haven't worked for him for many years, but you phone him to tell him you are going to East Berlin.'

'Yes.'

'Why would he be interested?'

Mark looked from one to the other. 'For the reason that I find myself here. I was afraid you might recognize me and assume I was working for them.'

The man stared at Mark. 'According to our sources, you are.'

'No.'

The man thumped the desk again. 'Don't lie! You were sent to make contact, pass messages. Who? Who are you trying to reach?'

'Nobody.'

The man gestured impatiently. 'Very well.' He nodded to the young man standing behind Mark.

Mark closed his eyes, anticipating another blow, but the young man suddenly gripped his shoulders and spun him round. As he turned, the man punched him viciously in the stomach. He was unprepared, and doubled over, badly winded.

'Get up.' The young man was leaning over him. He was smiling. Then he reached down and lifted Mark bodily, standing behind him and forcing him to face the table. Mark hung in his arms like a rag doll.

The woman frowned. 'This is senseless. You're not proving anything. Besides, we have drugs that . . .' She stopped in mid-sentence, and exchanged looks with her partner. It seemed to Mark that she was slightly uncertain. 'Why don't you tell us what we want to know, and have done with it?'

Mark shook his head, unable to speak. The young man holding him up, his arm clamped over Mark's chest, pressed the lower half of his body closer, as if to support him. Mark was aware that the man had become sexually aroused.

The woman spoke softly. 'Who are you trying to protect?' Mark shook his head, unable to speak.

The young man spun him round again, timing the next punch so that it struck him as he toppled and fell. The blow was less painful than the first, and Mark lay on his back, his eyes closed. He was vaguely conscious that his interrogators were talking in low voices, but he could not make out what they were saying. At length, the young man pulled him to his feet and, throwing Mark's arm around his shoulder, carried him out of the room. On the landing, he leaned Mark against the wall.

'Hold on to the stair rail. If you fall, it's your own problem.' He was breathing heavily from the effort of carrying Mark, and stepped back.

Supporting himself on the banister to take the weight on his arms, Mark slowly descended the staircase. His legs trembled with the effort and, for a moment, he sat on the stairs, waiting until his strength returned. Fear of falling made him grip the rail tightly.

The man was waiting for him at the foot of the stairs. He led the way to the cell. As Mark approached, the man handed him a glass of water. 'Here, you'd better drink this.'

The water was warm and tasted slightly bitter, but Mark swallowed it gratefully.

'I don't enjoy having to do this, you know.' Mark said nothing. 'If you tell them what they want to know, they'll let you go.' He leaned closer. 'You can tell me, if you prefer.'

'I've told them everything I know.'

The young man shrugged, and opened the door of the cell. Sigrid was still curled in a corner, where they had left her. Mark started towards her, but the young man halted him with a hand on his chest. Mark was too weak to resist the gentle pressure, and the young man smiled, his fingers caressing Mark's skin. 'It's her turn now, unless you have anything you want to add?' With the flat of his palm, he pushed Mark so that he fell against the wall, then walked over to where Sigrid was crouched.

Mark took a step forward as helpless anger welled inside him. 'You bastard!' His words were blurred. He tried to move, but his legs would not obey him, and he was having difficulty focusing his eyes. Then he remembered the bitter taste of the water. The young man was leaning down to lift Sigrid to her feet, but Mark could feel his senses slipping away. He closed his eyes, clenching his fists in an effort to remain conscious, but he was already falling. The last sound he heard was Sigrid's terror-stricken scream.

He awoke slowly. His mouth was parched and his lips were stuck together with dried scum. The back of his head pounded with a sickening throb that seemed to duplicate his heartbeat. As consciousness slowly returned and he recognized the brick wall of the cell, he was aware of changes. He was lying on a soft mattress, and was covered with a blanket. The surface of his skin felt slightly slippery and had a distinctive smell. Someone had rubbed vaseline on his back and shoulders. The room was pleasantly warm. His body still resisted when he tried to move, and he sank back into a confused sleep.

'Good morning.' Mark opened his eyes. The young man was standing over him. He was holding a large towel. 'I hope you slept well.' Mark watched him. 'Come, I have run a bath for you.' He smiled. 'We can't have you looking untidy.'

'Where is Sigrid?'

'Not far from here. I expect she will get up shortly.' He extended his hand. 'Can you manage?'

'Yes.' Mark rose to his feet unaided. It was painful.

'You'll feel better when you have bathed.'

'What happens now?'

The man looked surprised. 'Now? You're going home, I suppose. They asked me to look after you, and make sure that you have everything you need. Come this way.'

The bathroom was small and comfortable. The water was hot and, from the colour, Mark assumed that salts had been added. It stung his skin as he sat, but the effect was soothing. His clothes were hanging on the back of the door. They looked as though they had been cleaned and pressed. A hand-basin next to the bath was furnished with a fresh razor and shaving soap, neatly laid out. There was an unopened bottle of expensive after-shave on the shelf above the basin.

The young man was waiting for him in the hall. He examined Mark admiringly. 'You look like a new man . . . most elegant! Do you need anything else?'

'My watch.'

'Ah, yes.' He reached into a pocket. 'I had almost forgotten.' He handed it over. 'Anything else?' His tone was bantering.

Mark ignored him, checking the watch. The time was six-thirty.

The man led him to the door of the foyer. 'There isn't time for breakfast, or even a cup of coffee. Anyway, as you know, our coffee is not very good.' He opened the front door. 'There is a car waiting for you outside. Do you think you can manage down the steps?' Pale sunlight flooded the hall. From the angle, Mark guessed that it was early morning.

He stared at the young man for a moment. 'I hope we meet again.' The intensity with which Mark spoke took the young man by surprise, and he stepped back. Then he recovered his composure.

'I shall look forward to that. If I may say so, you displayed great . . . determination.' He bowed slightly and smiled, revealing white, even teeth.

A driver was standing by the car, smoking. When he saw Mark, he threw his cigarette aside and, like a well-trained chauffeur, opened the rear door. A second man was sitting in the front seat.

As Mark entered, he noticed that there was no inside handle at the back. Presumably, he was still a guest of the security men. The man in the front seat looked round and nodded politely.

'Where is Miss Wolpert?'

'She has already left. We will meet her at the border.'

'Which one?'

'The Glienicker Bridge. There is to be an exchange.' The man muttered instructions to the driver and faced the front. It was apparent that he did not propose to speak further.

Mark sat in silence, allowing himself to sink into the cheap cloth upholstery. His head felt clear, and although his body still ached, he had recovered surprisingly quickly. The car moved swiftly through empty streets, and he closed his eyes. He was still very tired.

He dozed for most of the journey, and was vaguely aware of the car stopping before he opened his eyes. The man in the front seat was watching him.

'We have arrived.'

A trio of people was waiting by the iron girders that marked the start of the bridge. Sigrid was next to the man who had interrogated him. Slightly apart, a uniformed border guard was staring across the bridge towards the Western zone. Beyond them, a pale mist was rising from the water, diffusing the rays of sunlight. It was a very peaceful scene.

When she saw Mark, Sigrid started towards him, but the interrogator held her by the arm. Mark was still too distant to hear what the man said to her.

'Good morning, Herr Holland. I trust that all your property has been returned to you?'

'Apart from a layer of skin that I left on the wall of your cell, yes.'

'Very well.' He blinked behind the thick lenses. 'I believe my government owes you a formal apology.' His insincerity was deliberate.

'Yes.' Mark stared the man down.

'In that case, it is formally offered.' For a moment, he hesitated. 'I find it difficult to believe that it was possible for you to withhold . . .' He left the sentence unfinished.

'I had nothing to hide. Perhaps that's something you and your animals don't understand.'

'Perhaps.' The man seemed unconcerned. 'I find it strange, nevertheless, that your Mr Sharpe should be so concerned with your return if – as you say – you are no longer associated with him. He was very quick to call us.'

'I expect it's because he has some idea of what East German hospitality involves.'

'Ah.' The man brushed the subject aside. 'We have taken this opportunity to arrange an exchange. Mr Sharpe was most co-operative. I am sure you are familiar with the routine.'

'I've seen it before.' Mark was aware that Sigrid was watching him, a puzzled expression on her face.

The man looked across the bridge, where three distant figures were visible. 'Then I suggest we proceed.' He raised his arm, like an official at an athletics event. One of the men opposite signalled back.

Mark took Sigrid by the arm, and they began to walk. The interrogator and the guard stayed several paces behind them. On the other side of the bridge, the three men followed suit.

'Tell me if I'm walking too fast for you.' Sigrid was clutching his arm tightly. The strap of her bag hung from her other hand.

She tried to smile. 'Not quickly enough! Oh Mark, why did this happen?' She kept her voice low.

'I wish I knew. I'm sure it had nothing to do with Karl or the music.'

'Then why?'

'I don't know. For some reason, they were convinced that I had been sent to make contact with someone on this side.'

'Who?'

He shook his head. 'There was no one. I never even spoke to Quentin Sharpe.'

'Who is he? I heard his name just now.'

'The opposite number of our friend behind us.' Mark stared ahead. 'If I'm not mistaken, he's waiting there to meet us.'

'But why did they think you had spoken to a man like that?'

'Well, I tried to, a couple of times. He was never there when I called.'

'But why speak to him at all? Mark, I don't understand. I thought you worked in the music world.'

'I do.' He tightened his grip on her arm. 'Believe me, I do.'

'Then why – ?'

'A man contacted me a few weeks ago. He was . . . wounded.' Sigrid was watching his face. She was walking slowly, and Mark reduced his pace to hers. The two men behind them kept their distance.

'Wounded?'

'Yes. The details aren't important, but the man worked for Quentin Sharpe.'

'How did you know?'

'I . . . recognized him.' One day, perhaps, he would explain the circumstances.'

'What did he want?'

Mark frowned. 'That's the curious part. He told me some crazy story about warning somebody in Dresden that he was in danger. It made no sense. The man he was talking about died years ago.'

'I don't understand what you're saying.'

Ahead of them, the faces of the three men were distinguishable. Mark recognized Quentin Sharpe. He was wearing a light raincoat. The other two were strangers. 'He asked me to tell Quentin Sharpe that a man in Dresden was in danger.'

'What man?'

'That's the point. I thought he said it was Richard Hyatt, but he died a long time ago. That's why it made no sense. So, I tried to call Quentin, but he wasn't there. I simply left the message and forgot about it. Sigrid stumbled, dropping her handbag, and Mark caught her as she started to fall. She smiled her thanks. Behind her, the guard retrieved the bag.

'I'm sorry. My foot caught against something.' She leaned closer. 'I don't understand why this wounded man came to you.'

'Neither do I, but it doesn't matter now.' He smiled ruefully. 'The police thought I was drunk!'

'Police?'

'It's a long story. Some time, I'll tell you all of it.' He looked up. 'We're nearly there.'

Quentin's party had stopped walking. They were standing about forty yards away, apparently awaiting a signal. Looking round, Mark found that the guard and the interrogator had also stopped. The guard had taken a heavy automatic pistol from its holster. He was still holding Sigrid's bag in his other hand, and she walked back a few paces to collect it. As she drew close, the interrogator suddenly reached out and grasped her arm, pulling her back. Mark turned towards them, but the guard raised his pistol, pointing it at Mark's heart. His hand was very steady.

For a moment, there was silence. Then the interrogator spoke. 'We agreed on a single exchange: one for one.'

'Let her go. She's not involved in any of this.' Sigrid was hidden from view, behind the guard's back.

The interrogator eyed him calmly. 'Later, perhaps, as part of another exchange. For the moment, Miss Wolpert stays with us. We only agreed to you.'

Mark stepped forward, and the guard raised his gun slightly. He was a young man, and looked nervous. 'Sigrid!'

She came into view, her arm still firmly gripped by the interrogator. Her face was pale. The man spoke. 'Don't be foolish, Herr Holland. Nothing will happen to Fräulein Wolpert. An exchange will be arranged on her behalf quite quickly, I assure you.' His eyes travelled past Mark across the bridge. 'They are waiting to begin the exchange.'

'I'm not leaving without her.'

Suddenly, Sigrid struggled loose and ran to him. The guard looked uncertainly from her to the man at his side. The interrogator muttered something, and the guard waited, his gun still aimed. 'If you try to take her with you, I'll order the guard to shoot her. Don't be foolish, Herr Holland! She would not have a chance.'

Sigrid clung to Mark for a moment. Her mouth was close to his ear. 'Go! You have to. Tell them to find someone for me quickly. Perhaps your Mr Sharpe will help.'

'I'm not leaving.'

'You must! Oh, Mark! Please tell them to hurry!'

'Not without you.'

'They won't let me go, but you can arrange things for me.' She smiled weakly. 'I'm not afraid anymore.'

The interrogator had joined them. 'You are being very sensible, Fräulein. No harm will come to her, Herr Holland. I will give you my personal guarantee. Ask your people to arrange an additional exchange, and it will take place immediately.' He waited. 'Are you ready?'

Mark nodded silently, and the man backed away, taking Sigrid with him. Once again, he raised his hand, signalling across the bridge. Mark looked at Sigrid, but she had turned her back to him. From the movement of her shoulders, he could see that she was crying.

'Please begin, Herr Holland.'

He moved slowly across the bridge without looking back. As the other man passed him, Mark did not glance in his direction. He walked mechanically, his eyes fixed on a distant point on the horizon.

Quentin Sharpe was waiting at the far end of the bridge, accompanied by a man dressed in an old sweater and dirty jeans. Quentin was standing with his feet apart and his hands tucked behind his back. The military cut of his raincoat added to the impression of a Guards officer attending a parade.

'Greetings.' He did not extend his hand. 'What the hell have you got yourself into this time?'

# 15

Quentin walked at Mark's side, his hands still locked behind his back. As a younger man, he had been handsome, almost pretty, but he had not aged well. There were dark patches under his eyes, and the flesh of his face had become loose and pallid. His hair was grey and thinning rapidly.

He glanced at Mark. 'I'm trying to avoid some cliché-ridden comment about old times!'

'Listen, before we talk, they're still holding the girl who was with me. I thought she was coming too, but they want to use her for another exchange. Will you help me get her out?'

Quentin gave an exaggerated sigh. 'There always seems to be a girl where you're involved! What's her name?'

'Sigrid Wolpert. She was with me on the bridge. They took her back at the last moment.'

'Sigrid?'

'She's from Munich.'

Quentin frowned. 'That sounds like a matter for Bonn to deal with. We're not involved with West German nationals.'

'It's important. Please, Quentin!'

Sharpe looked at Mark. 'I'm sure it is, but I've just used up one of their specials to pull you out.'

'I can't just leave her there. I was responsible for her arrest.'

'Are you sure of that?' When Mark did not reply, he continued, 'I'll see what can be done. If I can't help, I know a couple of people who might. The traffic's rather frequent here. Half the time, they don't know which side they're supporting. Perhaps we should have a talk first. I have a car waiting.'

'I'd rather walk in the fresh air for a few minutes, if you don't mind. It would do me more good.'

'If you wish. I'm taking a plane back to London at midday.' He looked at his watch. 'There's time.' They were walking along a tarmac road towards the Kleinglienicke palace, an ornate hunting lodge set in many acres of parkland overlooking the Wannsee. 'Why don't we take a stroll through there?'

'Thank you for your help. You must have moved quickly. They only grabbed me yesterday.'

Quentin was staring through the railings at the yellow and white façade of the palace. The fountains had not yet been turned on, and the two gold lions, from whose mouths the water spouted, roared silently in the clear morning air. He turned back to Mark. 'You were lucky. I happened to be in Berlin when the message came through. What's been going on, and why did you leave that cryptic message two nights ago?'

Mark reached into his pocket for a cigarette. He realized with surprise that he had not smoked since the previous day. For a moment, Sigrid's teasing smile haunted his memory. 'I wish I could tell you. I don't know what the hell it's about.' He lit a cigarette, inhaling cautiously. His body still ached, and he did not want to cough. 'I went into East Berlin yesterday for Konstantin Steigel –'

'The conductor?'

Mark nodded. 'He'd been contacted by some East Germans. They've discovered some unpublished Mahler scores, and want to sell them under the counter.'

Quentin smiled. 'Hold on! I'm not one of your musicologists.'

They were walking up a lane to the right of the palace. Tall trees shaded the grass. The park was deserted. 'Mahler died in 1911. Many musicians consider he was one of the greatest composers of the first half of the century, but he's only become popular with the public in the last thirty years or so.'

'I know who he is. I think I've heard some of his music. It's a bit on the heavy side for me.'

'Me too, if you want the truth. Anyway, it's been known for years that he left behind a number of scores that were never published. Everyone thought they were lost. The last time anyone saw them was in Dresden in the 1930s.'

'Why didn't they publish them then?'

'Probably because his music wasn't very well-known or very popular in those days. There could have been other reasons: squabbles between publishers, arguments with his widow. They disappeared, and it was always assumed that they were destroyed in the Dresden raids towards the end of the war. A couple of months ago, someone found them – or thinks he found them – in the basement of an old house in Dresden, and contacted Steigel. He's a Mahler specialist, and they wanted him to have the first offer before the authorities caught on.'

Quentin's eyebrows were raised. 'That sounds a bit risky.'

'It was, but not very serious. Konstantin called me in Geneva, and asked me to help him smuggle the music out. He was afraid that, as a well-known conductor, the East Germans might be suspicious if they saw him crossing the border with a large sheaf of handwritten scores under his arm.'

'Do you think they would have?'

'Frankly, no, but Steigel's an old man who's lived within the music world for a long time. He doesn't have much idea what the real world is like. He was very excited about the discovery. He's been dreaming of those missing scores for nearly half a century. I think he was also intrigued by the idea of a cloak and dagger operation to whisk them out of the country.'

'And you went along with it?'

'I said I'd help him. I also persuaded him not to take any large amounts of money with him. The plan was that he would examine the music to verify it, then pass it to me to bring across the border. I was there in a car. That's where the girl came into it.'

'I see.' Quentin walked in silence for a while. 'Who is she?'

'Her brother's the one who offered the music. Steigel is supposed to pay her, and she'll pass the money on.'

'And she lives in Munich?'

'Yes. Her family split up. She moved to the West when she was a child, but her brother stayed behind.'

'Hmm.' Quentin was thoughtful. 'It's an ingenious plan.' They were walking along a path under the trees. The mist had risen from the water, which glittered in the sunlight. In such a pastoral setting, Berlin might have been a thousand miles away. Mark was reminded of Sigrid's telephone call. Had that only been twenty-four hours ago? Quentin's voice cut across his thoughts. 'All right. I think I'm with you so far. What happened yesterday?'

The path curved towards the water, past a mausoleum constructed in the classic Greek style. As they walked, Mark described the events of the previous day, from the moment he had been taken prisoner at Checkpoint Charlie. Quentin listened in silence. From time to time, he glanced at Mark's face, but he did not interrupt.

When Mark had finished, Quentin led the way to the water's edge. There was a thin spattering of mud on his highly polished shoes, and he wiped them fastidiously on a clump of grass. 'You appear to have had an . . . uncomfortable time.'

'I've been through worse. The girl was badly shaken. There's a vicious little blond bully-boy with a sadistic streak who took pleasure in beating us up. They also fed me drugs while I was unconscious. God knows what they contained.'

'What did you tell them?'

'Nothing.'

'Are you sure?' Quentin was watching him carefully.

'I didn't know anything.' Mark's face was grim. 'Hence the brute force. When I started to talk about the music, they weren't interested. They seemed to be convinced I was trying to contact someone in East Germany. They kept asking me, and when I told them there was nobody, they brought out the blackjack and a hypodermic.'

'But you mentioned no names?'

'I didn't have any names to give them, Quentin. Who the hell do I know? I don't think I mentioned Karl, Sigrid's brother, unless I talked about him when they drugged me. They didn't care about the Mahler scores anyway. What shocked me was that they believe I'm still working for the Department, and that you sent me in.'

'Good Lord!'

'Exactly. I had the feeling that they were surprised when I told them nothing. I suppose they thought it was impossible to hold out against the drugs and beatings.' Mark watched Quentin closely. 'You look worried.'

'I? No, I'm just surprised.'

'Incidentally, you'd better have your people check out the telephone operators in the Kempinski. They knew I'd called you. That's why they thought I was still active.'

'I'll look into it.'

'Speaking of phone calls, why did you never respond to my messages from Tokyo and San Francisco?'

Quentin's face was expressionless. 'Your report was very detailed. There was no reason to come back to you.'

'Is that all you have to say? I saw Bailey die, for Christ's sake!'

'I know. That was a bad business. I don't know how they got on to him.'

'Who?'

Quentin's mouth was a thin line. 'That information's restricted.' He smiled wryly. 'Besides, in view of past history, I didn't think you were that eager to talk to me!'

'What was it all about?'

Quentin stared across the water. 'I'm sorry, but I really can't discuss it.'

'Bullshit! I'm not about to tell the world. What was all that crazy business about Richard Hyatt? He's been dead for years.'

'Yes.'

'As a matter of fact, I was in London the day of his funeral.'

'Were you?' Quentin stared at him. 'I didn't know that.'

'I was passing through, and looked in on Alex Beaumont. He told me about it. I think he was a little pissed off that he had to mind the shop while everyone else was down in Sussex for the funeral.'

'It was long before my time, but Alex has mentioned it. Hyatt's buried in a village called South Burton, not far from Arundel. I happen to know because I was in that part of the world, and the name rang a bell.'

'Why did Bailey think Hyatt was in Dresden?'

Quentin's eyes met Mark's for a moment. 'I don't know. We never worked that one out. It made no sense to us, either.' He looked away. 'We never found his body. Presumably, it ended up in the Japan Sea.' He hunched his shoulders. 'He wasn't a bad kid. I had the job of telling his family.'

'I only met him a couple of times. I forgot to mention something else. On the way back, I stopped off to see Ernie Sullivan in San Francisco.'

'Who's he?'

'He was CIA, before he retired. He'd worked with Hyatt in the old days. He didn't understand Bailey's message either. In fact, he was the one who suggested I pass it on, for what it was worth, and forget the whole thing.'

'That was good advice. Why do you mention Sullivan?'

'Because someone was photographing us while we were talking.'

'Really? Are you sure?'

'No, not positive.'

Quentin looked dubious. 'Then it may not be anything. If you'd just arrived there after the business with Bailey, you could have imagined it. We're all inclined towards paranoia.'

'Maybe. Actually, it was Ernie who spotted the man.'

'What do you think it means?'

Mark stretched. His aching muscles felt better. 'I don't know. I just had the feeling that my movements were being monitored. It was a strange coincidence that the scores showed up in Dresden.'

Quentin shrugged. 'Not if you're talking about East Germany. Isn't there an old joke about a tourist who tells the frontier official that he wants to visit East Berlin, Dresden and Leipzig, and the man says: "OK. What do you want to do in the afternoon?" Anyway, I thought you said the Mahler scores were last seen in Dresden.'

'Yes, they were.'

'Then it's not so coincidental.' Quentin looked thoughtful. 'Did you mention Bailey yesterday?'

'No. I never thought about it.'

'I see.' He was silent.

'Do you think it could have been related?'

'No, I don't see how it could be.'

'I certainly didn't associate one with the other. Bailey must have got it wrong about Hyatt.'

'Yes. It was all before his time – mine too.'

'I'm still surprised you didn't call me back.'

'Actually, I did try once, but you weren't there. I thought it was more discreet not to leave messages. It's better to let that sort of story die.'

'That was Ernie's opinion, too.'

Quentin was silent for a moment. 'It's not much of an epitaph for Bailey, but the fewer the people who know his name, the better.'

'I mentioned the incident to Sigrid.'

'Oh? When?' Quentin seemed suddenly alert.

'When we were crossing the bridge, just before they took her back. Your name came up in conversation, and she wanted to know who you were.'

'Why?'

'As far as she's concerned, I'm in the music world. She was curious to know why I would be calling someone in your line of business.'

'Did you tell her?'

'Not really. I explained that I had tried to call you several times in the past month.'

'What exactly did you say?'

Mark shrugged. 'Just that a man had asked me to contact you and tell you that Richard Hyatt was in danger. I told her that he'd been dead for years, making the whole thing senseless.'

'I see. What did this Miss . . . ?' He searched for her name.

'Wolpert. Sigrid Wolpert. You've got to help me get her out of there.'

'I'll see what I can do. What did she say?'

'I don't remember. I think it was when she tripped and nearly fell. They gave her a bad time, Quentin. I saw the bruises.'

'Quite. I'll call my friend before I leave Berlin.' He looked at his watch. 'I hate to cut this short, but I really ought to head back to town, especially if I'm going to help your Miss Wolpert.'

'Of course.'

'Would you like to see a doctor? We've got a good man here, who can check you over.'

'No, thank you. I'll wait until I'm back in Geneva. I'd like to find a phone and call Steigel. God knows what's happened to him. We were supposed to meet yesterday afternoon.'

'I'll drive you back to the Kempinski.' Quentin led the way. 'Did Miss Wolpert tell you what they did to her?'

Mark avoided Quentin's eyes. His description of the events had been general. 'They beat her pretty badly. Their muscle-man enjoyed himself. He doesn't like women.'

'What did they ask her?'

'She didn't really say. It was enough that she was with me.' Mark watched Sharpe's face. 'You look very pleased with yourself, Quentin.'

'Do I?' He laughed weakly. 'I'm just glad to see you back, all in one piece.' Quentin walked on in silence, and Mark had the impression that he seemed very relieved.


As soon as he reached the hotel, Mark called Steigel.

The old conductor was furious. 'Mark, where have you been? Heidi and I have been calling all night, trying to learn where you were. What happened to you? We waited at that damned café for nearly two hours!'

Mark thought quickly. 'I'm terribly sorry, maestro. We ran into trouble at the border.'

'Trouble? What sort of trouble?'

'There was some sort of mix-up over our papers. It may have been because Miss Wolpert was a West German. You know how difficult those border officials can be.' He extemporized easily. The Department had trained him well and, like riding a bicycle, it was a skill one never forgot.

'Heidi and I have been extremely worried.' His anger was diminishing.

'I'm sorry. The border guards detained us for hours. I think they do that sort of thing deliberately.'

'That's outrageous!'

'It was nearly midnight before they let us go, and I didn't want to call you so late. They wouldn't allow me near a telephone while I was there.'

'You mean to say they held you prisoner?'

Mark smiled grimly. 'Yes, I suppose you could put it like that.'

'That's appalling! I hope you are going to lodge an official protest. How dare they do something like that? I know the cultural attaché here in Berlin. I think you've met him, too. Would you like me to talk to him for you?'

Despite everything, Mark found himself close to laughter. The cultural attaché was a small, mild-mannered man with a lifelong dedication to Renaissance choral music. How would he take on the blond boy from Gleimstrasse? 'Tell me about the scores. Did you see them?'

There was a long silence. When Steigel's voice returned, the disappointment in his voice was apparent. 'They were rubbish, Mark. Ridiculous! Any third-year music student could have done a better job!'

'What do you mean?' Mark felt a sudden coldness.

'They were fakes, my dear, and not even good ones. It was an insult to the intelligence!'

'Are you certain, maestro? What happened?'

'Of course I am certain! I will tell you exactly what happened. Heidi and I went to the Pergamon Museum, just as we had arranged. At least that was worthwhile. I had forgotten the magnificent treasures on display. We spent about an hour there, and then we waited by the Babylonian arch, as I said we would. This horrid, dirty little man approached us. He was vulgar and obsequious, and called me "Professor" every time he spoke. I finally told him I was a Doctor of Music, and not a teacher, but he simply smiled and bowed and picked at his dirty fingernails!

'After ten minutes of inane conversation, I suggested we go to examine the music, and he drove us to a filthy apartment somewhere near the Immanuel-Kirche. I used to know that area quite well, but they have changed all the names of the streets. Everything was Karl Marx this and Lenin that!' He grunted. 'I remember when poor Kurt Weill told Brecht he was not prepared to set *Das Kapital* to music! That was a mild complaint, compared with the situation today! What a sad place it is, my dear. When I think of those stately streets and grand buildings that I used to know . . .' He lapsed into silence.

'And the music?' Mark tried to hide his impatience.

'The music? Hah! He took us through this shabby little building. It stank of boiled cabbage and urine! I was ashamed to subject Heidi to such an embarrassing situation. Then, with the air of a magician producing a rabbit out of a hat, this impertinent little charlatan produced ten pages of handwritten score. Someone had copied out part of the third movement of the Sixth Symphony, in handwriting that bore not the slightest resemblance to Mahler's own. It was disgraceful! They had not even done an accurate job. There were mistakes in the viola line, and the fool had omitted the horn parts on one page altogether! As soon as I saw the first page, it was quite evident that the whole thing was a cheap confidence trick of the most transparent incompetence. The paper on which it was written looked suitably old. I would guess that it was the only genuine part of the whole shoddy presentation. How could they think that I would be taken in by it?' He hesitated. 'I must thank you for your wise advice, Mark. Thank God I was not carrying very much money with me. For all I know, the man intended to steal it from us.'

'What did you do?' Mark's brain was racing. He scarcely listened to Steigel's reply.

'I made no comment. While he watched me, I pretended to read the pages slowly, taking my time. When I had finished, he rubbed his sticky little paws together and said: "Well, Herr Professor, what do you think?" I would like to have told him there and then what I thought: of him, of the music and of the whole amateur concoction, but it seemed wiser to make our way back to the safety of the café, so I told him I would like to think about it and check some scores of my own before making a final decision. He offered to let me take several pages, and hinted that a down-payment would be appreciated, but I told him I did not feel it would be necessary. To be honest, my dear, I could not wait to take myself and Heidi out of that drrreadful place!' The rolling of his 'r's had become more pronounced. 'Then, he drove us to the café, and with a great deal of bowing and scraping and "Herr Professors", he took his leave of us. We waited for you until six o'clock, then told the driver to bring us home.'

'I'm very sorry, maestro.'

'It was not your fault, Mark. There was no way that you could have foreseen what would happen. You were the one who suggested caution on my part.'

'But I'm sorry I wasn't there to meet you. It must have been aggravating.'

'You had your own problems.' He sighed. 'It was a pity. I had foolishly hoped . . . well, it's too late for that. You know, perhaps it was never intended that we should see those scores. As I grow older, I begin to have a greater belief in divine providence. But then again, they may still be there, awaiting discovery at some later date by another generation. Maybe God has decided that we are not yet ready to see them.'

'Maybe.'

'In the meantime, I would like to see that disgraceful little man punished. I realize that my own activities in this affair were not entirely above suspicion, but he should be brought to justice.'

'Yes. Did he definitely identify himself as Karl Wolpert?'

'Certainly. As well as being tastelessly unctuous, he went to great lengths to give the impression that he was a bona fide musician. He even produced an identity card, somewhere around the third "Herr Professor"! When we drove to that hideous apartment, he kept up a running conversation that pretended he had some musical knowledge of a somewhat shallow academic standard. No wonder the East Germans have produced so few artists of any interest, if he is a typical example of their training! Frankly, I don't believe that even he really thought the scores were genuine. He couldn't have hoped that I would be taken in.'

'I see.'

'That young woman must have been part of the scheme, Mark. She must have known. Where is she now?'

Mark hesitated. 'I'm not sure. I left her some time ago.'

'You take my word, when she learns that I was not to be misled, she will disappear as quickly as she arrived. We should try to find her as soon as possible. She must have been part of this plan to relieve me of a substantial sum of money. I should have been more suspicious. The amount they proposed was far too low for an unpublished Mahler score. Obviously, they did not know what they were talking about. It's very sad. She seemed like a charming young woman. But then, credibility is their stock-in-trade.'

'You don't think she was equally taken in by her brother?'

'Not if she has been regularly in touch with him, as she claimed. Don't forget, we were supposed to give the money to her.'

'That's true.'

'It was she who organized the whole venture. When she suggested you should come to Berlin –'

'Sigrid suggested it?'

'Certainly. I didn't think it was necessary for you to be present. I'm not a baby!' He paused. 'On the other hand, I have been more than a little naïve. Anyway, when we first talked, Miss Wolpert suggested, almost insisted, that you should be there as my manager, to make sure that everything was in order. It was her idea that you should drive with her into East Berlin, so that I could hand the scores to someone less conspicuous. I proposed that she should take them, but she was nervous, so I agreed to call you. What a stupid wild-goose chase! Hello? Mark, are you still there?'

'Yes, maestro, I'm still here.'

'I'm sorry, my dear. You must be exhausted after your experience at the border. That was unbelievable! I will call the attaché before we leave.'

'When are you going?'

'I am expected in Paris this afternoon. A car has been arranged for the airport at eleven o'clock. It is much too early. It only takes twenty minutes to Tegel, but Heidi gets flustered if we have to hurry at the last moment.'

'Then I don't think we'll have time to talk.'

'No. You must rest. Why don't you call me in Paris? I'll be at the Meurice all week. There are a number of matters I want to ask you about. The Vienna Philharmonic wants to discuss a tour, but it doesn't sound very interesting. Between you and me, I think they want me to fill in for a cancellation. And London keeps calling. Can't we do something about their fees? If they're not prepared to give me an adequate number of rehearsals, then they should at least make it worth my time and effort.'

'I could probably come and see you in a few days, and we could go through everything.'

'That would be better still. I am embarrassed to propose it, after this fiasco.'

'Please don't worry. We didn't know it would be a waste of time.'

'We should have suspected something fishy, my dear. I suppose I was so excited that I was prepared to accept anything they said. What idiocy!'

'I'm very sorry, maestro. You must have been disappointed.'

'Yes, it was an unhappy experience, and quite awful for Heidi. Fortunately, I was too angry to be depressed. And Mahler was not the only composer. You know, I have been looking through some pieces by Alexander Zemlinsky lately. He was a good conductor, but I never bothered much with his music. Some of it is not bad at all. Maybe it is time to revive one or two of the better works.'

'That sounds interesting.'

Steigel's good humour had returned. 'There is always something new, my dear. That's what makes my work rewarding. Besides, at my age, I would like at least one more encounter with Beethoven or Brahms or Mozart. They offer consolation enough for the works I never saw. Please call me when you have the chance.'

'I will.'

'And try to find that Wolpert girl. She may lead us to the others.'

Mark replaced the receiver slowly. Konstantin had to be right. If the scores were such bad fakes, Sigrid and her brother must have dreamed them up together. But why go to such trouble to drag an elderly conductor across the border when it was evident that he would identify the forgery immediately? Poor Konstantin! He was more offended than angry that they had hoped to dupe a musician of his training and experience with such obvious imitations. Why on earth did they do it?

He crossed the bedroom to run a bath. The skin on his back and shoulders still smarted, but the walk in the Glienicke park had eased his aching muscles. Then he stopped. The answer seemed to be staring him in the face.

Konstantin had never been their quarry. They did not care how quickly he identified the music because, by that time, they would have achieved their purpose. The story about the Mahler scores had been concocted with one aim: to make sure that when the conductor crossed into East Berlin, his manager would be there, too. Sigrid had insisted on it. She had even chosen the time when they would be at Checkpoint Charlie. He had been their target from the beginning.

Mark sat on the edge of the bed, putting together the events of the past twenty-four hours in a new context. His captors were convinced that he had been chosen to contact someone on behalf of the Department. They knew about his visit to Sullivan and his call to Quentin in London, which meant they had been watching him for several weeks. And when he had told them nothing, despite the drugs and the beatings, they had shown an almost grudging admiration. Did that mean he had convinced them that they had arrested the wrong man?

He frowned. Sigrid must have been a part of their operation. Was that why she stayed behind? It had been a convincing performance, but then, a few bruises were easy enough to create, together with red-rimmed eyes. On the other hand, she couldn't have afforded to be with him when he spoke to Steigel. She needed to remain on the other side. Quentin Sharpe had been very curious to know what they had asked her when she was interrogated. Why?

His mind shifted to Quentin. Why had he moved so quickly to obtain Mark's release? After such a long time, he would not have expected the Department to show such immediate interest. When he had phoned, Quentin was never available. There had been something odd about his comments, and when Mark had told him the East Germans were convinced he was still working for the Department, his surprise had been unconvincing. And how had he described the Mahler story? An ingenious plan. It was almost as though Quentin already knew that the scores were false.

The water was hot and soothing, and Mark lay back with his eyes closed. He needed time to think.


At Tegel airport, the driver stopped his cab at the road leading to International Departures. There was a large board on which all flights and their destinations were posted.

'Which airline?'

Mark hesitated for a moment, scanning the list. Then, as if coming to a decision, he said, 'British Airways, please. The London flight.'

London, 1986

# 16

The pretty girl at the car-hire desk smiled pertly. 'I've put a cross against the boxes you initial if you want full insurance coverage.' She leaned forward confidentially, displaying generous cleavage. 'Don't tell them I said so, but it's hardly worth it, and it bumps up the costs. How long will you be needing the car?'

'I'm not sure. A few days, probably.'

'Well, we automatically work out the best rate for you. It depends on the mileage. Sometimes, the weekly rate's cheaper.'

'Thank you.' Mark initialled the boxes and signed the form. 'Do you have any road maps?'

'Only London, and not very detailed. It depends what you want.' She looked at him. 'I know London pretty well myself, if you need help. As a matter of fact, I go off early today.'

'That's very kind, but I'm on my way down to Sussex this morning. I'll need a local map, showing some of the smaller villages.'

'We don't have anything like that. You might find something in the bookshop upstairs, but I wouldn't guarantee it.'

'I'll try a garage on the way.'

'They're not much better, these days. If I were you, I'd take the M25 from here, even if you do go a bit farther round. It's better than fighting your way through south London. You go left instead of right at the roundabout.' She checked the form. 'You did say you'll be at the Westbury Hotel this evening?'

'Yes.'

The girl grinned. 'I bet you're in the property business. I can always guess what my customers do!' She seemed almost unwilling to complete the transaction. 'Are you looking at a house?'

'No. As a matter of fact, I'm hoping to visit a grave.'

The smile vanished. 'Oh. Well, if you'd like to come this way, sir, I'll show you where to pick up the car.' She preceded Mark out of the terminal in a cloud of heady perfume.

The lush slopes of the South Downs basked in the morning sunlight. Despite their perennial grumbles, the English were enjoying old-fashioned summer weather, of the kind Mark always associated with past times. Why did he never remember the rainy days? He drove slowly, choosing smaller roads when they were available. He was in no hurry, and allowed his sense of direction to lead him south towards the coast, passing between neat, well-trimmed clusters of houses with picture-book village greens and travel-brochure inns. The outlying farms looked as though they belonged to a model train set, and the green and gold rectangles of carefully tended wheat and barley gave way to a sudden field of brilliant yellow rape flowers. It was like driving back into his childhood. At times, the countryside looked familiar. As a teenager, he had stayed in a country hotel somewhere to the north of Pulborough. It had been rather grand, with an ornamental lake and antique furniture in the reception rooms. He no longer remembered the name of the village. Could it have been Bedham or Strood Green? The names were as appropriate as the peaceful landscape.

In Berlin, he had slept for most of the day and through the night – a deep, dreamless sleep, during which the drugs in his system had exhausted themselves – and had awoken early in the morning, feeling refreshed. An occasional twinge of pain in his back and shoulders was a sharp reminder of his blond tormentor, but his skin no longer suffered from the tiny cuts and scrapes that criss-crossed its surface.

He wondered what had happened to Sigrid. Now that her cover was blown, she would not risk returning to Munich. Mark felt no rancour towards her. She had made a complete fool of him, but that had been her function in the operation. She was a professional, as he had once been, and she had been good at her job. If anything, he felt a slight admiration. She was quite an actress! He wondered idly whether the blond boy had taken pleasure in inflicting enough damage to produce the welts and bruises that had scarred her body. For a moment, Mark's eyes narrowed. One day, he would confront that young man again, on different terms.

Outside Lower Horncroft, he stopped the car to consult his map. He was only a few miles north of Arundel, and there was a West Burton, on a minor road off to the right, but no South Burton. He would have to ask at the next village. Mark paused to light a cigarette, opening the window of the car to let in the sound of birds. He stared vacantly through the windscreen. He was still not sure what he expected to learn, but he knew that the answer lay somewhere in England. Why not start with Richard Hyatt's grave?

He came upon the village quite suddenly: a row of houses, a post office and, just beyond, a small church nestling behind a clump of trees. The cemetery looked old and badly kept. There were thick weeds covering the weatherbeaten slabs of stone, green with age, and grass was steadily reclaiming the path leading from the rusted metal gate to the main door.

Inside, there was the smell of dust and disuse. Several postcards with curling edges lay on a battered table by the entrance, next to a hand-printed sign requesting visitors to leave the correct money in the wooden box provided. The lights had been turned off, and the trees outside shadowed the windows. For a moment, Mark thought he was alone, but a sound caught his attention. A man was removing dead flowers from the altar steps and stuffing them into a plastic rubbish bag. He was dressed in old dungarees and a torn pullover. He looked up from his work and nodded to Mark.

'Hello. Have you come to have a look at the church? It's a rather good example of English Perpendicular, middle–fifteenth-century, although the foundations are supposed to go a long way further back. They're Norman, but the external buttresses fell off somewhere round the 1400s. The walls are thick enough.' He seemed to be relieved to stop working. 'Those are yew trees outside, which suggest an ancient pre-Christian sacred grove used by the ancient Britons.' He smiled. 'For all we know, there were all sorts of high jinks going on in those days!'

'I suppose so.'

The man wiped his hands on his dungarees, and Mark had the impression that they came away dirtier than before. 'To be perfectly honest, I don't know the first thing about church architecture, but you pick up the jargon as you go along.'

Mark walked down the aisle towards him. The stone floor was

gritty with dirt that had been trampled into it. 'I was hoping to find the vicar.'

'That's me.' The man smiled apologetically. 'My name's Simpson. Sorry about the mess, but I only manage to come here now and then. I look after two other churches, and they're very much busier. This place has come to a standstill. It wasn't only industry that had its cut-backs in the past few years.'

'I see.'

'It's a pity, really. This is my favourite, but nobody wants to come here anymore. The parish covers a fairly wide area, and those people I do see prefer to drive on the main road. This one's off the beaten track. Besides, there's little left of the original village. Just about all the houses have been sold off as weekend cottages. A few of the older residents have hung on, but their children are more interested in the cash value of the buildings. I'm afraid Sunday mornings are for reading the colour supplements and waiting for the pubs to open. I used to hold an evening service here every fourth Sunday, but the congregation dwindled down to me and one other person, so I gave up.' He spoke cheerfully.

'That's a shame.'

'I suppose so. All my regulars have gone, so my work seems to consist of seeing the last of the locals off the premises, so to speak.'

'How long have you been here?'

'About twelve years, give or take. I don't know where the time goes.' As he drew closer, Mark realized the man was not as young as he had thought. There were traces of grey in his receding hair, and deep lines cut into the sides of his mouth. Despite his smile, they gave him a look of permanent disappointment. 'Let's see. I must have started at the end of 1973. This was my first solo effort.' His eyes took in the church for a moment. 'I was all set to conquer the world in those days, but it's not so easy to achieve when you're on a limited stipend. Is there anything I can do for you?'

'Yes, I think there is. I'm anxious to have a look at the grave of Richard Hyatt.'

'Hyatt? That's a good local name. We've got half a dozen of them buried here. When I first arrived, and had more time on my hands, I did a lot of work on the graveyard, cleaning up the stones and sorting out all the old records. I was thinking of writing a sort of village history, by tracing the lives of the local families: where they came from, and where they moved to.' He saw the expression on Mark's face. 'There hasn't been much time for that in the past few years. It's one of those unfinished projects that I always meant to follow up. Something else usually has to take precedence.'

'I expect you'll remember Richard Hyatt.'

'No, but my memory's like a sieve these days. I certainly recognize the name. What's your interest, if I'm not being too nosy?'

'He was my uncle. I've been living overseas for some years, and I thought I would pay my respects. I don't often come to Britain, and when I do, I'm normally stuck in London.'

The vicar regarded Mark oddly. 'Your uncle?'

'Yes, on my mother's side. I was very fond of him.'

'I think you've got the wrong place. If my memory serves me correctly, the last Hyatt buried here died around 1920. I could be wrong, but I don't remember any others.'

'Are you sure of that?' Mark felt a sudden tenseness.

'Not absolutely, but we can have a look at the records. I seem to think the notes I started are somewhere in the vestry, too. It shouldn't be hard to check.'

'Then you don't remember a funeral in the spring of 1976? Quite a lot of people came down from London for it.'

The man frowned. ''Seventy-six? That was during my tenure. No, I don't recall anything like that. As a matter of fact, I don't remember any funerals during my first few years. It's funny, but I had to look up the order of service the first time I was called on to officiate.' He smiled. 'This is a pretty small place, you know. A lot of people prefer the crematorium over at –'

'Do you think we could have a look at those records? It means a great deal to me.'

'Of course. Are you sure you haven't got your churches mixed up? Perhaps it was West Burton.'

'No. I'm certain it was South Burton.'

'Well, that's us, all right.' He started back down the aisle, towards a small door on the left. 'Why don't we take a look?'

'Thank you. I'm sorry to be a nuisance, but it's important.'

The man turned to look at Mark. His expression was puzzled. 'So you said.'

'I was very fond of him.'

'I hope I can be of help, but I still think you're in the wrong place.' At the door of the vestry, he paused. 'It's lucky you caught me in. As I mentioned earlier, I don't come here often. They're talking about closing this place down one of these days.' He smiled. 'That's why I gave you the speech about its architectural background.'

'Can they do that?'

'Good Lord, yes! They've pulled down dozens in London over the past twenty years. There's a very fancy block of flats in Paddington in place of the one where I was christened.'

'How depressing.'

The man shrugged. 'Not much point in keeping them open if nobody uses them, and the land alone is worth a fortune. You did say Richard Hyatt, didn't you?'

Mark returned to London by the fastest route, travelling down the outside lane as quickly as the traffic would permit. By concentrating on the road, he was able to assemble his thoughts. There had been no trace of Richard Hyatt. They had searched the records thoroughly, and found nothing. Seeing Mark's frustration, the vicar had offered to call the local Registrar.

'I know him quite well. We have occasional professional dealings, in a manner of speaking!'

'No. I don't want to bother you.'

'It's no trouble, and it could cut through a lot of red tape if I make the call. You know what it's like if you start asking for back information.'

'Yes, but I must have made a mistake after all. I imagine there are several other counties with villages called Burton.'

'Good Lord, I hadn't thought of that! There must be half a dozen.'

'I'd better contact someone in the family, to make sure. Thank you for all your help. How certain are you that they're going to close this church?'

'I'm afraid it's pretty definite; possibly before the end of the year, if the rumours are true. I tried to get up a petition to save it – protected building, and all that sort of thing – but nobody showed any interest. The trouble is, the moment people see the local vicar walking up their garden path, they suspect a collection or a favour, and pretend not to be in!'

So Richard Hyatt was not buried in South Burton, as Quentin had said. Had he made a mistake over the name of the village?

Furthermore, this particular church was soon to be closed. Did Quentin know that? In which case, why had he gone to the trouble of telling him where the grave was? Except, of course, that he did not expect Mark to check so soon. The road narrowed, and he pulled behind a heavy lorry as oncoming traffic blocked the way. If Richard Hyatt was not buried in South Burton, where was he?

His thoughts switched to Bailey. There had been no doubt about his message. According to him, Richard Hyatt was in Dresden. How could that be? Quentin Sharpe had seemed equally puzzled by the suggestion. It was meaningless. But there had been something odd about Quentin's behaviour in Berlin. Neither his questions nor his answers had rung true. Mark accelerated as the road opened up again. He needed to talk to Quentin.

He was crossing the foyer of the hotel when a voice called his name.

'Mark Holland?' The man looked familiar, but Mark could not place him. 'Don't you remember me?' His accent was American. 'Don Graham. We met in Buffalo, when maestro Steigel was guest-conducting.'

'Yes, of course.' Mark vaguely remembered a party after the concert in a large house belonging to one of the orchestra's board members. Steigel usually attended such receptions for a regulation fifteen minutes and left, relying on Mark to hold the fort. After a few years, all the houses and the faces began to look alike.

'I decided to go after a solo career after all, as we discussed. Say, it's good to see you!' His handshake was hearty. 'Do you live in London?'

'No, I'm just visiting for a day or two.'

'Oh.' Some of Graham's enthusiasm diminished. 'That's too bad. I'm making my European debut with a recital at the Wigmore Hall on Friday, and I hoped I could talk you into coming.'

'I don't think I'll still be here.'

The man nodded. 'It's tougher than I expected to find someone to represent me. I've been doing the rounds of all the agencies, but they don't want to know. It's worse than New York, and there seems to be less choice.'

Mark looked at his watch. It was almost five o'clock. 'Yes. London's difficult.'

The American did not move. 'I've got this great girl presenting the recital, and she's really worked on the press to come and hear me. She's an angel, but what I really need is a good, full-time manager. I suppose I couldn't interest you in the idea?'

Mark smiled professionally. He was anxious to go to his room and telephone. 'My agency is very small, and we're based in Geneva, which wouldn't serve your cause. You'd be better off with a London manager.' He could not remember what instrument the man played. 'What's your programme?'

'Oh, the usual stuff, I guess: Mozart, Dvořák and Brahms. I don't see any point in doing off-beat pieces.'

'I suppose not.' The reply did not help.

'It's like when they picked on Zubin Mehta at a press conference for not playing enough contemporary music.' Graham smiled. 'He told them not to bitch at him because he planned to play a Brahms cycle. It was because he loved those symphonies that he became a conductor in the first place! I guess I feel the same way. I saved a couple of dazzlers by Sarasate for the encores.' Mark nodded. The man had to be a violinist! 'Listen, are you sure you couldn't stay over through Friday? I'd really appreciate your opinion.' Like all musicians, he seemed convinced that travel schedules could be altered to accommodate his recital.

'I'd love to hear you, but I have to be back in Geneva by then.' Mark moved towards the lifts at the end of the foyer, and the American kept pace with him.

'I guess Steigel keeps you pretty well-occupied?'

'Most of the time.'

Graham laughed. 'He's a wily old character! Did he tell you what happened with Jack Markowitz in Buffalo?'

'No, I don't think so.' Mark pressed the button for the lift. Musicians loved anecdotes and, under normal circumstances, he enjoyed them, too. Konstantin had reached the age when a whole folklore of stories, true and apocryphal, now surrounded him.

The American was not to be deterred. 'We were playing Mahler Five and Saul – that's our first Horn – wanted to take the evening off. It was his wedding anniversary, or something like that. Anyway, he knew Steigel would never let him go, so he asked

Jack to sit in for him, and they cooked up a great plan to fool the old man. Jack wore a grey wig of curly hair, just like Saul's, and the same, thick horn-rimmed glasses. From a distance, you couldn't tell them apart!' He chuckled at the memory. 'So, the concert takes place, and Jack sits in Saul's chair and plays like a dream. Believe me, I was there, and I could have sworn it was Saul playing. Jack even stood up and took a solo bow at the end. I guess it would have been even better if the local reviewer had given him a special mention.' The lift doors opened, but Graham placed a restraining hand on Mark's shoulder. 'Jesus, I was killing myself, laughing! When we went backstage, heading for the dressing-rooms, who should be waiting in the corridor but maestro Steigel. He goes over to Jack and pats him on the shoulder, and says, "Bravo, Mr Markowitz. Please tell Saul how well he played!" Then he looked at him for a moment, and added, "The wig and the glasses really don't suit you."' Graham laughed. 'And poor old Jack thought he'd pulled off the stunt of a lifetime! I tell you, nothing gets past that old buzzard, least of all a spot of make-up.'

Mark smiled. He had heard the story before. Konstantin had told him about it. The conductor had recognized the horn player's tone within a few notes. A second lift door opened. 'You must forgive me if I run. I want to make a phone call before my office closes.'

'Sure.' The American gripped his hand. 'Maybe we'll run into each other again? I'll be in the hotel mostly, practising. I'm in Room 302, if you feel like grabbing a bite to eat.'

'I'll remember.' Mark made his escape, and pressed the lift button. It was a good story, and the man was right. Nothing escaped Konstantin's hawk-like attention, and the tone of an instrument was as identifiable to a musician as a fingerprint. A spot of make-up would never . . . He paused. Make-up!

When the voice on the line answered, he did not ask for Quentin Sharpe. 'Can I speak to Mr Bailey's secretary, please?'

There was a pause. 'Who's calling?'

Mark hesitated. 'This is Cartwright, in Accounts.'

'Just a moment. I'll see if she's still there.'

After another pause, a girl spoke. 'Hello?' She sounded cautious.

'Oh, hello. My name's Cartwright. I'm in Accounts. Are you Mr Bailey's secretary?'

The girl did not reply immediately. 'What did you want to know?'

'It's quite simple, really. We're making up cheques for next month's payroll, and Mr Bailey's tax deductions show a sudden drop. I think it's something to do with an increased mortgage payment.' He paused, but the girl made no comment. 'The thing is, I don't want to reduce his deductions if the information's wrong, because it means we'll have to make it up next month by taking off a whole lot more. People hate that.'

'I'm afraid I can't tell you anything about it.' Her voice was coolly professional.

'Well, I'm only trying to be helpful.' Mark sounded aggrieved. 'You'd be surprised how angry people become when we need to make up back taxes. Anyone would think we were keeping the money for ourselves!'

'Yes, I suppose so.' The girl wavered.

'I just wanted to keep my records straight, if I could. You wouldn't happen to know if he's moved recently, would you?'

'Not as far as I know.'

'I suppose he couldn't have, could he? Otherwise, he'd have given you a new contact number for after hours.' Mark kept his voice friendly.

'Yes, that's right.'

'So it looks as though I've picked up a mistake this end. That's the third I've found in two months! I hate these bloody computers!'

'I didn't know the payroll was computerized.' Her voice was warmer.

'Yes, we've been using them for months now, but we're still trying to get all the gremlins out. They say machines are infallible, but we never had this trouble before.' He sighed. 'I'd better check it out.'

'Thanks.'

Mark paused. 'I take it he's still at the same address?'

'Belsize Park?'

'Yes, that's the one. I can't think why the damned computer's made such a cock-up. Somebody must have pushed the wrong button. Damn it! It'll take hours to check through the whole list, in case there are any other wrong entries. These things have a sort of domino effect once you set them in motion. I'm going to be here all hours!'

'I'm sorry.'

'It's not your fault, but thanks anyway. At least you've helped me sort this one out. What's your name, by the way?'

'Tracey.'

'I'll remember. Maybe I can stop by and have a chat some time.'

'I'm on the second floor.' She sounded pleased.

'I suppose there's no chance the machine didn't make a mistake, is there? He's still at Belsize Park? Number . . .' Mark hesitated, as though checking his list.

'Number ten. It's a block of flats, and he's on the top floor.'

'And you're sure he hasn't moved? He's still there?'

She giggled. 'He certainly was two nights ago.'

'You sound as though you know.'

'Don't be cheeky!'

'I was just joking.'

'Well, we're not amused.'

'I didn't mean to offend you. My name's Bob, by the way. Look, in case he has made any new arrangements, I'd better call back some time when he's in. Maybe I could stop by, and have that chat. OK?'

'All right. I told you where to find us.'

'Second floor. I haven't forgotten. It'll be nice to meet you in person.'

'I'll be here.' Her voice was friendly.

'Do you expect him in tomorrow?'

'Yes, I think so.'

'What time?'

'Any time after nine.' She lowered her voice. 'He's usually in before I am.'

'OK. I'll look in and see if I can get this thing sorted out. Thanks for your help, Tracey. I'll look forward to meeting you.'

Mark returned the receiver to its cradle and sat, staring into space.

# 17

It was raining when Mark left the hotel, a fine drizzle which developed into a steady downpour. English summer weather! He had waited until after seven o'clock before leaving, in the hope of missing the worst of the rush-hour traffic, but the streets were blocked by vehicles edging their way through the rain. London always came to a standstill when the weather was bad. It took nearly twenty minutes to reach Regent's Park. To pass the time, he played with the tuning dial on the car radio, which sputtered a welter of regional accents at him: London, Geordie, Irish, Scottish, Yorkshire, Lancashire, phoney American. Standard, BBC English seemed *démodé*, almost a music-hall caricature, except for the news bulletins.

He avoided the queues of cars in Camden Town by skirting the park, and drove through Primrose Hill and the quieter network of avenues beyond until he reached Belsize Park. Most of its solid rows of Victorian and Edwardian houses, too large for single families, had been converted into luxury flats, as the estate agents claimed. He found a parking place almost directly in front of Bailey's building, which seemed a little newer than the others. The main entrance door was closed, and there was a Yale lock. It looked shiny, and a panel of illuminated buttons next to a metal grating indicated that there was an intercom to each apartment and an electrically controlled locking device. There were too many people passing in the street to risk forcing the lock.

After a few minutes, a woman in a plastic raincoat, carrying a heavy shopping-bag, climbed the steps to the entrance. Mark stepped quickly out of the car and followed her, waiting while she fumbled in her purse for a key.

'Can I hold your shopping while you do that?'

For a moment, she was startled, then smiled gratefully. 'Thank you. Sorry if I jumped. I didn't see you standing there.' She handed him the bag. 'I hate to put it down, in case it tips over. What horrible weather!'

'Dreadful.' Always the traditional opening gambit!

She fiddled with the key, rattling it in the lock. 'I can't get this damn thing to work properly. Ever since they changed it, I've had to jigger it back and forwards before it fits.'

Mark nodded. 'I've had the same trouble with mine. They must have cut bad keys, or the lock itself is faulty. It probably needs a drop of oil.'

The woman grimaced. 'Knowing this place, they probably bought it on the cheap! I'll get my husband to have a look at it.' She glanced at Mark. 'I haven't seen you round here before.'

'No. I only moved in recently. Top floor. I'm staying with Mr Bailey until I find a place of my own.'

'You probably missed the break-in.'

'Break-in?'

She nodded. 'Thieves. It's getting terrible round here. Our building was the third in the past month. They didn't leave a trace. That's why we all insisted they change the lock. You can't trust anybody, these days.' The door finally opened, and she led the way into the foyer. Mark returned her shopping bag. 'Thank you very much. I expect we'll run into each other again.' She nodded towards the rear of the hall. 'We're at the back, on the ground floor. You must drop in for a drink some time. I think people should be more neighbourly, don't you?'

'Of course.' Mark hunched his shoulders. 'I'd better go up and change. It was so bright this morning, I didn't bother to take a raincoat.' He started up the stairs.

'Perhaps you'd like a cup of coffee?'

'That's very kind, but I'll be going out again shortly.'

'It's no trouble, especially after you helped me. I'll just unpack first.'

'Please don't trouble, but thank you all the same.'

There were two flats on the top floor. The one facing the rear of the building had a small printed plate inscribed 'E. Bailey' next to the bell-push. What did the 'E' stand for? Edward? Mark had never known his first name. He tried the bell, and heard a two-tone chime from within. He stood very close to the panelling, his fists clenched, ready to move quickly.

No one answered. The flat was silent. He risked a second chime, glancing over his shoulder at the door of the other flat. He did not want to disturb Bailey's neighbours. After a further silence, he reached into a pocket for a thin strip of plastic, and inserted it in the ridge between the doorjamb and the door, pressing downward. He hoped Bailey had not double-locked the mechanism. For a moment, he felt resistance, but increased the pressure. The tongue of the lock slid back to open the door.

It was a small flat, neatly converted out of two large rooms at the back of the house. A tiny foyer led, on one side, to a living room and kitchen, with a bedroom and bathroom on the other side.

He tried the living room first. It was sparsely furnished: two easy chairs and a sofa in matching colours, arranged in a half-circle with a glass-topped coffee-table between them. There was a dog-eared copy of *Playboy* on it. A folding table stood against the wall, with two cane-seated wooden chairs, and there was an amateurly painted bookcase lined with paperback thrillers. The top surface held an expensive-looking record player and two small speakers. The walls were decorated with framed posters in brilliant colours, advertising rock concerts, and there were Greek scatter rugs on the varnished floorboards. At the end of the room, a counter separated the kitchen area, which was closed off by a bamboo screen.

He walked through to the kitchen and opened the refrigerator. It was almost empty. There was half a bottle of milk on a shelf inside the door, and an unopened carton of orange juice. He checked the label on a packet of bacon. It had been purchased within the last few days. Hanging from a hook above the counter, there was a key-ring containing two keys. He took them. In a drawer of kitchen utensils, he found a short, sharp-bladed knife, which he placed in another pocket. It might prove useful later.

At first sight, the bedroom revealed little more. It was tidy but characterless, as though its owner spent little time in it. A double bed occupied the centre of the room, and there was a fitted wardrobe in one corner and a flap-top desk in another. On a bedside table, next to the telephone, there was a small, leather-framed photograph. Mark recognized the snapshot of Bailey immediately. He was sitting at an outdoor restaurant, squinting into the sun, his arm around the shoulders of a pretty, dark-haired girl wearing a swimming costume. The setting looked Greek or Italian. Another item caught his attention. In the waste-paper basket under the desk, there was a discarded copy of the *Evening Standard*. It bore yesterday's date. Someone was living in the flat and, if Tracey was right, it was Bailey.

The desk revealed surprisingly little. There were several unpaid bills, some letters from a woman who signed herself 'T' (Tracey?), a diary with no entries, paper and envelopes, and a small address book, which he pocketed. The contents were as bland as he remembered Bailey to be. There was nothing in the pockets of the clothes he found hanging in the wardrobe. A cheap nylon suitcase was stored on the top shelf. He appeared to be a man of few interests and fewer possessions.

Mark sat on the bed, debating whether to await his return. It was more comfortable than the car, but the woman downstairs had threatened to arrive with coffee, and he did not know whether the owner of the flat across the landing was a friend who might call. He felt the keys in his pocket, and decided it would be safer to return later.

He met the woman at the foot of the stairs. 'Hello. I was just coming up to invite you over for a drink.'

'Oh. That is nice of you, but I have to go out again.'

'We'll make it another time.' She looked at Mark. 'You didn't change your clothes.'

'No. I seem to have dried out.' He looked at his watch. 'I'm a little late.'

'I won't keep you. Now that you know where we live, don't forget to give us a call.'

'I won't.' He closed the front door carefully.

He returned to the car and, tipping the driver's seat back, settled down to wait. His body was still tired, but his mind was fully alert. The rain had reduced to a sporadic drizzle, and he opened the window to allow cool air to circulate. Keeping the volume low, he turned on the radio. They were relaying a concert from the Festival Hall. Occasionally, cars swished past on the wet tarmac, their lights bright in his eyes. The heavy clouds had made it grow dark early.

The traffic seemed to increase slightly after ten-thirty, and he assumed it was because the theatres and cinemas were closing. In a little while, the last of the late evening diners and drinkers would drift home, after which the street would be deserted. Mark settled himself deeper in his seat, hoping that his presence would not attract attention.

A taxi stopped outside the building, its diesel engine muttering. The occupant was a young woman, and he watched her as she leaned into the front cab to pay the driver. Then she walked quickly up the steps of the house next door.

He was becoming sleepy, and lowered the window further. Tiny droplets of rain blew on to his face. On the radio, there was a programme of avant-garde music from Holland, and he turned it off. The street outside seemed unusually quiet.

Shortly after eleven, he heard footsteps. Someone was approaching from behind, and Mark adjusted the rear-view mirror, trying to catch sight of the newcomer. The man walking towards the car was the same size and build as Bailey, but Mark could not identify him for certain. He was dressed in a raincoat, the collar drawn up around his cheeks, hiding his features. The pale, overhead glow of the streetlamps illuminated him momentarily. Mark closed the window slowly, and let the seat-back fall until his body was completely hidden. He kept his eyes on the mirror. The man drew level, pausing at the foot of the steps. Mark did not move. Then, as the man climbed towards the entrance of the building, Mark brought his eyes level with the edge of the door-frame. There was a light in the foyer and, as he opened the front door, Mark saw the man's face in profile. It was Bailey. A moment later, the door closed, blocking out the light.

Mark remained in the car, motionless, forcing himself to wait. He estimated how long it would take Bailey to reach the top floor of the building and let himself into his flat. He checked his watch. It was eleven-ten. He would wait a further twenty minutes before making a move. He wanted Bailey relaxed and prepared for bed before he arrived.

At eleven-thirty, he left the car and moved to the top of the steps. No lights in the windows of the building were visible from the street. A solitary car passed, and he waited until it had rounded a corner, out of sight, standing immobile in the shadowy entrance.

Bailey's key did not fit the door. Remembering the problems encountered by the woman, Mark gently worked it from side to side, twisting it, but it would not enter the lock. He tried the other key on the ring, but it was too thick to penetrate the narrow slit. Then it occurred to him that they must have been the ones for use with the previous lock.

For a moment, Mark hesitated, uncertain. He had no access to the building. He pressed a button on the illuminated panel.

Within a few seconds, he heard a voice. 'That you, Trace?'

Mark did not reply. He stood, watching the lighted panel, his shoulder against the door. After a moment, there was a buzz, and the door opened. The hallway was dark, and he moved on tiptoe, finding his way to the staircase. Looking upward, he could see a faint glimmer of light.

As he reached the top floor, Mark took out the kitchen knife, cradling it in the palm of his hand. He moved forward stealthily, ready to strike.

The door to Bailey's flat had been left open, its light spilling across the landing. Mark moved silently. He entered the empty foyer, pushing the door shut with his foot.

Bailey was in the living room, dressed in shirtsleeves and slacks. He was standing in front of the hi-fi, putting a record on the turntable, and did not look round.

'Hi! Thanks for cleaning up all the mess. I didn't expect you to. As a matter of fact, I wasn't sure whether you'd be coming over this evening.' He chuckled. 'After what happened last –'

His words were cut off as the crook of Mark's left arm closed over his windpipe with enough force to throttle him. Bailey started to struggle, his hands grasping at Mark's arm, and Mark brought up the knife in his right hand so that the blade pointed at the younger man's face. Maintaining the pressure, he spoke in Bailey's ear.

'Try anything and you're dead. Understand?' The struggle ceased, and Bailey nodded.

Changing position suddenly, Mark released his arm from Bailey's throat and kicked at his legs behind the knees. The man buckled, falling backwards with a groan. His head struck carpeted floor, and he lay for a moment with his eyes closed. Mark knelt at his side, his leg pinning down one of Bailey's arms.

The tip of the knife touched Bailey's throat, but he pressed gently, so that the blade did not break the skin.

'You're supposed to be dead already. Remember?'

Bailey opened his eyes, looking up into Mark's face. They did not focus properly. Then recognition registered, and he gasped. 'Oh Christ!' His face was ashen.

Mark rose slowly to his feet, stooping to keep the knife against the man's throat. 'Get up. You have some talking to do.' He moved back slightly, to allow Bailey to sit. 'Now!'

Bailey rubbed his throat, his eyes fixed on the knifeblade hovering a few inches away. Then he looked at Mark. 'How did you know?' His voice was hoarse, barely audible. 'Who told you?'

'Nobody told me, in so many words. Maybe if your boss

Quentin Sharpe hadn't tried to be quite so clever, I might have gone on believing your dramatic little death scene in Tokyo. That was a very convincing performance!' Bailey said nothing, and Mark stepped closer, the point of the knife again touching the man's throat. 'Now you're going to tell me what it was all about.'

Bailey shook his head. 'I can't.'

'Like hell you can't!' The tip of the knife scraped Bailey's chin, and he shrank back. 'You set me up as the target in some elaborate counterplay for the Department, and I want to know why. I've been kidnapped, drugged, beaten, had the shit kicked out of me by a sadistic little East German faggot, and you're going to start explaining. If not . . .' The knife moved forward.

Bailey was frightened. 'Look, you've got to believe me, I don't know what the whole plan was. I was told to find you in Tokyo, and –'

'Don't give me that "only obeying instructions" bullshit! How the hell is Richard Hyatt involved? He's supposed to have died years ago, except that . . .' Mark paused. 'What did you mean about warning him in Dresden?'

'I don't know. That's what they told me to say.'

'Who?'

'Sharpe.'

Mark watched him. 'Quentin told you to say that Richard Hyatt was in Dresden?'

'Yes.' Bailey shook his head helplessly. 'I don't even know who the hell Hyatt is. I never met him. Quentin didn't explain anything when he briefed me.' His eyes seemed to glance over Mark's shoulder for a moment.

Mark was about to speak again, when he was interrupted. 'Drop it!' The voice sounded slightly bored. For a moment, he did not move. Then he turned slowly, still gripping the knife.

The man standing in the doorway of the living room was of medium height but broad, his shoulders almost touching the sides of the narrow entrance. His face was misshapen and scarred as a boxer's. The black metal silencer on his heavy service revolver made the gun look like a sawn-off rifle. His eyes flicked to the kitchen knife in Mark's hand, and he smiled crookedly. 'Don't try anything clever, squire.' The gun moved slightly. 'This thing'll blow a hole through you quicker than you can think. Drop your tin-opener like a good boy, and stay there nice and quietly.'

Mark let the knife fall to the floor, and the man nodded approvingly. He glanced at Bailey with a look of contempt. 'You – get yourself out of the bloody way.'

Bailey scuttled sideways. 'Did you know he was coming here?' He sounded resentful.

'We thought he might show. I've been watching the house for the past couple of hours.' He seemed to ignore Mark, but the gun never wavered. 'You'd better have a chat with your randy girlfriend.'

'Tracey? What's she got to do with it?'

The man grinned unkindly. 'Little Miss Hotpants wanted to know a bit more about the nice man who chatted her up on the phone this afternoon, so she called a friend of hers in the typing pool.' He looked at Mark for a moment. 'When she learned there wasn't any Bob Cartwright in Accounts, she was sensible enough to tell us about it.' The contempt in his voice returned when he looked at Bailey. 'I thought she was supposed to be covering for you.'

'Shit! Does Quentin know about this?' Bailey's nervousness increased. 'He'll give us both hell!'

'Serves you right for knocking off the hired help. You'd better talk to her in the morning. Meanwhile, get Sharpe on the phone now. This thing's turning into a right old mess.' Bailey hurried through to the bedroom. When he had gone, the man sniffed with disgust. 'Stupid berk!'

'What are you going to do?'

'Me? Nothing, as long as you behave yourself. I'm just here to look after government property. We must be hard put to it if he's the best we can muster! Why don't you go and sit in one of those chairs? We may as well make ourselves comfortable.' His manner was almost friendly. 'And don't start asking me any of your questions. I wouldn't know the answers. I'm just a minder.' He settled himself in one of the armchairs facing Mark, and glanced at the magazine on the coffee-table. 'Trust him to read that crap!'

Mark relaxed into the chair. There seemed to be little else to do. 'What's the matter? Don't you like women?'

The man scowled. 'Of course I do, but I'm into sex, not gynaecology. Half those pictures . . .' He left the sentence unfinished.

Bailey returned, hovering in the doorway. 'He'll be here in a few minutes. He didn't sound too angry when I told him.' He turned to Mark. 'Tracey shouldn't have talked.' His voice was petulant.

'It was an easy enough mistake. Believe it or not, there was a Bob Cartwright in Accounts years ago, during my time.' Mark kept his voice casual. 'I meant what I said about Tokyo, by the way. That was an impressive piece of acting. You had me going.'

'It wasn't so difficult. It was dark, and you couldn't see me properly. The gunshots made sure you didn't come any closer.' He looked pleased with himself. 'I've done a bit of amateur dramatics.'

The man with the gun glared at him. 'Christ, in a minute you'll be showing us your bloody press cuttings! Why don't you just belt up? Have you got any coffee in the house?'

'Yes, I suppose so. It's instant.'

'Then why don't you go and make us a cup?' He shook off his raincoat, transferring the gun from one hand to the other as he did so. 'I've been standing out in the bloody rain, waiting for you.' He picked up the magazine and began reading it, seemingly ignoring Mark, but the gun in his hand remained steady.

Quentin Sharpe arrived twenty minutes later. When the doorbell chimed, the man put down the magazine and sat forward in his chair while Bailey went to the door. Mark could hear them talking in low voices in the foyer. A moment later, Sharpe appeared in the entrance.

'You're getting to be a nuisance.' His face was expressionless. 'Why didn't you go back to Geneva?'

'To wait for you to set me up again? Fuck you, Quentin! I want a few answers.' From the corner of his eye, Mark had the impression that the man with the gun, his back to Quentin, grinned briefly.

Quentin's voice was cold. 'What makes you think I'll give you any?'

'Because I'm going to keep digging until I get them. You can save a lot of time by telling me what I want to know. Why did you set me up?'

'I don't know what you're talking about.'

'Bullshit! How do you explain the mysterious recovery of the late Mr Bailey, Quentin? Yesterday in Berlin, you gave me a sob story about having to break the news to his parents. You'd better call them back and tell them there's been an unexpected development!'

'Perhaps. What else have you got?'

'You should have called back when I phoned you from San Francisco. It was out of character. That was your first mistake.' Quentin frowned. 'Your second was to pull me out of East Berlin at a moment's notice.'

'I told you, it was a lucky accident that I was there.'

'Rubbish! You didn't owe me any favours. You were there because you knew I was going to be arrested as soon as I crossed the border. The whole thing was a set-up from the start. There were no Mahler scores in East Berlin, Quentin. You knew that the moment I told you what had happened. What did you call it? An ingenious plan!' Mark stood, and the man with the gun was suddenly alert, but Quentin motioned him to relax. 'You knew they had made up that whole Mahler fairytale as a bait to lure me into East Berlin. I only realized it afterwards, when Steigel told me what he found, but you guessed immediately. Your behaviour was much too false when I told you about it.'

'And why was that?' Quentin's voice remained calm, but the muscles on his jaw were taut.

'Because you wanted me to be arrested. That was the set-up. It was you who spread it around that I was working for the Department again.'

Quentin had grown pale. 'That's a very interesting theory, but it's only guesswork. Why should I care whether you're arrested or not?'

'That's what I want to know.' Mark lit a cigarette. 'You were interested enough to want to get me out again as quickly as possible. You could only have had one reason for that.'

'Which was?'

'To find out what happened to me, and what I'd told them.' Sharpe sat on one of the hard-backed chairs. He seemed weary. 'That's when you made your next mistake, Quentin, telling me where Richard Hyatt was supposed to be buried.' Quentin looked up. 'I went to South Burton this morning. There's no Richard Hyatt buried there. I talked to the local vicar. He was working in the parish at the time of the supposed funeral. It never took place.'

Quentin said nothing. He was watching Mark cautiously. At length, he cleared his throat. 'Yes, that was foolish of me. I didn't expect you to go there quite so soon.'

'Because you knew the church was about to be closed?' Quentin's silence was acknowledgement. 'All right. We've established that Richard Hyatt didn't die ten years ago, or if he did, he wasn't buried in Sussex. Where the hell has he been ever since? In Dresden? That's what Bailey was instructed to tell me. If so, why? Why did you go to such elaborate lengths to tell me Hyatt was in danger?'

Quentin stood suddenly. 'That's enough! You've asked me all the questions I want to hear.'

'I'm still waiting for the answers.'

'You're not getting any.' He seemed to come to a decision. 'All right. You want to know what happened to you in the last few days, Mark? You were seconded back into the Department for a short term of duty.'

'Without my knowledge or consent? You're out of your bloody mind!'

'I don't give a damn about your consent! You should have read the small print in your release papers when you resigned from the Department, Mark, especially the clause about being brought back on active duty. And, I might add, the Official Secrets Act still applies. That covers you until the day you die.'

'Don't give me that shit! Are you really trying to tell me that I'm obliged to work for you, if you so decide, and get myself beaten senseless, without even knowing why? I don't work for the bloody Department, now or at any future date, willingly or unwillingly, and you know it!'

Quentin's voice was raised. 'At this point, there's damned little you can do about it. You *were* working for the Department, whether you wanted to or not. The job's done, if it's any consolation to you, so why the hell don't you get yourself back to your cosy little music world in Geneva and forget it?'

'No. I want the whole story, if only to protect myself in the future.'

'And if we're not prepared to tell you?'

'I'll go on digging, asking questions, until I find out for myself, even if it means asking a few old acquaintances on the other side.'

Quentin took a step forward, white with anger. 'If you try –'

'I don't belong to you, Quentin. I don't work for anyone except myself. That's why I chose Switzerland when I climbed out of your sewer. You can't touch me there.'

Quentin's eyes were cold. 'We're not in Switzerland at the

moment. In view of what you're saying, I think it's highly unlikely that you're going to find your way back there.' The man with the gun stood, and Mark sensed his tension. In the corner, Bailey whispered, 'Oh Christ!'

Mark watched Quentin's face. 'I think you might just be stupid enough to try something like that, but I can't believe you're also dumb enough to suppose I didn't take out a little insurance of my own.'

Quentin hesitated. 'What do you mean?'

'My telephone. It has a very useful little device. Everyone uses them nowadays.' Quentin looked puzzled. 'Have you ever noticed that, whenever I arrive anywhere, I always call the office in Geneva, to tell them where I am?' Sharpe nodded. 'I make two calls every time, Quentin. The first is to my office. The second is to an answering machine in another building. When I call that one, I name names and describe places, with an accurate, up-to-date account of everything that's happened to me. You'll be flattered to know that you've featured on it quite a lot in the past few days.'

Quentin was very still. 'What does that mean?'

'I have a friend who's a lawyer in Geneva, Quentin. You've never heard of him. In fact, very few people realize we know each other. Swiss lawyers are trained to be very discreet. I make a point of phoning that man once a week, no matter where I am, from anywhere in the world. He's the only other person who knows where my answering machine is. If he doesn't hear from me within ten days, he has strict instructions to transcribe all the information on the tape and, if he decides it would be . . . appropriate, he will send copies of those transcriptions to selected editors of newspapers in various countries, on either side of the Iron Curtain, inviting them to print the details. Each transcription, incidentally, is to be accompanied by a brief curriculum vitae covering my activities during the years that I worked for the Department. There are enough details to whet any newsman's appetite. So, if anything happens to me, and my lawyer isn't satisfied with the circumstances, that information will be on its way around the world within ten days of my . . . disappearance.'

Quentin looked thoughtful. 'I don't believe you.'

Mark shrugged. 'That's your choice. It's also your gamble. Perhaps I should add that, in view of the details currently sitting in my answering machine, my legal friend will have no hesitation in sending out the material. Whether he does or not is up to you.'

'You're very sure of yourself.'

'I know what's in the machine. Frankly, Quentin, I would have said it was in your interest to make sure that I stay in the best possible health until my next phone call to Switzerland.'

There was a long silence. When Quentin spoke again, his voice was low. 'What do you want to know?'

'For Christ's sake, Quentin! How, exactly, did I fit into your plan?'

'Very well.' Sharpe glanced at the other two men in the room. Some of his reassurance had returned. 'Put the gun away. Neither of you heard any of this conversation. Is that understood?' They nodded. He returned to Mark. 'You'd better come with me. You'll have to meet the man with all the answers.' He walked slowly to the foyer.

Mark followed him, ignoring Bailey and the other man. The bluff had worked. There was no secret telephone in Geneva. Perhaps Quentin had half-guessed it, but he was not prepared to take the chance. In the foyer, he asked, 'Who are we going to see?'

Quentin almost smiled. 'I would have thought that, with your marvellous powers of deduction, you would have worked that out by now. Alex Beaumont.'

# 18

There was a Daimler limousine waiting in the street. A uniformed chauffeur held the door for Mark as he entered. The upholstery was pale leather and, from the aroma, it was very new. With the doors closed, the interior was silent.

Mark smiled. 'You've come a long way since the days when you were running errands for Willis, Quentin. Is this part of life at the top?'

'I wouldn't know. I usually walk to work. You could have had the same, if you'd hung on.' He seemed ill-at-ease. 'I'd better phone ahead, to warn them we're coming.' Quentin fiddled with a small, portable telephone, picking at the digits with the tip of his index finger. 'I hate these bloody things! They should make the buttons bigger.'

'Where are we going?'

'Maida Vale.' Quentin concentrated on the receiver pressed against his ear, awaiting a reply. 'Hello, Patrick? I'm on my way over. I've got someone with me who has to talk to Alex . . . Five minutes, give or take.' He frowned. 'Yes, it is necessary . . . Then wake him up . . . No, I wouldn't suggest it if it weren't important . . . Very well, do whatever you have to.' He replaced the telephone, staring at the instrument for a moment, as though lost in thought.

'He doesn't sound very pleased to be disturbed.'

'No.' Quentin hesitated. 'Look, we don't have very far to go, so I'd better forewarn you. Alex Beaumont is in a pretty bad way. I'm afraid his appearance may be something of a shock. It would be kinder if you pretended not to notice.'

'Really? I seem to remember he's several years younger than I am.'

'Probably, but his lifestyle has been a little different from yours. He's hanging on by a thread, at the moment.' Quentin avoided Mark's eyes. 'There's a rather unfortunate disease that seems to be increasingly . . . fashionable these days. I hope you don't want me to spell it out. God knows, the Government has posted enough warnings about it. People always think it's never going to happen to them!'

Mark spoke softly. 'Alex?'

Quentin nodded. 'There's very little we can do for him except keep him as comfortable as possible. He can't last much longer.'

'Poor bastard!'

'Yes.' Quentin's voice was bitter. 'Believe it or not, there's a fanatical police chief in Lancashire who claims it's a kind of divine retribution. It must be very reassuring to have such a clear conscience!'

'I read about him in the Swiss press. Unbelievable!'

'We put someone in the house, to look after Alex. The rest is a matter of time.' He glanced at the telephone. 'Patrick's inclined to be very protective. He doesn't want Alex disturbed more than necessary.'

'I'm sorry. Would it be better to wait until the morning?'

'It doesn't matter. He's reached the stage where there's little difference between days and nights. To be honest, it's a good excuse to find a few more answers while we can. I thought it was better to let you know before we get there.' He stared at Mark. 'I take it you realize it's not contagious? If he wants to shake hands, there's no reason not to. I doubt whether he will.'

'You seem very concerned, Quentin.'

'He's still one of us.' Quentin stared out of the window, and did not speak again.

The car stopped outside a Victorian mansion-block near the Edgware Road. It was after midnight, and the building was dark, but a light burned in one window on the second floor. As Quentin approached the front entrance, an electric buzzer signalled that the door had been opened from within. Presumably, Patrick had been watching for them. Sharpe walked past an ancient-looking lift with a trellissed metal door and started up the carpeted staircase. He climbed slowly.

On the second floor, a slim young man stood in the open doorway to a flat. He was wearing a pale blue silk shirt, open to the waist, and designer jeans, and was barefoot. He watched them approach in silence.

'Hello, Patrick. This is Mark Holland.' The young man ignored Mark. 'How is Alex?'

'I told you he was sleeping.'

'Did you wake him?' Patrick nodded. 'We'll go through and talk to him.'

'No. He doesn't want you to see him lying in bed. He's putting on a dressing-gown.' He glared at Quentin. 'That takes him time to achieve! Is it absolutely necessary to come here at this hour of the night?'

'Yes, I'm afraid it is.'

'Very well.' He pouted like a child, folding his arms. 'You'd better wait in there.'

They entered a small living room cluttered with ugly furniture: dark mahogany and oak copies of antiques that were patently cheap reproductions from the 1930s. The pieces were ill-assorted, their surfaces chipped and stained. Dusty sporting prints decorated the walls, and the faded carpet was worn in several places. The furnishing was completely out of character for a man of Alex Beaumont's tastes, and there was something vaguely familiar about the room which triggered a memory in Mark's mind.

He turned to Quentin. 'Why is Alex living in a safe house? This place belongs to the Department. I seem to think I came here at one time.'

Quentin shrugged. He looked uneasy. 'It was more convenient. Alex lived in a mews in Kensington. There was no lift to the floor above – just one of those narrow, metal spiral staircases. He would have been stuck in one room, so we brought him here. I don't know how much more he'll be able to tell us. He seems to be deteriorating rapidly.'

Despite Quentin's warning, Mark was not prepared for the shock. Patrick pushed the door open with his foot and slowly entered, half-carrying a skeletal figure into the room. Alex Beaumont had wasted to a pitifully thin shadow of a human being. He had lost all his hair, and his pale eyes stared out of deep sockets beneath tautly stretched, pallid skin. He was unrecognizable. Supported by Patrick, Beaumont's slippered feet scarcely touched the floor, and his legs dragged awkwardly behind him.

'Hello, Alex. It's good to see you.' Quentin's voice was warm as he grasped the man's hand. A painfully thin arm hung loose from the folds of the dressing-gown. Beaumont smiled gratefully, baring his teeth like a death's head. 'I've brought along an old friend to see you. Do you remember Mark Holland?'

Beaumont spoke slowly and with difficulty. 'I remember you.' His voice rattled in his throat.

Patrick settled his patient in a faded wing-chair, placing an old blanket over his knees. Beaumont sat, waiting while the young man tucked the material around his thighs. 'Are you warm enough?' Alex nodded slowly, and Patrick kissed him gently on the cheek. 'I'll wait for you next-door.' He scowled at Quentin, and left the room.

Sharpe pulled a chair close to Alex, facing him. Mark sat nearby. Leaning forward, Quentin placed his hands over Beaumont's and, for a moment, their fingers locked. 'We want to talk to you about Richard Hyatt, Alex. It's important that Mark understands what we did.'

The tortured face became momentarily animated. 'Oh yes, I remember Hyatt. He was brilliant! He pulled off one of the greatest espionage coups of all time. Nobody thought he would get away with it, but he did!' Beaumont nodded enthusiastically. 'He tricked everyone!'

Quentin spoke as gently as a lover. 'It was a long time ago, before I met you. How did he do it, Alex?'

'We organized it between ourselves, Hyatt and I.' Alex began to nod, and Mark could not tell whether the movement was a muscular spasm. 'Some of the others knew what we were doing, but I was the one who looked after the details. I was the contact man.' He looked at Sharpe for approval, and Quentin smiled encouragingly.

'Tell me what you did.'

Beaumont was silent for a moment, as though gathering his thoughts. 'We announced that Richard Hyatt was dead – a heart attack. We planned it for a long time. Hyatt had told everyone that he was in bad health, and that his doctor had already warned him.' He giggled foolishly at the memory. 'So nobody was very surprised when they heard he had died suddenly. I found a doctor who filled in a death certificate for us.'

Quentin looked at Mark. Almost under his breath, he said, 'The doctor died a couple of weeks later. Hit-and-run accident.' He spoke so quietly that Beaumont did not appear to have heard him.

Mark leaned forward. 'I came to see you on the day of the funeral, Alex. Do you remember that?'

Alex turned his head slowly. 'Yes, I remember. You were supposed to give me some papers, but you never did. Hyatt was angry.'

'Where was the funeral, Alex? You told me everyone had gone to Hyatt's funeral that day. Willis and the others weren't in the office, because they were out of town. Remember?'

'Oh yes. I forgot about that.' He smiled at Mark. 'There wasn't a funeral – just a memorial service. I told you they were all away, because we didn't want you talking to anybody. You were only a field man.'

'Then there were some others who knew Hyatt wasn't really dead?'

'A few. Just the senior men.' He smiled again. 'They never believed he would get away with it.' The smile seemed to be fixed on his face. 'Please can I have a drink of water?'

There was a carafe and glasses on the sideboard, and Mark half-filled a tumbler. He handed it to Quentin, who held it to Beaumont's lips. He drank obediently, like a small child, his hands remaining folded on his lap. When he had finished, Alex stared at Mark. 'You left the Department.'

'Yes, a long time ago. It was soon after Hyatt was supposed to have died.'

For a moment, he appeared to be thinking lucidly. 'Didn't you go overseas?'

'Yes. I work with musicians.'

'That must be nice. I don't know anything about music. Patrick sometimes plays the radio for me.'

Quentin grasped Beaumont's hands again. 'Let's talk about Richard Hyatt, Alex. What did you arrange with him?' He stroked the lifeless fingers.

'He went over to the other side.' Beaumont's smile had returned, and he looked at Mark. 'He defected.'

Mark watched his face. 'What do you mean?'

'He defected, Mark. He went to work for the other side. I arranged it. The East Germans couldn't believe their good luck. Hyatt persuaded them. He was brilliant!'

Quentin turned to Mark. 'Alex is right. The Director General, a man fully conversant with security operations here and in America, crossed over, to work for them.'

'And you let him go?'

'Of course we let him go!' Quentin's voice was irritated. 'Hyatt was still working for us. We set him up in East Germany. Think about it, Mark! Our top man, planted in East Germany. It was an amazing opportunity.'

Beaumont nodded happily. 'I was his contact man.'

Quentin smiled at him. 'That's right, Alex. You passed information to him, and he fed material back to you.'

Alex giggled again. 'They never thought we'd get away with it.'

Mark was silent for a moment. 'What went wrong?'

Quentin sighed, his eyes never leaving Beaumont's face. 'Ah, that's another matter, isn't it, Alex?'

Beaumont's expression changed, and he looked at Sharpe fretfully. 'We don't have to talk about that, do we, Quentin? You said we didn't have to discuss that part again.'

Quentin spoke softly. 'Just one more time, Alex. You see, Mark doesn't know what happened.'

'But I don't want to talk about it.' Beaumont's face crumpled, and he looked as though he was about to cry. 'Please, Quentin!'

'It's all right, Alex.' Quentin stroked the hands again. 'Just explain some of it. Mark needs to know.' Alex was silent, watching Quentin's hands as they massaged the discoloured skin of his fingers, as though restoring them to life. His mouth moved, but he did not speak. 'Just tell Mark what happened.'

Beaumont turned his head away. His voice sank to a whisper. 'Hyatt wasn't working for us. He tricked us. He wasn't a double agent, working for the Department. He was working for the East Germans, from the beginning.'

Quentin's voice was soothing. 'How do we know that, Alex?'

'One of our people – Thomas Daub – escaped to the West.' His voice grew weaker. 'He told us that our . . . sleepers, in Dresden and Berlin, had all . . . disappeared. He knew that . . . at least two of them were . . . dead.'

Quentin nodded slowly, looking towards Mark. 'But what was the significance of that report, Alex?'

'Please, I . . .'

'You might as well bring it all out into the open.' Alex was silent, his head bowed, and Quentin continued, 'You see, Mark, we were still receiving regular reports from those agents. Alex filed them every month. It was only then that we realized that Hyatt had double-crossed us.' He stared at Beaumont. 'Alex is right. He tricked everyone!'

Beaumont looked helplessly from Quentin to Mark. 'I'm very tired. I'd like to go to bed now. Please, Quentin.'

'In a moment, Alex. You were going to try to remember other details.'

'I don't remember any other details, Quentin.' His eyes were pleading. 'You promised to leave me alone.'

Quentin smiled kindly. 'I know, but I hoped that seeing Mark again might help you.'

Alex shook his head, his eyes closed, and remained silent.

Mark watched Sharpe carefully. 'What happened next?'

Quentin leaned back in his chair. 'We were faced with a couple of difficult alternatives. Either we conceded that Hyatt had pulled the wool over our eyes, which was the most obvious course –'

'In view of what he'd done, it was also the most logical.'

'Perhaps. On the other hand, there was just an outside possibility that we could persuade the East Germans that we'd pulled the wool over theirs, and that Tricky Dicky had double-crossed them.'

'That would never work.'

'Why not?' Quentin turned away from Beaumont, who remained immobile, his head lowered. He might have been asleep.

'With the sort of stakes we play for, they would have accepted the idea that we'd been prepared to jettison a couple of local agents if it helped to establish Hyatt's credibility. They wouldn't hesitate to do the same to theirs.'

'Christ! And you wonder why I wanted to get out of this business!'

Sharpe ignored the comment. 'After assessing the situation, we decided that we had everything to gain, but we needed time. If we could slowly discredit Hyatt and make his colleagues suspicious – just the hint of a doubt, here and there – we could reverse the situation to our advantage and undermine their whole information network. You must admit it was worth a try.'

'If they bought it. That's a very big if.'

Quentin nodded. 'That's why we started more than two years ago. You know, it's not as difficult as you think, once you know what you're doing. It's a matter of simple misdirection. Watch any third-rate conjurer on television. He does it for a living.'

Mark was thoughtful. 'So you continued as before, as though nothing had happened?'

'Exactly. We kept Daub out of sight. Shipped him off to Canada, if you're interested. I understand he's very happy there.' He glanced at the figure huddled in the armchair. 'Of course, we were a little more cautious about the information Alex passed to Hyatt. We had to keep him supplied, but we made sure there was nothing too vital.'

'Except, maybe, the sacrifice of a couple more agents?'

Quentin's face was expressionless. 'We saved as many as we could. You've played chess, Mark. Have you never given away a pawn to trap an opponent's bishop?'

'Chess is a game, Quentin. We're talking about people.'

'They knew the risks they were taking. In the meantime, we made a few little mistakes on Hyatt's behalf – nothing too obvious, but enough to make his friends wonder. Doubt is a curious affliction, isn't it? It's a little like jealousy, gnawing away at the psyche, even when logic tells you it's unreasonable. By the end of two years, there was quite a formidable group of doubters surrounding Richard Hyatt, asking embarrassing questions that he was having difficulty answering.' He glanced again at Beaumont. 'And, of course, Alex was ill, which meant that Hyatt had lost touch with his most reliable . . . contact. It was a very long campaign, but it was beginning to pay off.'

'I'll bet you enjoyed it.' Mark leaned forward. 'Where did I come in?'

Quentin smiled nervously. 'I thought you would have worked that out by now. You were our *coup de grâce*, Mark. We went to a great deal of trouble to prepare you.' He looked relaxed, but his eyes were wary. 'You see, we had to find someone who really believed Richard Hyatt was in danger: someone who'd try to warn him, someone who would withstand interrogation if he was taken prisoner, rather than reveal what he knew.' He hesitated for a moment. 'You accepted Bailey's story in Tokyo, otherwise you wouldn't have tried to reach me on the phone. Richard Hyatt was in danger, and he was in Dresden. It didn't make much sense to you, but we established it in your mind.' He shrugged, apparently gaining confidence. 'Of course, in view of your past history with the Department, we could assume that you wouldn't be prepared to put up with extreme pressure. You had been told enough to make you crack when the treatment became –'

For an instant, Mark felt blind rage. 'You bastard! You double-crossing . . .' He was on his feet, his body tense, ready to strike, but Quentin slid from his chair and backed away, his hand reaching into an inner pocket of his jacket. His face was very pale. Alex Beaumont buried his head lower, closing his eyes.

The moment passed. Mark spoke in a low voice. 'So that's why you set me up! The scene in Tokyo was designed to make me believe . . .' Quentin relaxed slightly, but his hand hovered by the lapel of his jacket. 'You wanted me arrested!'

'I told you earlier, you were seconded back into the Department. We were entitled to do it.' Quentin kept his distance. 'You already guessed that we let them think you were working for us again.' He smiled weakly. 'I never doubted your intelligence, Mark. That's why they were watching you in San Francisco. Actually, they'd been keeping an eye on you longer than that. Don't you see how vital it was that they believed you? At the moment you were taken at Checkpoint Charlie, you became the most valuable element in our plan.'

Mark returned to his chair. His voice was filled with contempt. 'You can sit down again, Quentin. I'm not going to spoil your expensive jacket. God, don't you care how you play with people's lives? What would you have done if they'd finished me at the house in Gleimstrasse? Written me off as another pawn in your fucking chess game?'

Quentin settled on the edge of his chair. 'It was a gamble I had to take, Mark. Given different circumstances and a reversal of roles, you would have done the same. Don't fool yourself with any grand humanitarian illusions. It was a good operation, even if it nearly failed.'

'What do you mean?'

'You didn't tell them, despite what they . . . did to you. If I understood you correctly, you only told that Wolpert girl at the last moment, when you were crossing the Glienicker bridge.'

'Yes, that's true. I told her about Bailey in Tokyo, and mentioned Hyatt's name. That was just before she stumbled and dropped her bag. It must have been a prearranged signal.'

'Maybe. The moment you spoke to Steigel back in West Berlin, you would have known she was a decoy. What I can't understand is that you didn't crack when they interrogated you. Why didn't you give them Hyatt's name?'

'Why would I?' Mark looked at Quentin. 'I already knew he was working for the other side.'

'What?' In his astonishment, Quentin rose again to his feet.

There was a long silence before Mark spoke again. 'I knew Richard Hyatt was a double-agent. I'd always known.'

Quentin stared at him. 'Do you know what you're saying?'

'Yes.'

'Good God! How long have you known?'

'Since the day he was supposed to have died of a heart attack.' Mark's voice was calm. 'He killed a man in Hamburg called Harry Price, by the way. You may want to adjust your records. And, if he hadn't done his famous disappearing act that day, he would almost certainly have killed me, too.'

Quentin was white-faced. 'Jesus Christ, Mark! Why didn't you tell anyone?'

'There was no one I could tell, and no one would have believed me. I was more concerned with surviving.' He suddenly felt exhausted. 'You may as well hear the whole story. It started on a lousy, wet afternoon in Hamburg.'

He spoke, uninterrupted, for about twenty minutes, recounting the events in a monotone. This time, he included all the details, including the death of Jill in the car crash. Quentin listened in silence, moving to the window and standing with his back to the room, staring into the darkness. Occasionally, he looked up, and his eyes met Mark's in the dusty reflection of the glass. It was impossible to tell whether Alex Beaumont was aware of what he was saying. He remained, as before, slouched in his chair, his eyes closed.

When Mark had finished, the room was silent. Quentin, his hands thrust deep in his pockets, continued to stare into the night.

As though aware of the hiatus, Patrick re-entered. 'Have you finished with Alex? It's time he rested.'

Hearing the young man's voice, Beaumont seemed to come to life. 'Please may I go now, Quentin? I'm really very tired.'

Quentin glanced at Mark, his eyebrows raised. 'Do you want to ask him anything more?'

'No.'

He nodded to Patrick. 'Go ahead. Good night, Alex. I'll see you again soon.' Patrick scowled at him.

At the door, Beaumont turned towards Mark. 'Goodbye.'

'Goodbye, Alex. Perhaps we'll –' Mark's reply was cut off as Patrick closed the door.

For a moment, Quentin faced him. 'Well, now we both know everything.' He shook his head slowly. 'My God, Mark, if only you'd told us!'

'No one would have believed me. I'd been sent to Hamburg, Quentin, either to dry out or ship out. The only assumption anyone would have made was that I'd thrown in my hand with the other side. If they'd found Stratta's papers on me, I would have ended up doing life for treason. It would have been my word against Hyatt's. You heard Alex. I was only a field man!'

Quentin looked at his watch. 'We'd better go. I'll drop you off at your hotel.'

'In a moment. Several things bother me.'

'Oh?'

'Why did Hyatt decide to move the date of his supposed death forward? He went to a lot of trouble to hijack those papers from the Department, but he suddenly changed his plans so that I couldn't possibly deliver the papers before he disappeared. Why?'

Quentin was silent for a moment. 'We think it was the news of Harry Price's death. I found a memo from Willis to Hyatt, suggesting that the Department should treat Harry's fall as murder, and recommending a detailed investigation. There was a handwritten reply from Hyatt, saying that he was satisfied it was an accident. According to Hyatt, Price had a long history of drinking.'

'And?'

Quentin shrugged. 'I can only guess. Killing Harry Price was a mistake. Hyatt was being over-cautious. We think he feared that if an official investigation went ahead, and routine questions revealed that he had been in Hamburg a few days earlier, it might throw suspicion on his whole, extraordinary plan to disappear.'

'I'm amazed anyone believed it in the first place.'

Quentin nodded. 'That was the ingenious part. It was such an unlikely move that they fell for it.'

'Then why did he leave early?'

'Two reasons, as far as we can tell. First, to divert attention from the Price situation. Hopefully, he'd satisfied Willis, and the others would be too preoccupied with faking his sudden demise. The second was for his own personal safety. If Willis had soldiered on and set up an investigation, Hyatt would have been safely tucked away in his new nest, where we couldn't touch him.'

'Then the double-agent routine would have failed.'

'True, but he was still extremely valuable to the East Germans. It was a better choice than to stay behind and risk being caught as a traitor and murderer, so it was worth dumping you and the papers.' Quentin looked at his watch again. 'Shall we go?'

'No.'

'What's the problem?'

Mark spoke slowly. 'When I asked Alex if he remembered my being here on the day of the funeral, he said I was supposed to give him some papers. What did he mean by that?'

Quentin seemed uneasy. 'He must have assumed that you hadn't met Stratta after all. From what I read in the report, everyone believed the papers were destroyed in the car crash. They were written off.'

'And Stratta?'

'He tried to contact us several months later, but we were no longer prepared to buy. It seems that several other sources had come up with the same answers that Stratta had found, and we weren't in the market any more.' He smiled thinly. 'They threatened to expose him to his bosses in Milan, and that was the end of it. Why don't we go? We can talk in the car.' He led the way to the door.

'No!' Something in Mark's voice made Quentin stop. 'That's not what's bothering me. How did Alex Beaumont know I might be carrying those papers, Quentin? I was supposed to deliver them only to Hyatt. That's why I realized he'd changed sides. If Alex knew about them, he must have been working for Hyatt.'

'You could have misunderstood him, Mark. The poor fellow's hardly able to –'

'Bullshit! He knew what he was saying.' Mark looked round the room. 'You're keeping Alex in a safe house, with someone to watch him at all times. His health suddenly took a turn for the worse. When? About a year ago? Jesus Christ, Quentin! What have you done to him?'

Quentin remained by the door. He suddenly looked old. 'Hyatt had to have an accomplice, Mark. He could never have got away with it all alone. He was too visible. We can't prove it, but we think Alex was the one who finished off old Harry Price. He and Hyatt were working as a team. We only picked that up later. When we started to destroy Hyatt, we needed to keep Alex under controlled conditions. It's foolish, but even now he won't admit to what he did. He adored Hyatt, and nothing will ever persuade him to betray his hero, even at this late stage. Why do you think I brought you here, Mark? Alex couldn't tell you anything that I don't already know. I wanted to see whether your presence would make him say something that would incriminate him further.' He smiled sadly. 'He did, when he referred to Stratta's papers. I wondered whether you'd noticed, not that it really matters any more.'

'So you brought me here to play cat and mouse with a dying man. Thanks, Quentin! It doesn't take much imagination to guess how Alex became infected, does it?'

Quentin's eyes were cold. 'It was the most convenient solution to the problem. Until we could persuade the East Germans to eliminate Hyatt themselves, we needed to keep his London partner under wraps. We couldn't make him disappear under questionable circumstances, and we certainly didn't want the publicity of a spy trial. Hyatt was aware of Beaumont's sexual preferences. We needed a means of taking Alex out without arousing suspicion. The man's at a terminal stage. It's only a matter of days. I brought you here to see whether I could learn anything more, but I'm too late. It wasn't a game.'

'Wasn't it? Have you ever watched a cat with a mouse,

Quentin? It doesn't kill its victim immediately. It plays with it: sets it free to run away, then pounces on it and drags it back. The mouse dies of fear and torture.'

Quentin's voice hardened. 'Alex Beaumont is a spy. In a different situation, we would have eliminated him on the spot.' He sighed. 'In his case, perhaps that policeman has a point. I had an old nanny when I was a child, and when I misbehaved and hurt myself as a result, she always told me it was God's punishment.'

'Except that you're not God.'

They drove in silence to the Westbury, the car moving swiftly through the deserted streets. As they approached the hotel, Quentin said, 'If it's of any interest to you, Richard Hyatt was taken into custody this morning. One of our people was watching his house in Dresden. Two security men picked him up as he was leaving for his office. From the way they grabbed him and bundled him into the back of a car, it looks as though our long shot finally paid off.' He hesitated. 'I suppose we owe you our thanks.' Mark did not reply. 'You seem to overlook that you served your country.'

'Spare me, Quentin! Don't try patriotism. It's the last resort of a hypocrite.'

Quentin shrugged. 'Well, at least you'll have the consolation of knowing that the man who was the cause of your anguish now faces similar treatment. I wonder whether they'll use the same boy on him to extract his confession.'

'Do you know who he is?'

'Yes, as a matter of fact, we do. His name's Erich Huber, and he should have been put away years ago. The local police have half a dozen charges pending against him, but his bosses in Security keep pulling him out on State business. When he's not employed by the heavies for softening-up exercises, he works as a masseur in a health club next-door to the Metropol Hotel in East Berlin. He's there daily from nine to five, helping overweight foreign tourists remove their extra pounds. I don't imagine he's any too gentle with them, but that's all part of the service.' The car stopped in front of the hotel. 'Will you be going back to Geneva tomorrow?'

'Yes.'

'Is there anything we can do for you?'

Mark was thoughtful. 'Yes, I think there is.'

'All right.' Quentin waited.

'I need an extra passport for a day or two. I don't have access to that sort of thing any more.'

'Oh?'

'I'll send you the details in a few weeks, as well as a suitable photograph.' He saw Sharpe's expression. 'Don't worry, Quentin. The Department won't be involved.'

'I'm pleased to hear it.' Quentin smiled weakly. 'I do hope you're not planning to do anything illegal!'

Berlin, 1986

# 19

There were long queues at the checkpoint at the Friedrichstrasse station. Leaving the S-Bahn in bright sunlight, Mark joined the other passengers from the train as they filed down the staircase through tiled passages until they entered the large hall where the lines formed. It was still summer, and the majority of those waiting patiently were tourists from many parts of the world. Mark heard Swedish, French, Italian and American within a few feet of where he was standing. Most of the visitors were in their late teens and early twenties, dressed in jeans and a variety of sports shirts and brightly coloured tops. They spoke in low voices, slightly overawed by the dour presence of the border guards and the prospect of finding themselves on the other side of the Iron Curtain. A few laughed and joked in loud voices, but he had the impression that they did so to bolster confidence. Here and there, visible in their formal clothing, businessmen in dark suits perspired impatiently, constantly checking their watches and complaining that they would be late for important meetings.

Each of the lines entered a narrow passage, where uniformed guards seated behind glass screens stared at prospective visitors, examining passports and apparently photocopying the information. Their expressions never changed.

After waiting about half an hour, Mark found himself undergoing inspection. He handed over his new passport, and waited while the guard looked him over, comparing him with his photograph. His recently grown beard and moustache felt prickly and uncomfortable, but he was glad that the hall was out of the hot sunshine. He was not sure whether the dye he had applied would begin to run if he sweated. His shoulder-blades felt sticky.

The guard seemed to take a long time with the passport, and Mark gazed stoically at a point above the young man's head. The document identified him as Harold Watkins, and his occupation was listed as Trade Union shop steward. It was probably unnecessary to choose an appropriate profession. He doubted whether the German read or spoke English very proficiently. Mark's chief concern was whether there might be hidden metal detectors concealed somewhere in the passage down which he must walk. Strapped to the calf of his right leg, the long, thin-bladed knife, its edges honed to razor sharpness, might cause a warning bell to ring.

At length, the passport was returned, and the guard transferred his unblinking gaze to the next visitor. Mark moved to the next point, to pay for his visa and East German currency. It was the same routine as Checkpoint Charlie, and the woman who counted out the paper money might have been the sister of the one who had served him before. Moments later, he had passed into the East German side of the station. No warning bells sounded.

He came out of the station and turned right, walking slowly among the crowds of pedestrians making their way towards the Unter den Linden. The kiosks offering cigarettes and cheap souvenirs were busy, and an old woman selling bunches of flowers had almost exhausted her supplies for the day. It was just after eleven o'clock.

About fifty yards up the incline on which he was walking, Mark turned right again, crossing a small, open square towards the solid modern block of the Metropol. It was one of the newer hotels constructed for East Berlin's growing tourist industry, similar in design to half a dozen others that had sprouted in the past few years.

He entered the lobby of the hotel and turned left, in the direction of the upstairs restaurant. The receptionists at their line of desks ignored him. The Metropol was a popular meeting-place for Western businessmen to entertain their East German partners in the over-priced dining room, and the staff in the lobby were accustomed to casual visitors.

Instead of continuing up the staircase, Mark entered the men's toilet. It was deserted, and he went into one of the cubicles and locked the door. Once inside, he unstrapped the knife from his leg and slipped it under the right-hand cuff of his shirt. The material held it in place, but by flicking his arm downwards, the narrow haft slid comfortably into the palm of his hand. He flushed the strapping down the toilet, and returned to the lobby.

Glancing at his watch, as though checking the time of an appointment, he strolled nonchalantly into the street. He stood for a moment, then moved to his left. He had seen the sign advertising the health club earlier, when he was crossing the square. Mark quickened his pace, wondering whether he would need to make a reservation for a massage. Perhaps Erich Huber would be free to take him immediately.